Derek's Good Relations

Relations and Relationships - poor Derek has far too many of both.

He has a book to write - a mother he has only just met - a wife about to give birth and a poodle who hates him. Life had been so different a year and a half ago. Back then it had been a life before ET and Mom and a heap of other people interfering with his good intentions.

In Mac Black's fourth Derek book the plot thickens and Derek tries to be devious, as he blunders from disaster to disaster, making us laugh all the way!

Current titles by Mac Black

Please... Call Me Derek
Derek's in Trouble
Derek's Revenge
Derek's Good Relations
Derek's Secrets (2014)

Why not check the publisher's website www.uppublications.ltd.uk
or follow Mac on www.macblack.info

First published in Great Britain in 2013 by U P Publications Ltd
Head Office: 25 Bedford Street, Peterborough, UK. PE1 4DN

A CIP Catalogue record of this book is available from the British Library

ISBN 9781908135421

Also published for Kindle by U P Publications under ISBN 9781908135438

FIRST PAPERBACK EDITION

Published by U P Publications - Printed in England by The Lightning Source Group

www.uppublications.ltd.uk
www.macblack.info

DEREK'S
GOOD
RELATIONS

Mac Black

U P Publications

2013

1

An important piece of furniture in any household is a bed.

Many other things, of course, are essential to maintain a happy home for a young couple: deep and meaningful things – like love and understanding of your partner, tolerance of each other's eccentricities, having a little money left after paying the monthly instalment to the mortgage company – to mention but a few. Without these things, relationships could eventually founder and collapse.

Two exist in Toozlethwaite Manor – beds, that is! Can their importance be denied? No. By the way, in case you are not already aware – Toozlethwaite Manor is the fanciful name selected by Derek for the cosy little cottage, where he and Sally live. However, back to the beds!

Comparing the two, there is the one that is used all the time by the young couple, which sits slap-bang in the middle of the main bedroom and is both large and extremely comfortable. Both Derek and Sally consider this expensive, robust, king-size, double bed to be very important, especially at night when they snuggle close together. It may have cost a lot, but to them it was a very wise buy.

As for the other – the single bed – it is definitely not nearly as comfy as their large one. It sits in the spare bedroom, deliberately single, and with a new mattress. The new mattress was cheap, and less pleasant to be lying on than its predecessor. Sadly, its predecessor had to go – too comfy; ended its life in the Municipal Skip serving Newingsworth, Slatterfoot, and surrounding districts, and all done for a very good reason, and not due to chance, or economics.

Derek had recently learned the lesson that, if visitors are made to feel too comfortable, they forget to leave. Mr Hamish Macintosh was a perfect example of that. He's been gone for a while now, thank goodness, but his departure seemed the perfect moment to change arrangements: a safeguard for the future. At the time, Hammy's residency had seemed a distinct possibility of becoming permanent.

Tonight, Sally was first to bed, but experiencing only limited pleasure at the luxury of the clean sheets, even though these were sheets that she had not been required to wash, or dry, or iron.

She'd been in bed now for six hours.

It was shortly after midnight before Derek changed into his pyjamas. This was even later than normal for him. Double pillows: he fussily removed one before lying down flat on his back, staring at the ceiling, saying nothing. *At least, for once, she is not complaining about me coming late to bed and waking her*, he thought. However, Sally wasn't asleep and it was a probability that neither would be getting much shuteye tonight. They were now both in bed – but not the same one! Aha, you say, what in the name of heavens is Derek up to this time? Was he banished to the spare bed? If not, whose bed is he in then?

Derek was many hundreds of miles away to the north, in Inverness, Scotland, to be precise, in Mrs Morag McDougall's bed. Well, he was in one of them, in a homely little establishment where Mrs McDougall catered for 'bed and breakfast', and wishing that he was not. He should be with his wife, especially at a time like this. It was very obvious to him that this occasion would be one that would not go unnoticed and, in turn, not likely to be forgotten the next time she was feeling a little out-of-sorts; this night would be remembered. It was likely to be used against him one day...

The sheets on Sally's bed were specially marked along the edge, 'Property of NHS Marsdonfield'. She was in the Marsdonfield General Hospital, the local hospital for Newingsworth, Slatterfoot, and surrounding districts, although, when in a rush to get here, with Hammy at the wheel chuntering away about the other road users, it had seemed a long way to travel – and anything but local!

Enjoyment at the thought of impending motherhood was not happening. Unfortunately, these serene thoughts were being spoiled a little by the discomfort of the becoming-much-more-regular labour pains.

"I don't care what you think," her mother was telling her, "I say that Derek should be here, by your side, holding your hand. That's what husbands are for. I am most disappointed in Derek! And does Millie have to continually keep rushing in and out of the room?"

Her mother was obviously tired and beginning to feel the strain. Shouldn't that be my problem, Sally asked herself? Knowing that help would be at hand the moment she pressed the button, she would have been happy being in the room on her own with the earphones on, listening to middle-of-the-night music, but she couldn't say so to either her mother or her mother-in-law. It would be most unkind.

Her mind turned to her husband – wasn't it so like Derek, though, to miss out on this?

The rain had not stopped in Inverness and was playing rhythmically on the dormer window of Mrs McDougall's attic bedroom. No stars to be viewed tonight.

With the sound of the raindrops just loud enough to be attention seeking, he was lying staring at the ceiling with thoughts tumbling around in his head. Hearing the rain pitter-patter was not sleep inducing at all for Derek – Sally was having his baby – his son. He was about to become a father ...the father of an alien!

The darkness was dredging up worries; was it such a good idea that they were about to call their little boy *Edwin?* That name surfaced many months ago – it was still a lovely name, but....

It was just regrettable that after they'd informed everyone what the little fellow was to be called, they realised that the initials might be a tiny bit problematic in the future – Edwin Toozlethwaite – *ET?*

They had considered giving him his grandad Alexander's name as a middle one, but having the initials EAT didn't seem to add anything worthwhile, so that inspiration was abandoned. His other grandad, the I-wish-to-remain-anonymous James Hoist was also considered, although reluctantly. By adding James, Edwin's initials would then have become EJT, and, while that would have been acceptable, and an improvement, as far as Sally was concerned, to Derek it was not.

Since being acquainted with Hammy, a lot of bletherings in his ear had given that organ the ability to understand the Scot's tongue. All his years, Derek had grown hateful of nicknames, and a word was lurking there, he could tell, it was just waiting, and full of Scottish potential: *Eejit!* In Hammy's company a well-used word! A momentary lapse of clear thinking on Derek's part, or maybe even a bold contradiction of a ridiculous statement of Hammy's, and the Scotsman would have no hesitation with his response... "Naw, naw, naw! Yoo urr jist talkin like a big eejit noo!" So, no! The 'village idiot' was not a complimentary Scot's term, and no son of his was going to go through life burdened with it!

Forget a middle name – ET will remain plain and simply 'Edwin'.

Goodness, he wasn't even born yet and, sadly, the future daddy was already into the habit of referring to their little boy as ET, so what chance was there of him avoiding it at school? In the future, this sweet little child was destined to be alienated, in a nice way hopefully, whether he liked it or not!

Derek had taken great pains to point out confidently to his wife, about the 'nickname' thing, that he'd been through all that; their son would cope. He'd had that problem all his life, he said, which was stating the obvious to Sally, and, he asked her, did it worry me being called Sweaty? Of course not...

He was choosing to forget that it was only in this last year he had been successful in discouraging most people from being tempted to call him by his nickname. It was something Sally knew only too well. It was she who had worked in the background on their friends encouraging them to call him Derek instead, and, if she'd wished, she could have justifiably claimed most of the credit.

"And it didn't do me any harm..." he was proclaiming pompously.

His wife knew that to be a little less than the truth.

Of course, the son that was about to be born, was not the only addition to the Toozlethwaite household. Sally already had Jilly, sweet little Jilly – wasn't it a pity that Jilly hated Derek...

2

Life had been so different a year and a half ago.

Back then it had been a life before ET and Jilly, or Mom, or Twister, or Sam and Angelina. No-one could have foreseen the way each of these little dramas would be unfolding for Derek and Sally, and how the unfolding would begin at the party...

That Saturday evening had certainly been life changing. What had been carefully planned – a simple opening of a restaurant, a simple announcement of an elderly couple becoming engaged, and a simple introduction for a book (which had still to be written), plus a few songs from an ex-rock sensation – turned out to be a very complicated getting-to-know-you affair.

Although it was obvious that one person had *not* enjoyed himself, everyone else did, once they had learned and understood their relationships, of course, but if the laughter and happy crying could be considered a measure, it was a very successful party, though, as with all good things, it had to come to an end.

The breaking up was in the early hours of Sunday morning and the less-than-sober participants noisily left Anton's 'New Astoria Eating House', wending their merry ways to their respective destinations, leaving Anton, his son Peter, and the new chef, Tommy, to do the clearing up.

Another busy day ahead was destined for these three stalwarts. The Saturday night party had been for the private opening, with no public admitted, and thankfully, other than severe knife damage to one wall, the place had survived relatively unscathed. Vacuuming the tartan carpeting and wiping down surfaces, cleaning glasses and dishes, and generally rearranging tables and chairs was all that was required.

When you are already tired after a busy day, it is sometimes difficult to enthuse about the next challenge, and that was the way they felt. The adrenalin had flowed for the first occasion but it would have to happen all over again – for the public. The New Astoria Eating House would be opening to the good citizens of Newingsworth, Slatterfoot and surrounding districts, at lunchtime on Sunday, which seemed only a few hours away!

"Letsa getta feenished, an' getta the heck outoffa here," suggested Anton.

Anton was now wishing he'd chosen Monday...

Still feeling the effects of shock at her sudden appearance and the knife throwing act, Mr James Hoist had been driving for an hour when it occurred to him – he'd rushed off without bringing his guitar and his coat, and his wallet. Now, the wallet he could not do without!

Carrying his wallet in his back pocket was the normal way for him, but last night he put it in the pocket of his coat. In his trouser back pocket it would have spoiled the shape of his rear when he was performing ...well, that was the theory!

In his earlier years, when he'd been a big star and in the spotlight, he'd never carried anything in his pockets. Wearing his tight trousers, the female fans preferred seeing only the shape that they liked – the real him, and no artificial help needed. He'd always considered objects such as keys, money, or a wallet to be distractions. In those days, he'd been pernickety, in much the same way a female is with the smoothness of a dress, but – and it was a rueful thought – maybe now he wasn't the same attractive shape he'd been in his younger days.

Careering along the motorway at ninety miles an hour going south, he had been desperate to put as much distance as he could between himself and Newingsworth, but now, what should he do? The miles he was adding by the minute were putting him further and further away from his money, which was not a good idea!

He had little choice. He'd have to go back. All his credit cards were in the wallet, and come to think of it, there was a fair amount of cash in it too. The coat was expensive, though it didn't matter all that much, but the guitar, that cost a fortune and it was his favourite. So, at the next motorway service station, he pulled off.

Might as well have a break, he decided.

A solitary can of coke was purchased using the few coins kept in the car for emergencies. Disturbingly, it was the only money he had; a very unusual situation for him to be in, and it made him feel even more vulnerable than he had back at the Eating House.

What was needed was a good strong black coffee, but he'd tasted the stuff they serve in the motorway cafes and it didn't appeal at all tonight, so coke would do. He went to a table in the corner away from everyone, and looked around. It always surprised him how many people chose to move about the country at this late hour – or was it early? The place was busy. He wondered how many of these drivers had started out, and then changed their minds about where they were going. Most likely, he was the solitary idiot who had.

There was little alternative. He would have to go back, but he couldn't return while they were all still there. He felt a fool, not just for leaving his essentials behind, but regarding the whole affair.

Damn Derek Tee! He was the organiser, and the one who'd encouraged him to perform; 'like the old days' had been the comment. Did he set me up? Or did he simply want to ensure there would be good headlines for his frigging book?

If he ever comes near me again...!

It would take an hour to get back up the motorway; the country roads could be slow, but the party would probably still be on the go, and all laughing at him, no doubt; wouldn't want to arrive there too soon with them all still there. Sit here a little longer, maybe. When they all leave, and while the clearing up is being done by the staff – that would be the time to get back in and grab his stuff.

The whole episode annoyed him, but it was also exhausting him. Not being as young as he used to be – he fell asleep in the chair...

"Are you all right, mister?" asked the cleaning lady, reaching for his crushed empty can.

He woke with a start.

Where am I? What happened? Why am I...?

"What time is it?"

"It's 'alf past one..." she told him.

"I've got to go!" he blurted out, and then jumped up too quickly and caught his foot on the chair leg and fell over.

The cleaner stopped her work and stood holding the brush.

"Are you sober enough to drive?" she asked, looking down at him.

"I have not been drinking," he responded angrily, and the cleaner decided it would be a wise move to leave cleaning of the area until after this one left.

It wasn't until he was back in the car that he noticed the pain in his leg, particularly when he first used the clutch, but he had to get on the move quickly and couldn't let a little thing like that hinder him. He couldn't afford to be too late. He had to get there before they closed the place, and gallingly, he had to go back exactly the way that he'd travelled only a short time ago and at such speed.

With little to hinder him he was able to continue on his way in top gear, and avoid using his left leg, and thankfully the motorway police force made no appearance to stop him pushing it. Anyway, going slowly was for old men with cloth caps!

The pain in his left leg seemed to have eased – until he changed gear as he left the motorway exit. Ouch! It continued to make him suffer all the way along the twisting country roads. The more pain he suffered, the more blame he put on that bloody Derek Tee!

Parking a fair distance away, in case anyone saw him again, he went on foot along a totally deserted Newingsworth Main Street – to find the New Astoria Eating House in darkness!

No, no, no...!

Peering through the glass, he could see his guitar sitting where he'd abandoned it on the raised platform, and it looked like his coat was still where he threw it when he did his 'star's entrance'. It was hanging off the chair, but at least both were still there. No one had pinched anything, though he couldn't tell if the wallet was still in the pocket.

He knocked on the glass doors, which hurt his knuckles and had no effect inside. He picked up a small stone from the gutter and tried with that, and though it made more noise it still brought no-one to help him. They'd gone home...

What about the door lock? It didn't look particularly strong to him. A gentle push would probably get him in, so, he pushed... No success: a little harder maybe? So, he pushed a little harder...

RINGINGINGINGINGINGINGINGINGING ...and on it went!

Failed! Damn! Painful leg or not, he moved quickly. What temporarily deafened and frightened the life out of James Hoist was the highly-sensitive quality burglar alarm that Angie Schwarz had very wisely arranged to have installed during the refit. Not only did it frighten him severely, it totally removed any little bit of self-respect that remained.

He hobbled quickly along the main road and down the side street, and made it back to his car, scrambling in and cowering down just as the local police patrol car roared passed with the blue light flashing menacingly. There he stayed, glad that he'd parked far enough away to be out of range of any checks being made by the police.

Anton had only just pulled the duvet up to his chin and placed his head on the pillow when the phone call came. The burglar alarm had to be switched off, the policeman told him. They had contacted his son, but he'd informed them that it was his father who had the piece of paper giving the instructions for resetting the new alarm; would you please come and fix it, he was requested. They were very polite about it and apologised for waking him, and said they would wait until he arrived.

"We would be 'ighly obliged if you could 'urry," the nice policeman said, because they were late for their rest break.

A short time later, when the police vehicle passed the end of the road where James was parked, he could see this time the blue light was not flashing. He got out of the car, winced with pain as he put pressure on his left leg, and limped back along towards the scene of his crime.

Inside, the light was on this time. He could see Anton, who'd obviously given up any thoughts of returning to his own home, and who appeared to be making himself up a bed on the floor near the platform using some loose cushions. As he watched, the older man looked around, noticed the coat hanging from the chair, lifted it and rolled it up. Bending down awkwardly, he laid his weary body on top of this makeshift bed, using the coat as a pillow...

Now wait a minute – that's my good coat...

James crossed the road, went to the glass door, and tentatively knocked: tentatively because he was afraid the burglar alarm would go off again the moment he touched the glass. It didn't; and it didn't attract Anton's attention either, possibly due to him being extremely tired...

A pebble was used again, and success this time: the door was opened.

"Anton..." said James.

"Yea, whatta you want thees time of night? We no open untilla the morning an I deserva somma sleep. Go backa home, or standa quietly iffa you wanna be first in queue..."

"Anton, it's me... Twister, James Hoist... I was here earlier," he pleaded.

"Why shoulda I knowa you now? You werra verra rude to me when you werra here!"

"I'm sorry Anton. I apologise. It was unusual circumstances for me and, in my hurry to leave, I left some things behind: your pillow for starters, and my guitar."

"Oh, comma in then. Never let ittabe said that Anton, the Beega Italian, could notta forgive a rude-a-man. You wanna bacon an' egga, yea? I no getta any sleep oanywy..."

So eventually, when James left a few hours later, he had made friends with Anton. When he put on his coat, he checked and found his wallet was still in the pocket. He lifted his guitar and made a silent vow not to perform in public again, even if Derek Tee got down on his bended knee.

Anton closed the glass doors behind the retreating figure, sat on a chair, and fell asleep in an upright position. He remained that way until his son, Peter, arrived – after what seemed like only minutes. The new working day was beginning, it would soon be lunchtime, and the New Astoria Eating House was now really opening.

3

Before leaving the house, his solemn promise was that he would only be having soft drinks at Derek's party. He did not want to suffer a repeat of Daisy's torturous criticism of him after the Bowling Club night: the night that he and Hammy had been absolutely blotto!

Tonight, he vowed, he would show everyone that he could control himself.

"Only soft d-d-d-drinks, G-G-G-Gran, so d-d-don't you forget and start g-g-g-giving me alcohol," he instructed as he closed the front door at 12 Blytheton Road.

"Hector, we have been married how many years? And, for how many of these years have you been told, my name is Daisy? And how many times a day do you continue to call me Gran?"

"Which answer d-d-d-do you want f-f-f-first?"

It was Daisy who arranged for the taxi home; Hector failed – he was stewed. Thankfully, as far as she was concerned, her husband was lying in the backseat of the vehicle, with his mouth open but fast asleep and silent. She did not want a repeat of three weeks ago...

How well she remembered the events that followed the Bowling Club function: that particular evening, being a special all-male affair, very certainly lacked the restraining influence of female wives and partners. The males let their hair down, figuratively speaking of course, because, with only a few younger members present, hair was in very short supply. Hector certainly enjoyed himself, they both did, him and Hammy, with Hector insisting afterwards that Hammy would return home with him.

They'd walked from the club, or rather staggered, in the early hours of the morning, singing their heads off all the way. Sound carried well that night. Daisy was in her bed when she first heard them from at least two streets away, taking turns to sing solos followed by lusty duets, at a volume that successfully wakened many of the neighbours. Of course, being encouraged by one very late night-owl – out having a last cigarette at his front door before turning in – who stupidly requested a particular song, caused their progress home to be even slower. They obliged him by singing what they knew of it and, surprisingly, several verses poured out, word perfect.

It did surprise Daisy to hear the extent of Hector's repertoire; he even knew most of Hammy's Scottish songs! And thank goodness they had tolerant neighbours but, anyway, he had a nice singing voice and it was a strange fact that, when singing, his stutter vanished. He rarely sang when sober. For some reason that Daisy couldn't understand, that night, it brought a little tear to her eye.

Nearly everyone laughed about it the next day, but it was still a little embarrassing for Daisy, thanks to snooty Mrs Jemima Brodie two doors along. She was the only one to comment critically. Daisy always thought of that one as Mrs Puddleduck – the only other Jemima she'd ever heard of and, anyway, it wasn't as if Hector made a habit of that sort of drunken behaviour. Misbehaving the odd time was acceptable to Daisy.

With him driving again, he was keeping off the strong drink; being totally against drinking and driving, he'd been especially well behaved since he bought the scooter. This was pleasing to Daisy. However, with them using the taxi tonight, he had avoided driving – and it was happening again; a second time in only three weeks. Daisy knew exactly what he would claim tomorrow; she'd failed to control him. It was perhaps not surprising considering the circumstances, but at least, on this occasion, she was with him to assist his return.

For Daisy, it was highly desirable that there should be no noise. She didn't want Mrs Puddleduck getting excited again, but he was sleeping like a baby, his head on her shoulder. That would do just fine...

To be fair, it had been one of those special nights: the sort of occasion when Hector could not possibly have kept his vow. It wasn't every night that their only daughter surprised them by returning home – in fact it was only once every thirty-odd years, so tonight had been more than a surprise, it had been a shock! On top of that, they'd discovered that they had another grandchild – who was female – and that she was an American!

The taxi stopped at the gate.

"I could do with some help, please," she said to the driver, who wasn't in the habit of leaving his cab at this time in the early hours but who could see these two old folk would be in the back of his cab all night if he didn't assist.

Moments before, it was perfect, Hector being asleep; now it wasn't and he really didn't want to be awake. As he was almost carried up the path by the driver, his legs seemed more flexible than they ought to have been. "Would you help me into the house with him please?" Daisy asked.

"Of course," the taxi driver replied, which was most out-of-character for him. He was glad none of his mates could see that he could be a nice guy sometimes. He didn't behave like this for everyone, you know. It was to do with appearances. This older woman reminded him of his dear departed mother, the mother who left him and his father twenty-two years ago to vanish to somewhere in Spain with the next door neighbour. She would probably look like this little old woman now. He still missed her...

He had to support the old guy for a few minutes at the doorstep while she rummaged in her handbag for the key, and then they were in, and through to the living room, and the old guy was dumped on the settee. The driver had probably missed at least one valuable fare in town because of this but what the hell; helping was a good feeling – sometimes. An inner peace was still with him as he left the house, closing the door quietly behind him, having refused to accept any tip for his assistance. He did this for his dear long-gone mother – bless her soul...

Daisy looked down at the figure lying there, already fast asleep again. There was a contented smile on his face. It seemed a shame to move him – anyway, it would probably make him grumpy. She took the tartan blanket from the cupboard in the hall, brought it back and placed it carefully over him, switched off the light and left him to sleep it off.

Upstairs she went, changed into night attire, glad that she'd had only a couple of glasses of wine, climbed into bed and was instantly asleep. It had been an exhausting party for everyone, with maybe too many surprises in one night, and perhaps a little too much alcohol for some. It was obvious that someone would be having a sore head in the morning!

She was not overly pleased at being woken up.

What time is it? Only eight o'clock! What had awakened her?

The curtains had been opened wide and the sun was shining straight into her eyes, and standing at the foot of the double bed, looking down at her, was Hector: washed, dressed, and with a big grin on his face.

"B-B-B-B-Breakfast t-t-time, D-D-D-D-Daisy d-d-d-dear," he said cheerfully. "Aren't you g-g-g-getting up to m-m-m-m-make it?"

4

It was a great night, but why after so much enjoyment does there always have to be a day of reckoning? This morning, the morning after, it was Sally who answered the phone, mainly because her head, though painful, was less so than Derek's and anyway she wasn't in bed.

"Hello," she said weakly into the mouthpiece of the house-phone.

If she had still been in bed the phone would have been left to ring even though, as she knew from experience, a pillow over the head fails to deaden totally its infuriating sound. The phone in her hand was purchased over a year ago and Sally would have loved to be able to make adjustments to it but had no idea how, and although she'd asked Derek to sort it, as usual, it was still the same. The ring from this house-phone was piercing.

Moments ago Derek's uncomfortable sleep had been ended by the noise. He was lying with his head covered, and moaning, although the ringing had stopped. He was regretting not looking for the instruction book for the darned thing each time Sally asked.

Anyway, she'd only struggled out of bed to fetch a glass of water, not to answer a phone. Her throat and head were feeling very rough, and she was going to have to talk...

"Hello, darling, how are you. What a wonderful party that was last night, wasn't it?" Holding the receiver at arm's length, failed to reduce the screeching sound her mother's voice was making in her head this morning. "Sally, Sally... Are you there, darling...?"

Her mother wasn't going to give up. Sally would have to speak – but could she? She tried moving her mouth – nothing happened, then she tried activating her brain. She tried once more.

"Mother..." It came out as a strange sound to her ears, and obviously, had the same effect at her mother's end in Cloverton.

"Sally, darling, what's wrong?" an anxious mother asked. "You have been to bed, I hope... Have you?"

"What time is it?" asked her daughter.

"Almost noon."

"Oh, yes, well that would be ...let's see – three hours of sleep. Yes, I have been to bed ...thank you, Mummy."

"But we all left just after two o'clock. That's when Anton locked up the outside doors, and I'm sure he would have checked that no-one had been left behind. Oh, Sally, you weren't locked in the toilet were you?"

"No, Mummy. Derek and I did a lot of talking when we got home."

"You haven't kicked him out again, have you? I did notice, he drank rather a lot."

"No, Mummy. He'd had too many surprises last night – as well as too much to drink. Neither of us could sleep. We talked a lot, and we are very tired now."

Why can't you take the hint and go away again, she thought uncharitably, but her mother continued. As she stood in the living room, holding the phone, Sally tried to recall what she and Derek had actually talked about, but that was more than could be expected of the tiny part of her brain currently functioning.

"Your father had too much to drink as well. He can't resist consuming it freely, especially when it's someone else paying – but I'll let you sleep – speak to you later..."

"Right, Mother..."

"Tell Derek, I really enjoyed it. I can't wait to meet his mother again. She's some woman. Oh, by the way, your father isn't with you, is he? I can't find him in the house. He's probably gone out for a walk – to clear his head – though that's not like him. No matter ...enough, bye for now." Sally replaced the receiver on the charging stand and made her way back to bed. She was sound asleep almost before she pulled the covers back over her head.

Even though it was a portable device, the receiver was left in the living room. If she had taken it to the bedside table and it rang again, it could have been answered without anyone rising, couldn't it? We have to suppose, giving her the benefit of the doubt and the state she was in, she probably just hadn't thought. Or, had it been left there deliberately? It could be that she didn't care if it rang again, she would certainly not be answering it – so who would?

Derek replaced the pillow under his head, without opening his eyes because that would have let in the light; he wasn't asleep.

"Muriel ...annoying woman, he grunted to himself, "mother-in-laws ...huh! Phoning in the middle of night..." As he turned over, his head seemed to stay behind; was it actually facing backwards – the wrong way on his body now? It felt like it. His head throbbed painfully. The rest of his body was numb. He tried again.

In a tentative effort to move his head to where naturally it should be, by accident he opened his eyes at the same time. This caused part of the room to become glaringly and frighteningly bright, and to wobble – seriously. Shouldn't have had that naughty thought about Muriel, he told himself, made my head feel bad – of course, nothing to do with excessive alcohol – and when he thought he couldn't feel any worse, the phone rang again.

"Sal... Sally," he tried.

The figure beside him remained still. If he'd been able to focus, he might have seen that there was a deep-sleep-induced-contented smile spread right across her face.

"Sally ...the phone ...it's ringing. It's very noisy," he slurred, but Sally wasn't listening.

The pillow went over his head but, as before, failed to do what he had hoped. The phone continued to ring... A loud piercing ring...

"I'll get it Sal. Don't you worry – I'll ...get it..."

He struggled to untangle himself from the bed sheet, and as he hit the floor the pain in his head suddenly felt less as he realised there was now a greater pain in his elbow.

"I'll never drink again," he vowed, as the head pain returned.

The phone was still ringing...

5

Alexander was having difficulty focussing. An eye-test recently became essential and then led on to what he had been hoping to avoid – the prescribing of reading glasses. Unfortunately, at this precise moment when they were needed, he couldn't find them.

The light should have been bright enough on his mobile to enable him to see, but, to his eyes, the figures displayed on the screen just looked fuzzy. He peered at what looked like the incredibly small letters of the directory listing, and then found what just might be 'DerandSal' – and dialled. This was done with considerable hope, and a throbbing headache. Help had to come from this call – he needed it! He didn't feel well, but thank goodness deliverance was only a phone call away and the system was attempting to connect. The intermittent buzzing sounding in his ear wasn't helping his headache. Of course, a simple solution would be to stop the noise by giving up...

"Hello...?"

"Ah, Derek – at last – I knew I could rely on you."

"Alexander?"

"Yes, of course it is, Derek. Who were you expecting to call? (Hic) I need your help. Listen very carefully, please... WHERE AM I?"

"What?"

Alexander cleared his throat, and tried to control the words. He could appreciate himself that he was not enunciating with his usual clarity – and tried again. "Derek, please don't have me repeating myself... I said, WHERE AM I?"

At the other end, Derek felt he didn't deserve this. He had his own problems, thank you very much. He couldn't remember removing all his clothes last night and tumbling into bed without pyjamas. That wasn't his style at all and he felt vulnerable standing in the middle of the living room, naked, talking to his father-in-law, who sounded the worse for wear too.

"Derek... Derek, talk to me, please..."

Derek blinked. He was suffering a severe hangover, lacking sleep, and standing there with no clothes on, and his father-in-law was asking him stupid questions. "Where are you? Yes – Uhmmm... Are you giving me any clues, Alexander?"

Alexander looked around him. He was somewhere inside, there was glass, and there was leather, there were dials – and there was a steering wheel!

"Yes... I'm in a car," he replied triumphantly.

"Good, then you've answered your own question, haven't you," the sarcastic voice said.

"Derek, you are not being very helpful."

"All right then, what colour is the car?" The voice was now humouring him.

"How would I know? (Hic) I'm on the inside. Hang on a minute..."

"WHAT THE...?" said the face, which appeared through the half-opened door. Andy Woodstock, who opened up his car door only to collect the bag he left by mistake overnight in his vehicle, reacted as any normal surprised person would, by banging his head on the edge of the car's bodywork as he pulled back in shock.

"Ah, it's all right Derek," said Alexander into his mobile. "You haven't helped much, but I think I'll manage now. (hic) It looks as if the cavalry has arrived." Alexander ended the call and looked up. He recognised the young policeman from last night's party, standing outside holding the car door open and rubbing the back of his head. He looks a little bit unsure of where he is too, thought Alexander.

"How did you...?" Andy began to ask...

"Don't know..." Alexander, immediately – and confidently – was able to respond.

Not the most helpful answer was it?

This morning, Andy was sober as a judge and ready for duty. Last night, he had been one of the few at Derek's 'get together' who all evening pretended to enjoy soft drinks, and only because later he was to be driving Sophie home, so he had to resist being tempted by any alcohol. He also knew very well the effect a drink and driving offence could have on career prospects in the police force and as he planned to continue being a policeman for a long while yet, very sensibly, sobriety had been the watchword...

Having a clear head to start the day was always the best way to approach law and order, Andy believed, and this morning he felt in top-notch condition and ready for anything – or rather, had been – until he opened the car door.

Sally's father, the bank manager that he met for the first time last night at the party, had ended up accompanying Sophie and him back here in the rear seat of his car. It had happened without them knowing, but, decided Andy, discovering how was not going to be achieved while Mr Alexander Davidson sat slumped inside and he stood outside like an idiot.

Discussing it upstairs in the flat seemed a more sensible way to get to the truth. Maybe even an 'interrogation' face to face at the kitchen table would be required!

Only one person, other than Andy, could claim to have remained sober last evening, and that was James Hoist, or Twister, as he'd been known in those heady rock-star days. It could be said that it was uncharacteristic for him ever to remain sober on a night out, so, last night at Anton's, his remaining almost teetotal was not intentional. He had one glass of wine, and that had been only to loosen up his tonsils, and to reduce the nervous feeling, but the wine hadn't helped much.

Being seven years since the last time he performed, the appearance of confidence exuded by him last night was an act. He'd never been confident performing, though he knew he looked it, but this he'd kept secret from the others – nor was anyone aware that he was very superstitious. Carrying his lucky key ring, the skull, had always been an essential, clipped to his belt. He never went on stage without it. He'd expected to be able to find it last night and clip it on his belt before leaving home for Newingsworth – but could he find it?

No... And did it turn out to be a lucky night? No, again, and definitely not for him! A disturbing feeling of impending doom had been present from the moment he entered Anton's. Though he could think of no justification at the time for such a mood, other than the absence of his lucky charm, he had tried to shake it off. The feeling proved to be prophetic.

Having a glass of wine may have helped his nerves a little when he'd begun to perform at last night's gig, but when he left his nerves felt totally shattered. He had been desperate for something stronger. Escaping had been a much more powerful primeval requirement. The realisation was there, the moment the knife whizzed by, of how easily Millie's little act could have gone wrong. He had been eager, and greatly relieved, to exit Anton's – thankful to have all parts intact.

Normally after performing on-stage in his younger days, a bottle of Scotch would have been consumed rapidly as he relaxed, chilling-out in an anonymous hotel bedroom but, last night, he'd left the place in a panic, without his coat, guitar and wallet, hadn't he? So, no Scotch, a hurried departure, then an extra journey; instead, he'd had to make do with fresh bacon and egg cooked by Anton in the early hours of the morning.

He'd had to admit to himself, as he travelled south for the second time on Sunday morning, thanks to Anton's surprise breakfast he felt more comfortable with life. He even had pleasant memories of the early days with Millie, and felt more satisfied with his musical performance at Anton's, prior to Millie's interruption, of course.

There was one thing he couldn't get out of his head – it was probably unjustified and being unfair, but he couldn't stop feeling that Derek Tee was to blame!

Alexander's legs were doing funny things all the way into the lift, and along the corridor, and then into the flat. He was trying to walk straight, of course, but this fellow wasn't helping, pushing one way, then another – and he was pretending to be the sober one? Alexander was happy to drop into a soft seat when he arrived inside the flat, and there he sat with the stupidest of grins, looking up at the policeman towering above him.

It was only the mobile phone that Alexander had trouble seeing, the close-up vision; the frown lines on the policeman's face were as clear as you like! Why was he not happy?

"I was sure I got into a taxi last night," he explained, speaking through teeth which seemed loose, even though they were all his own, "...But it was very dark (hic) and I think I maybe had a few drinks last night – I just can't remember..."

"You climbed into my car by mistake, obviously," said Andy drily.

"Oh! Very sorry ...Andy, isn't it?" said Alexander. "Could you poshibly oblige with a cup of coffee, I'll drink it and get on my way. I can walk back eashily enough, thank you."

Alexander's slurred speech was a bit difficult for Andy to understand, even though his ears should have been tuned-in due to a working experience dealing with drunks. These were slightly different circumstances. Normally a recalcitrant body would be dumped in a cell until sober, and that could still be worth considering... No, this is Derek's father-in-law.

Andy Woodstock was dressed in his police uniform, because he would be starting his duties in three-quarters of an hour. He would have to leave soon if he was to maintain his reputation for good timekeeping. A serious interrogation of Alexander was not going to be possible; he didn't have time, which was disappointing. He looked into the bedroom.

"Honey, are you getting up shortly? We have a visitor who badly needs some black coffee. I'll have to go now. Could you do the needful, please?"

He turned to Alexander, who had lost interest in his surroundings and was flopped out in the comfortable seat, beginning to doze. Andy reached down and tapped Alexander's arm and then regretted it as, suddenly, Alexander leapt convulsively awake.

"You ok?" Andy asked the bleary-eyed older man.

He felt guilty and suspected that it was unfair leaving this problem behind for Sophie to have to deal with, but he didn't have a great deal of choice if he were to reach the station on time.

"Sophie will get you the coffee. I have to go to work. Hope you make it home successfully, Alexander. We'll maybe see you again. Bye..."

As he left, he shouted into the bedroom.

"Bye Sophie. See you later, sweetheart," and the door closed.

Why did he call me sweetheart, Alexander wondered? "Sophie. Sophie? I knew a Sophie once," he murmured to himself. "Oh, she was a wicked one – she got Derek into trouble, she did... That Sophie was some gal (hic) though, worth getting into trouble for..." The thought brought a smile to his face, the type that to a knowing onlooker could be verging on being described as a leer.

The figure in the flimsy nightdress, and wearing fluffy slippers, was slipping tanned arms into the silk dressing gown as she came out of the bedroom. She said nothing, only glancing briefly at the back of the head of the dozing shape in the chair, and continued through into the kitchen. The usual noises of activity came from there, water burbling to the boil, cups clinking, spoons hitting china and very soon, two cups of freshly brewed coffee were carried into the room by the vivacious little blonde.

"There we are, Alexander. That should help a lot," she said. "You must have had a great deal more than me to drink last night, but it was a great party though, wasn't it?"

Alexander perked up when she spoke. He blinked a few times and that helped a little. It seemed necessary to sit up straighter in the company of a lady, but there was panic as she reached out to hand him his drink. It took great concentration to avoid overbalancing the cup and saucer now in his hands. Instinctively he knew she would not be pleased to have coffee spilled all over this lovely chair.

"Oh... Were you there – at the party?" he responded. "I don't remember seeing you." He tried to focus more. He could see a female, a blonde female, a very pretty blonde female, sitting opposite him.

"You don't remember me? How disappointing. We talked about Derek's plan for the book..." she replied with surprise, because it was unusual for her not to be noticed, and remembered, by males.

"I think you are wrong," he replied. He was trying hard to articulate the words properly, but finding it very difficult. "The only person I talked to about Derek's book was his editor, a Mr Brown, a charming chap – maybe a bit effeminate – but charming all the same."

"There you are – you do remember..."

"No, no... I talked to a chappie – a fellow – a male person – with a moustache..." insisted Alexander, "and he looked nothing like... *hmmm...*" and the memory of the fellow from last night was now quite clear, but he took another long stare at the figure before him.

"Yes, I did have a moustache," she said.

A stupid grin appeared on Alexander's face as she said this. How ridiculous! ...And then the penny dropped. "What? Oh... So you... (Cough) Muriel was... It was you who came out of the... (Cough)"

"Yes Alexander?" she prompted, teasingly. "I came out of the what?" It was coming back to him now – Muriel's comment, *'Mr Brown is a very strange man...'*

"...Ladies toilet!"

"Oh, you did notice then," she giggled.

"That was you?"

"Yes," and she giggled again.

"Great heavens... You convinced me – and Muriel – and Sally. And you are the same Sophie – *Derek's* Sophie. Who'd have believed it? (Hic) Did Derek recognise you? He's not very bright at times, you know..."

"Oh yes, I think he knew who I was all right," she said with a wicked smile.

"It's all coming back to me now... I remember you very well. You are Sophie Clerkenwell-Brown and I've met you before at the cottage, after you and Derek... *ahummm...*"

He was beginning to feel the effect of the coffee, and it was a vast improvement on his earlier condition, but his speech still sounded out of control. "...And my daughter, Sally, she came into the house when you had no clothes on – and caught you – and Derek. I drove you to the station, later – had to get you out of there!"

He was now well awake. Who'd have believed it? She had been 'Mr Brown' ...and he had been talking to him – to her, last night. How could he have failed to see that she was most definitely a real woman? There could be no questioning that. She was very attractive, and yet he hadn't even remembered... Oh, oh, could this be the first signs of premature senility?

To disprove that disturbing thought, Alexander's mind wandered – in his imagination he began to remove Sophie's dressing gown...

"Your daughter, Sally – she over-reacted that day. And as for poor Derek – she made him suffer," Sophie replied, "...and all for no reason. Poor Derek, but anyway, that's in the past."

At this point Alexander's conscience kicked in, made him replace her dressing gown, and told him to stop behaving like a dirty old man... "But we'll have to decide how we are going to get you back home," Sophie said.

"Don't worry about me," Alexander replied bravely. "I'll stagger back, or get a taxi. I didn't know that you were living in Newingsworth now. When did you move? You used to live in London."

"I didn't move, Alexander – you are in London."

6

Not a sound could be heard. Even though it was Sunday, there was remarkably little activity for an establishment, which, twenty-four hours ago, had been declared open for business. In truth, there was no-one to be seen or heard moving anywhere in the building.

This was the New Farmhouse Hotel, Newingsworth, and, other than the majestic tick-tock of the grandfather clock in the entrance hallway, the place was silent. Five minutes earlier, if someone had been around and listening, they would have heard the chimes of that very same clock inform them that it was twelve noon.

If it can be appreciated that, last night, the hotel's only three inhabitants had been willing consumers of the flowing wine at the opening of the New Astoria Eating House, perhaps the tranquillity might be more understandable. It could be said it was lucky that anyone was inside the hotel at all.

When they'd arrived back together last night – Thelma, Hammy and the one guest, Millie Schwarz – it was Hamish Macintosh who should have been the one to produce the key to open the main entrance door, but he couldn't find it on his person.

Firstly, he was sure that he had put it in his trouser pocket. Thelma pointed out to him that for this evening's outing it was a kilt he was wearing, and having his trousers currently sitting folded on the chair inside the hotel did absolutely nothing to help the situation.

It must have been the sporran it was put it in then, was his next claim, which of course when he looked did not contain anything other his name and address in case he got lost on the way home. That didn't help the situation either, and then he remembered that, earlier, being last out of the hotel he had locked the place carefully and put the key under the doormat in case he lost it ...and that was where it was; of course, strong drink did nothing to improve matters.

Although the 'Hazelnut Room' had been booked by Derek for the important performer, Mr James Hoist, the gentleman who was to star at his 'book' pre-launch party, today it lay unoccupied. That gentleman had decided, for his own personal reasons, not to enjoy the new hotel's hospitality. This had been a little disappointing for the management, especially with the place having been only newly opened, but, no matter, three rooms *were* in use.

The 'Chestnut Room' was occupied. It contained the hotel's solitary guest, Derek's new Mom, Millicent Schwarz. That room had been booked in advance by her daughter, Angelina, although not paid in advance. The other two rooms in use were in the main building. No names were allocated to these rooms as they were for staff accommodation only. Today at this late hour, one was occupied by the Manager, and the other by the Assistant Manager / Housekeeper.

Whether it was necessary to use two separate rooms had been debated when they'd returned last night. The Manager had been of the opinion that, being newly engaged, "it would mak an awfae lotta sense" if the Manager were to share the Assistant Manager's room – and bed – and save disturbing his bedclothes.

The Manager went to bed sorely disappointed!

Although Hammy tried to wheedle his way into his new fiancé's room when they'd arrived back home, he had been vigorously repelled.

She made it so very obvious that standards for the older generation were considerably higher than those of the modern youngsters.

"You may have become engaged to me," he was reminded, "but you haven't made an honest woman of me yet!" Only engaged, and a deal was a deal, he was told. "You'll have to wait!"

Hammy had hoped ...but he couldn't be bothered arguing about it, and so, rejected, he went off to his own room feeling slightly huffy, and in any case – rather tipsy. Actually Thelma had been a bit disappointed in him. She'd hoped that he might have argued a bit more; she might even have given in!

To the embarrassment of the management team, and just before the grandfather clock had the chance to strike 'one', it was the solitary guest who moved first and made her presence known by banging on the doors of her hosts.

It seemed sensible to her that she should remind them that someone else was in the place and that it was now early afternoon on Sunday. More importantly – not only was she a paying guest, she was starving.

Incredibly, Millie wakened after enjoying a sound sleep, having zonked-out from the moment her head touched the never-been-used-before pillows, and woke totally refreshed. She'd showered, applied the essential make-up, and now appeared almost as if she had been teetotal the previous evening, though she'd been anything but...

The banging on the door certainly roused Thelma from some unpleasant dream involving Hammy, who, out of spite, was trying to stop her leaving her room by bricking up the doorway. Though appreciating leaving her nightmare behind as she hurriedly dressed, she did not relish the embarrassment of facing the solitary guest so late in the day.

The only thing to be done she decided was to offer sincere apologies to the guest for the poor service displayed by the hotel staff, especially as this was a first-time visitor. At the same time, she felt it important to emphasise that the problem was more the fault of the manager, Mr Macintosh, than herself, and then she promised a reduction in the bill. This delighted Millie; she had only done it for a laugh. She regretted telling them that later because Hammy immediately offered to reinstate the original higher figure, "If it would mak ye happier." He was immediately told to "Shush!" by Thelma.

However, getting to know each other last night at the party removed any formality from this morning's occasion in the kitchen, and, anyway, having the restaurant back in Detroit meant Millie felt at home in that department. Food preparation came as second nature to her and she was pleased to roll up her sleeves, offering help with a make-shift meal.

With the three of them sharing out the duties, in no time at all they were sitting at a dining table like a happy family, getting tucked into a hot breakfast – although a little later than was traditional for that meal: more of a 'brunch' the three agreed. To satisfy their thirst it was decided unanimously, after the excesses of the previous night, that sparkling water would suffice.

Of the three, Millie was the only one who was bright and energetic, exactly the opposite of Thelma and Hammy. Excitement and activity would definitely not have been their choice today.

The trolley, carrying the coffees, was grabbed by Hammy to give him much-needed support as they left the dining area. The hotel lounge was targeted; in Hammy's mind, preferably the farthest distance to be ventured today. Millie sat down with them for the coffee, and together the trio began watching a Sunday afternoon movie on Sky. For the two mature barely-engaged persons sitting in the plush comfort of the new settees, this mediocre film with the sound playing at low volume proved more soporific than any medication.

However, Millie was wide awake and left sitting twiddling her thumbs, so she poured herself another cup of coffee and wondered what she should do. She couldn't just sit around doing nothing; that was for old folk but, with the hotel being not a great deal more than a hefty stone's-throw away from the home of her newly-found son and daughter-in-law, it occurred to her that, perhaps, any time now they would be putting in an appearance here. Obviously, they would be eager to see how she was coping, but so far no sign. Of course, they could be under the weather, like this pair snoozing on the settee.

Just look at them ...newly engaged, holding hands in their sleep ...doesn't it look sweet? Unfortunately, the romanticism of this idyllic scene was lessened by the grunts and snorts coming from Hammy.

Millie wandered back into the hallway. No-one else was in the place. Wasn't it peaceful? Everything was new and perfect, and showed it. There was not a spot of dust to be seen anywhere and not an ornament or picture out of place. The only room where anything had been disturbed was the kitchen, and even there the three of them had cleaned up afterwards. When the part-time staff returned tomorrow, would they have anything to do?

Wasn't it nice being able to look out of the windows and see the fields stretching into the distance? So different from Detroit, but she could see no sign of her newly discovered family rushing to be with her again. Should she do something – like ring them, Derek and Sally – or wait until they make contact? I hope I haven't offended them, she thought ...that fuss in the restaurant, but seeing James Hoist after all these years! It was nice surprise though, wasn't it? Wonder if he's recovered...?

The grandfather clock began to chime again.

A flicker of life was actually beginning to show in Toozlethwaite Manor – due to the ruddy phone ringing once more. Sally couldn't understand why the noise, which woke her and was continuing at a high volume, had failed to wake the snoring lump lying beside her. On, and on, and on it went and, as the ringing did not appear to be going to stop of its own accord, she rose.

"Hello," she said, expecting it to be her mum to tell her that Dad was back, and not to worry.

It was a female voice, but not her mum.

"Hello, could I possibly speak to Mr Derek Tee?"

"You want Derek? Who is calling him please?"

"This is Soph..." and the voice hesitated.

It's not exactly a mastermind question thought Sally, understandably irritable after very little proper sleep. She tried unsuccessfully to stifle a yawn... Come on... Spit it out...

"Who did you say it was?" she prompted once more.

"Err... This is Mr ...*uhmm* ...Brown's secretary speaking. Mr Brown ...my boss, would like to talk over some aspects of Mr Tee's story. Is he there?"

"I thought Mr Brown would have talked it to death last night. He and Derek were head to head for a lot of the evening."

"Apparently not..."

"Hold on then."

Sally went back into the bedroom and unceremoniously whipped the bedclothes from the prone figure. The prone figure snored on.

"Derek... Wake up... Mr Brown's secretary is on the phone. Mr Brown wants to speak to you – again."

Derek stirred.

"Mr Brown...? Who's Mr Brown? Oh, that Mr Brown ...but she doesn't... I'll get it!"

"Hurry up, she's waiting," said Sally. "I'll put on the kettle."

As Sally went into the kitchen, Derek realised who it probably was, and he was correct.

"Sophie, what are you doing ringing here?" he hissed as quietly as he could.

"It's your dear father-in-law," Sophie hissed back. "He's sitting on my sofa, pissed as a newt, as they say."

"I don't understand..."

"He was in the back of Andy's car when we drove home last night. We just found him this morning. I gave him coffee, and that sobered him up a bit. When I told him where he was he was shocked, so I stupidly offered him a large whisky to steady his nerves, which he readily accepted and swallowed in a single gulp. I shouldn't have offered the alcohol – I realise that now – it set him off again..."

"Sophie, where are you?"

"I'm at home – in London. Where do you think?"

"And Alexander ...he's with you? ...Does he know you are Mr Brown? Does he know you are a female?"

Suddenly, Derek's mind was filled with unpleasant thoughts. Exposure of their little ruse came to mind, together with self-preservation, and the potential for blackmail; suicide also had to be considered.

"Yes – and – yes – and – yes," responded Sophie.

"Oh..." he simply said, although '*work brain, work*!' was bouncing inside his head to no avail.

"So, what do I do about it? Dump him in the Thames?"

"Yes, if you can lift him. No, be sensible. I'll have to phone you back. Speak to you shortly."

"Please, don't be too long. Bye."

As Derek replaced the receiver, there was a knock at the back door, and suddenly he was aware he was again standing in the middle of the room – naked. Sally obviously hadn't heard the knocking. She was still in the kitchen.

"Sally," he shouted, as he turned and made his way back to the bedroom, but stopped and had to return to the living room to shout again. Sally obviously still hadn't heard the knocking, and she apparently had not heard his shout either. His glance went to the window. The curtains were open and there was a face looking in.

It was Mom – she had come to visit.

7

"I've only just gotten here and already, Derek, I've seen an awful lot of you..."

Derek felt uncomfortable, even though he was now sitting with a dressing gown securely wrapped around him. He wasn't sure he properly knew this woman yet, even though she was a very close relative. Yes, it was true that they had been corresponding by email about the rock band, and it had been nice meeting her face-to-face last night, and there was no denying that it had been fantastic learning who she really was – but for her to have seen... well! It was one thing, your mother bathing you when you are three or four years old, and being knowledgeable of all your little bits and pieces, but he was almost thirty-three...

"You can see we've just tumbled out of bed," explained Sally, "but you look as if you slept well, Mom." Sally was not fully at ease saying the word 'Mom' to this woman, particularly after having seen her almost skewer Derek's dad with a carving knife. That memory would last a long time she reckoned. She'd known Millie only for the length of time they'd been together for the party last night. There had been a lot of chat and they'd become acquainted a bit, but it didn't feel like a relaxed relationship yet. Anyway, as it was Millie who insisted that she be called Mom by 'her family', so be it. Who am I to argue, Sally decided?

"Yea, it's real comfortable in Hammy and Thelma's hotel, but I'm the only one there," she told them. "They won't make their fortune like that, surely?"

"There would have been some company, but you chased it away, didn't you? Would you have liked Twister to be there with you?"

asked Derek, "...because that's where he was supposed to stay last night."

"Jumpin' jellossiphats – no!"

The phone rang...

"I'll get it!" Derek shouted out.

He was quick to claim the call, and stood up, but Sally was nearer, and quicker. She lifted the handset, and listened, then turned to Derek with a quizzical look.

"It's Mr Brown's secretary she says – for you again."

"I'll take it outside, Sal, so you and Mom can get to know each other better."

It was a nervous-looking smile he gave them as he carried the phone out to the back garden...

"Sorry Sophie, I was waylaid by Millie – Mom, as she wants us to call her – and she has just appeared and I can only apologise. I haven't managed to..."

"Derek, listen, it's about Alexander. I had to call an ambulance. It's probably just a false alarm, at least I hope it is – but he's on the way to the hospital."

"What? What happened?"

"He threw up all over my living room carpet, but then took a funny turn. I didn't want to take any chances."

"Oh God, what am I going to tell Sally – and Muriel. Why would you, or Mr Brown's secretary, or my publisher, or whatever you are calling yourself, phone me about my father-in-law? ...and him in London – and now in a London Hospital? How can I explain that to them?"

"I don't know Derek. I'm just a simple publisher with no brain, obviously. You are the writer. You should be good at making up stories. I'll leave it with you. Speak to you later."

He didn't want to go back inside. What was he going to tell Sally? Why life had to go round in large circles, and small ones, Derek could not understand, always returning to the same part – where he landed so deeply in the soft stuff? Exactly how Alexander came to be in London was absolutely nothing at all to do with him, but somehow he could feel that the blame would be coming in his direction. More seriously, Alexander had come face-to-face with Sophie again, but this time it was the real Sophie! Would he squawk?

Just standing outside like this was doing no good; he'd have to go back in, but what could he tell them? Think, man, think...

He went inside.

"Everything all right, Sweaty?" asked Mom sweetly. "You look very guilty..."

Thanks Mom, he thought, particularly for using that name, and for the heartfelt sentiments. Now, she had made him feel guiltier still!

"What's wrong, Derek?" asked Sally.

"It's complicated..." he responded, thinking fast, "...your dad – he took a wrong turning last night it seems. Finished up going into Andy Woodstock's car, probably was aiming for a taxi, but his sense of direction was a little off apparently. He's in London."

Derek, grateful that hysterics hadn't kicked in immediately, remained tense. Save the hysteria for later...

"Is that what Mr Brown's secretary was phoning about then?" queried Sally.

"Yes..." said Derek, already regretting being involved in this whole business.

"How did she know?"

"Eh... She's friendly with Andy Woodstock ...and he is on duty today." You are doing all right Derek, he told himself, but what next? There will be more questions, inevitably. If I just guide them in the correct direction I'll be out of the wood. "...And they've had a major emergency in London!" Oh no, that had come out with a rush. He regretted saying it; wrong direction – but he would have to continue... "Yes ...a bomb scare! And Alexander couldn't phone me – didn't have my number, so because Andy is involved in this major security alert, he phoned Mr Brown ...and asked him to tell his secretary ...to pass on the message."

"And why didn't Alexander phone you himself?" asked Mom, "And does Muriel know?"

"Has he contacted her?" Sally added, because surely her father would have been thoughtful enough to have contacted his wife right away.

Derek was outnumbered, and that was not fair. He struggled enough when it was only Sally, but now she was getting assistance from Mom, no, not fair at all, but he had to keep going...

"No, because the bomber took him hostage and stole his phone." *Why did I say that?* He could have kicked himself. What was wrong with telling the truth? Tell them about the hospital ...but somehow, he couldn't. He was on a roll. "Yes, but they'll keep me informed of the situation. They said not to worry," he rounded off, and heaved a sigh of relief. He had reached a conclusion. He had not mentioned Sophie, and they had believed every word. That was quite good for an off-the-top-of-the-head tale, he told himself. He could relax again...

"They said not to worry?" exploded Mom. "It's a hostage situation, for heaven's sake!" Mom's sudden outburst made Sally realise that she hadn't really been listening to Derek.

"My dad, a hostage... Oh no! We'll have to tell my mother," said Sally.

"No, no, no..." said Derek. He had probably been correct earlier. There was a lot he shouldn't have said, and he was becoming surprisingly skilled at making his world go pear-shaped.

8

Derek should have thought it through properly before rabbiting on, but they'd pressured him!

Of course, Muriel was distraught when Sally phoned her – her Alexander – he was in the hands of villains, or terrorists! But why was Derek doing the negotiations? What's wrong with the Metropolitan police – they hadn't made contact with her yet – why not? Should she get on to them right away? What was the national emergency number for terrorist attacks anyway? We don't know? Then what's the name of our MP again? He's the one I'll ring. He should be doing something...

It started to unravel for Derek the moment Muriel received the phone call directly from her husband. Now sobered up, and released from hospital having been pronounced fit and healthy, but at the same time, accused of using up valuable NHS facilities unnecessarily. Some wise advice was offered to him by a steely-eyed nurse – go easy on the booze!

Now he was starting to regret having phoned his wife. She was putting him under considerable pressure and expecting answers he was unable to supply. When she asked if he had escaped, or if the police had secured his release, he was baffled. Alexander could not recollect having experienced any hostage situation, and admitted thankfully that he must have blanked out during that time.

Anything could have been happening to him – he hadn't even known he was in London. No, he hadn't lost his phone, it was in his hand. Muriel asked him why the police hadn't taken it from him as evidence of his kidnapper's fingerprints.

Mac Black

"Derek told me the terrorists took it from you – well, didn't they?" she prodded.

Poor Alexander stood in the middle of the pavement totally bewildered by the questions. How did Derek get involved? Oh yes, he'd asked him for help, he could remember that much. Maybe this was him helping then. He had his own phone in his hand and that's what he was using, having asked a fellow pedestrian to assist him in selecting his own home telephone number on that silly fuzzy screen, so the terrorists must have given it back!

Why did you leave your glasses behind anyway, Muriel asked? Alexander was relieved to hear that his new glasses were sitting on the kitchen table in front of her. He wanted to get back home. He felt safer at home. The next available train from The Big Smoke going to Newingsworth, or even near there, will be carrying yours truly, he promised her. However, at the station, he was disappointed to learn of the reduced service on Sundays – he'd missed the last one. He'd have to tell Muriel he would be delayed. Ten o'clock Monday was the first departure. So much for work on Monday but they'd manage fine without him.

So that became another worry for his wife. "Oh dear," she said when he phoned again, "you'll be in the big city all night. How you will you manage – in London – you'll be on your own?"

What a silly question, Alexander thought after the call, how will I manage? Imagine asking me that – me, a highly responsible, and capable, bank manager. Does she think I'm stupid...? Then he remembered how he'd arrived in London in the first place. She was right. How would he manage? Did he still have his wallet? Yes, thank goodness for that. So he'd have to find a bed for the night.

Now, wasn't it fortunate that Sophie had slipped her business card into his pocket as the ambulance men collected him and carried him out of the flat, and wasn't it fortunate that he found the card and hence her mobile number? Even more fortunate, that when he phoned her, she agreed that he could return to her place – for one night. He would be welcome to sleep on her sofa, now she had cleared up the mess he created earlier.

Derek was under pressure and having to think fast. No villains or terrorists after all, but he couldn't admit that it had been his imagination working overtime, nor could he say it had been Sophie who'd called. If Sally learned he was involved with her, even though it was only for business, it would lead to instant decapitation, or worse. Sophie might be a hot bit of stuff, but she was his publisher, he told himself, trying to justify it in his own mind. The trouble of course is, once you start lying...!

Sally was happy enough all these weeks ago, when she'd learned about the exciting prospect in hand for his story. The news, when she was told that a publisher had promised a contract, was also received with delight. By not offering a name he had succeeded in avoiding a downright lie about who the publisher actually was.

"Just as long as it isn't that blonde tart," Sally had said.

"Oh no," he'd responded. Technically, it wasn't really a lie either, because he didn't think of Sophie as a blonde tart – though he knew that wouldn't stand up in court, and then came the lie! He told her it was a male, a bloke called 'Brown' who had made the promise of the contract. That's what he said – because that's what she wanted to hear, he assumed, and last night, at the party, Sally had believed she was actually meeting him – Mr Brown, his Publisher. Sally hadn't twigged, apparently, that Mr Brown was a Miss, but if she had known it was Sophie... Sophie was definitely not trusted by Sally. In fact, Sally hated the woman even though she'd seen her only once ...apparently!

When the questions started coming from Sally and Mom about the earlier phone calls, Derek had to tell them that maybe he'd misheard the message, or else, he added, it could have been Andy Woodstock – kidding him on.

"That copper, he can be a right idiot at times," he said with a forced laugh.

It was very obvious to Derek that his wife believed not one word of his explanation. Of course, it did not help that Mom was staying with them for the evening and was also obviously finding his tales questionable too. He guessed he would have to get used to that.

There was another worry: what might Alexander say when he returned home? Had he already found out that Sophie was one of the party guests – with a moustache, and if so, was Muriel told when he phoned from London?

No... He couldn't have told her. If he had blabbed, Muriel would have told Sally right away. They didn't keep secrets. Exactly the opposite with them – they made sure secrets were shared... And if Sally had been told, he wouldn't have been permitted to stand here, upright, trying to rationalise it all like this, would he?

Relax ...but Alexander would have to be contacted – some pressure would be needed to be put on him not to talk. Derek would tell him, we males must stick together, and just hope he agreed.

Meanwhile, in London, it was late Sunday night – well, the early hours of Monday morning. Sophie was in her bed, having completed some homework by reading a few chapters received recently from a budding author. Pieces of paper now lay scattered on the floor. Disappointment for her and for the author who'd wasted her time with a lousy submission, but at least it had served a purpose – it put her to sleep.

Alexander was in the other room, stretched out on the sofa covered by a blanket. To be honest he was finding his temporary bed surprisingly comfortable, and pleased that his attractive hostess had not offered any more to drink. He knew he would have succumbed. It was sufficient that exhaustion gave him the pleasure of knowing he would be falling asleep very quickly.

For Sophie, and for Alexander, apart from the hospitalising activity, it had been a totally non-productive day. However, not everyone had been twiddling their thumbs just because it was Sunday. Some people had had to work.

Having completed an exhilarating extended shift on the streets of London, '...chasing yobbos an' yooves, as usual,' Andy was in the building and on his way up in the lift. After almost continual trudging around, he was looking forward to getting his feet up, having a hot drink and a sandwich, and the chance to watch some late telly for a spell, rubbish though it was at this time of night. He could just relax. Sophie would be asleep anyway.

Alexander was dozing seriously, and at any moment would be dead to the world. He had succeeded in tiring himself out by walking from the hospital to the station to find that no trains were suitable. On foot then to Sophie's flat – to be met with no answer. So, he'd gone wandering again, found a cafe that stayed open, had a plate of stodgy macaroni and a soft drink, before continuing walking, passing Sophie's every so often until eventually the lights went on.

As a consequence he had become very sober...

The lift opened in the hallway. Being late, Andy considerately tiptoed along the passage so that he would not disturb the neighbours, but Andy Woodstock could not enter Sophie's flat quietly...

There was a ritual. His bag was chucked into the corner, as he switched on the main ceiling lights. Sitting down on the chair in the hallway beside the door, his boots were removed, each of which clattered onto the floor, to the annoyance of the neighbours below. The kitchen door was then banged open, some bread inserted noisily into the toaster, and the kettle switched on to start boiling. The cupboard door was thrown open to remove a mug, which rattled on the hard kitchen surface, and all the time tonight he was merrily whistling the hits from the Sound of Music, the show that he and Sophie attended last week.

This was a side of Andy Woodstock that Sophie did not like.

Many arguments had occurred between them about his thoughtless and careless behaviour when he returned after work at night, and the threat of his eviction loomed large many times. Sophie failed to make him change, and his habits remained, so, a solution had to be found...

On shifts when he would be arriving home late, she had resorted to using ear plugs before going to sleep. Nothing could be heard once they were inserted, therefore there was no longer a problem. It caused less friction with this approach, and Andy was permitted to stay. Of course, every so often, he was reminded of whose flat it was – and it wasn't his.

As for Alexander, the way Andy entered you'd have thought he would be wide awake again, but no. He was undisturbed – he was out for the count, with no ear plugs required. The poor man had exhausted himself earlier, fit though he would claim to be. However, when the overhead light went on, because he was lying on his back, in his sleep Alexander instinctively pulled the blanket over his face.

In one hand, Andy carried a tray with a plateful of sandwiches, a mug of tea, and a bag of his favourite curry flavoured crisps. He pulled the kitchen door closed with a bang, came through to the main room, walked over to the television, switched it on, watched it warm-up, adjusted the sound, and turned around – *and saw the body!*

Now, you are thinking that he probably dropped the tray in surprise and spilled tea all over the same area that Alexander had already messed up earlier in the day, but no, Andy Pandy Woodstock was made of sterner stuff, he was a policeman...

With a steady hand he laid the tray down on the occasional table and tiptoed over to the bedroom door, very respectful of the dead...

"Sophie," he whispered, as he switched on the bedroom light, "I didn't think he was that bad. When did he give up the ghost? Anyway, why didn't you phone me and tell me he'd snuffed it? Have you contacted an undertaker? I could have helped you."

Sophie sat up, dazzled by the light, only partially awake. She gazed at the big policeman standing at the foot of the bed whose mouth was moving.

"Yes, ok, come to bed then, but it'll have to be a quickie," she said, "I'm tired..."

She lay down again, desperately wanting to go back to sleep, but firm in her mind to stay awake – and think of England, as Andy reached over and removed an ear plug.

"Sophie, you have a body..."

"Yes, I know – and you like it a lot. I know that too. And you'll probably have cold feet. Hurry up, please," she replied sleepily.

"...A dead body in the living room!"

"What?"

She was up like a shot and rushed straight through.

In the meantime, with the main room-light still on, Alexander had wakened. He felt refreshed, as if he had been asleep for hours – and he'd wakened with an appetite. Look, on the table. How thoughtful of Sophie to have left me supper, he said to himself – sandwiches and tea – and crisps!

He also appreciated the sight of Sophie, standing there in her flimsy nightdress, but he behaved like a gentleman and looked the other way, which was a wise move with her big policeman boyfriend standing right behind her.

"Is anyone else feeling peckish?" Alexander asked...

9

Monday, 8.00 am, and Derek and Sally have overslept, which shouldn't be surprising after the extremely rough weekend enjoyed by all and sundry, and, with last night turning into another early morning finale the late rising was inevitable.

Mom didn't leave until after 2.30 am and, as she had not returned to the cottage, Sally was assuming she'd made it safely back along the road. Although she was invited to stay overnight and use the spare room Millie insisted on returning to the bed that was waiting for her in the New Farmhouse Hotel.

Last night, saying farewell on the cottage doorstep when Mom departed, Sally was filled with guilt. It was very dark out there, and a distance of almost a mile and a half for her mother-in-law to walk alone. It would be alongside the stream and, when the moon was hidden by thick clouds, dark nights became pitch black. A torch would have been of considerable help but, having found one, when Sally switched it on it gave a weak little flash and the battery died.

Sally apologised to her mother-in-law; she was so sorry to be sending her out to walk along the lane on her own. Derek should have gone with her of course, being her son but, having over-indulged again, both he and his mother would have finished up in the stream. He was sprawled out on the sofa – totally incapable of escorting anyone anywhere, and probably incapable of reaching his bed without some assistance.

"Think absolutely nothing of it, Honey," Millie retorted. "Remember, I'm from Detroit."

It occurred to Sally later that there was a dynamo on her bike. If she had taken her bike to walk Mom back to the hotel, she could have cycled back on her own in no time at all and she wouldn't be feeling so bad about it.

The other way would have been to give Mom the bike to cycle back on her own, but as Sally wasn't sure of Mom's prowess on a bike, it might not have been a good idea; Derek had finished up in the stream a couple of times, and landing in muddy water could turn out to be a family failing...

Yes, it was morning and they were late! They were awake but only just, having forgotten to set the alarm for 7.00 am. Derek surfaced quicker than Sally when his mobile sounded, and was glad that his wife was reluctant to wake, being afraid it could be Sophie again! He forced himself to leap out of bed rather quickly to answer it. It seemed wiser for Sally not to have the chance.

Annoying though it was to be roused this way, it was fortunate the call came; his deep sleep would have continued otherwise, for several more hours, but where was the damn phone? It seemed to be ringing forever.

"Ah, yes – hello..." he said, eventually finding it and hurrying out of the bedroom into the bathroom. Sally mustn't hear this. He closed the door gently.

"Hello, this is The Fort Knights Music Agency, we are here to help you – musically..."

"What...? Oh, hello, I was expecting someone else..."

"I'm so sorry to disappoint you, because we always aim to please. Is that Mr Derek Tee, the soon-to-be-famous author?" the voice sang out. He should have recognised the voice immediately. It was James Hoist's secretary.

"Yes, it is, and it is Mabel isn't it? Good morning, how could I mistake that cheerful musical voice? You have brightened my day." He said these words with enforced cheeriness, trying to smile at his reflection in the mirror – he had read that was the way to make your voice sound bright and cheerful – and anyway, he could relax a bit now that he knew it wasn't Sophie.

He looked again in the bathroom mirror. Was that the usual mirror? Surely not! He did not like what it was showing him. Looking straight back was an unshaven, youngish man, but obviously the worse for wear, and ageing over-rapidly. He grimaced and the reflection looked even worse. Not pleasant to see at all.

"Oh, you remember me," Mabel giggled, "and what have you been doing to my dear Mr James at the weekend, you naughty boy? I should warn you, he is in a really foul mood this morning. He stomped into the office five minutes ago, and then yelled at me to get you right away. He doesn't yell very often. Today, he is sounding more like my husband..."

"Oh! You'd better put him on then, I suppose."

Derek wasn't looking forward to this. His head was still pounding and he just knew this was not going to be a quiet chat.

"That's him now... It's Mr Tee," he heard her sing out to the other office. "Now just calm down and don't you be nasty to him..." and then Mabel sang into the phone, "I'm putting you through now, Mr Tee..."

There was a moment of silence.

"Hello," Derek offered tentatively.

"Yea, hello," came a snarling response. "Did you set me up?"

"What do you mean?" Derek replied, with a voice sounding as angelic as he could muster.

"Millie, you arranged for her to be there to humiliate me, didn't you?"

"Of course I didn't," Derek replied indignantly. "What kind of a guy do you take me for?"

"One who's getting no more help from me, Sunshine!"

"Just a moment – that's not fair... I..."

"When was life ever meant to be fair?"

"Now just you listen to me – I didn't know she was going to be there. Anyway, how would you have liked it if your mother had suddenly appeared out of the blue after thirty-two years and made you call her Mom, and then started calling you Sweaty – eh? And then appeared outside your house, looking in your window – catching you in the bare buff?" Derek blurted out with annoyance and frustration.

"What? Say that again..."

"I'd rather not," Derek replied huffily.

"You said she was your mother? You – you are Millie's son?"

"Yes, so she told me."

"Thirty-two years ago?"

"Yes – well, she told me all about it the other night..."

"So, that means...! What's your real name?"

"It's Derek – Derek Toozlethwaite."

"Oh my God..."

"Yes indeed. So should I call you Mr Hoist, Twister, or just plain Daddy?"

There was silence at the other end; the conversation was over.

10

This was not good news – and Derek wasn't thinking flesh and blood. Yes, it could be bad for him to have a non-existent relationship with a father he hadn't even known still existed, but he could live with that. Much more importantly, the man who had replaced the telephone prematurely on him was the one who knew the facts, and the gossip, and the insider tales about 'Rabid Revenge' – this man was his main source of the information he needed for the book!

Why should misguided animosity interfere with the business of his writing? Derek didn't want to seem overly self-pitying but, he asked himself sadly, why does the smelly stuff always seem to come in my direction? What should I do – give up, or call him back? Maybe asking Sally would help; she would offer inspiration.

Unfortunately, his wife was still lying supine on the bed with the covers pulled up to her neck, barely awake, and reluctant even to think. "Oh dear..." was all she added – so Derek dialled back.

"Hello, this is The Fort Knights Music Agency, how can we help you – musically..." and, as ever, the female voice sang in his ear.

"Could I speak to him again, please, Mabel?"

"Are you from the Tax...?"

"Mabel, it's me, Derek..."

"Oh sorry, Derek, of course – oh, and Derek, I heard it all. You have my sympathy. I know I shouldn't have been listening, and it was naughty, but he left his loudspeaker-phone on and I couldn't help myself."

"Ah... any ideas then Mabel, that might help the situation?"

"If I were you, I would offer to set up a meeting for him with Millie, your mother. Maybe they could settle their differences.

Perhaps they'd even get together again. Maybe they are still in love..."

She offered the advice sincerely, Derek could tell, and her voice sounded quite emotional, as if she really cared about what happened to his father – obviously a dedicated secretary: one who was also obviously unaware of the whole story.

"She threw a knife at him, Mabel. What happened was done with the wrong type of feeling..."

"Oh, I didn't know that – a knife? Maybe she didn't mean to kill him though – perhaps she just wanted to cut him up a bit. Could it have been intended for someone else...? No, maybe not. I'd better put you through to him. Good luck."

There was a longer delay this time – an obvious reluctance on James Hoist's part to talk to him again, Derek guessed, but eventually they were linked.

"Can we start again, please," Derek asked nicely.

"I'll talk to you only if you call me James, or Twister – right?"

"Fair enough, and firstly, I didn't know she would be there, secondly, I didn't realise she disliked you enough to want to kill you, and thirdly, I thought you were doing a great job with the entertainment – until you left hurriedly, of course. You got home safely then?"

There was another lengthy silence. So, Derek continued. He would have to work harder.

"I don't have to use your real name in the book if that's what's worrying you. I could refer to you only as Twister, if it suited you? I still need to write the book, you realise, but I could be discreet ...even though it would take a lot of the spice away."

"That would help, I suppose..."

"I didn't find out until later, you know. After you'd gone Millie told me you were my..."

"Don't say it..."

"And do you know that you missed the chance to meet your daughter?"

"I don't have a..."

"Are you really sure, before you deny it? And Angelina would probably have been pleased to meet you – she may even have been surprised – she grew up thinking another gent was her dad."

Silence... Derek was afraid he might hang up again and was thinking madly about what else he should be saying. As long as he could keep him talking, or even just listening, he might have a chance...

"Have you ever thought of sitting down with Mom, and discussing things in a sensible and safe way?"

"Are you crazy, Derek? Did you see what she tried to do to me?"

"I guess Saturday night was not the world's best reunion, was it? It might have just been jet-lag of course; I've heard it can affect people in different ways, but if I was to win her over and she agreed to meet you, would you appear?"

"Not without body armour. You don't know her yet, son. She's a tough woman."

"But if I did succeed?"

"Hmmmm..."

"And will you help me complete my book?"

"We'll see..."

"I'll settle for that. That's great! Thanks Dad – oh! Sorry..."

There was a smile on Derek's face as the conversation ended. It turned out better than he could have predicted. He was happy and hungry. It was now time to eat.

"Sally, do you fancy a fry-up?"

There was no reply. Sally had washed and dressed hurriedly and already cycled off to work on her own. Sally was a touch more conscientious than he was obviously. For her, make-up would come later – she would spend another half-hour in the office toilet, but at least she would be on the premises.

Late though it was, Derek sat down and had breakfast and when he eventually departed, even later still, he was able to tell himself, life wasn't so bad. For a change, Derek was happy.

11

For thirty-odd years, he'd been the junior member of a family consisting only of himself and his grandparents – that was the way it had been, and the way it seemed it would remain – a home consisting of Mr and Mrs Smith and the young Mr Toozlethwaite – just the three of them. Derek had been quite happy that way – for most of the time.

His learning to read at an early age made his gran and grandad really proud. All thanks to a caring grandma for the encouragement and guidance she gave him before he started school. Initially it may only have been fairly simple words with pictures, but it was reading. With Daisy prodding away he became quite proficient and enthusiastic. Hector wanted to assist too, and would have helped more, but resisted for fear that his grandson might end up with a stutter like his.

As Derek grew, it was difficult for them to keep him supplied with reading material; the local library, the school library, the town's only bookshop, in fact anywhere that material was available to read, Derek would be a regular there. When he became engrossed in a good story, nothing would distract him.

When he was ten he began to think about the people who created the stories that he so avidly devoured. How could they do it? Were they very special? Was it easy? Then, one day, he asked of himself, could I do it? Could he use words to create exciting pictures in people's minds? So, he gave it a try, and...

"I can!" he declared cockily to his grandma one day. "I am going to be a writer."

And he meant it!

Though he was warned by her at that early age that it could be a solitary and frustrating occupation it became the one thing he aspired to. His was a modest ambition: to be world famous, creating stories that lesser mortals would clamour to read, and with that fame would come the fortune. He'd read that bit somewhere and it was very appealing, even at an early age.

It didn't quite work out that way, however, but the need to use words was partly satisfied by the job he eventually did – he became a journalist: one who was more than competent and much appreciated by his editor. However, Derek discovered that, in this field, fame and the fortune were not included. Though his work was done conscientiously, and with enthusiasm, he never gave up on the dream of becoming an author.

The daily routine satisfied for a long time, but gradually frustration came creeping in. Reporting: recording facts and other people's words, that was all that he was doing – at least that is the way it struck him – and he wanted more. He wanted to create...

There was a confidence and self-assurance during that period of his life; young, single, ambitious, with a target to aim for. He was seeking the opportunity to use his own imagination, and reaching for a different level, and, at that time Derek was sure he could achieve it. It had to be *his* story and be original too; ideas were bouncing around in his head; ideas that were desperate to be set loose...

This all sounds so conceited and big-headed but, wisely, his thoughts were never spoken aloud, and definitely not to his colleagues. Those working around him were happy having bread-and-butter daily routines. They were receiving good money at the end of each month, and in their eyes only a fool would give that up.

Life continued in its normal humdrum way, with him chasing around town digging up material related to all aspects of life: domestic upsets, sporting events, council business, house-fires, planning disputes, which villains went to court this week and why, obituaries, etc, etc, etc, until... That was it – he'd had enough!

He succumbed to his dream – the urge to give it a go, to become a free spirit. It was so strong that he gave up his good job at the Slatterfoot Evening News – much to the disgust of those he worked with who advised him not to – but he had decided.

It was time for Derek to become a *real* writer...

And he failed!

Oh dear...!

While successfully creating all the time in the world to release his ideas by giving up the day job – somehow, and at the crucial moment, he lost his sense of direction, his confidence, his inspiration, and all his computer files; for a short and worrying time, life began to go downhill fast.

There was a knock-on effect for his poor grandparents. They felt bad, but could only watch him suffer until, with perfect timing, someone came on the scene! She was the one for him ...and writing became considerably less important for a spell. Other matters took over; his family group was no longer to consist of just him and his grandparents. Sally arrived: a new, third person in his life, and a very important one too.

It was inevitable, written in the stars as they say; they married. In a flash, he became a family man with responsibilities, back in a job again and earning a living, although married life wasn't easy. After being both single and looked after by a fussing gran for such a long time, having to adapt to living with Sally was a challenge to Derek.

It wasn't only two young strangers sharing their lives that Derek struggled with. On the big stage of life, others became involved. Additional personages were waiting in the wings, because, courtesy of the law, marriage has its hangers-on: Sally's relations. Suddenly the family circle was bigger; a mother-in-law, a father-in-law, and Aunt Thelma – all acquired by him at no extra cost, there on the instant he said, "*I do*..."

Wanting to concentrate on writing, when young and single, was one thing but, although still young, marriage made a big difference.

Now there was little choice.

The need for reliable earnings became dominant. He had married into a well-off family, and Sally had lived a comfortable life, so a lot was expected of him and, in particular, a regular income was a must.

The writing, the personal fame and a fortune, would have to wait a little longer.

There was something else Derek had longed for when very young. It started at his Primary School; playing together and hearing the chatter of the other young children, he began to appreciate that his life was different. Yes, he loved his gran and grandad but he could hear his little friends talking happily of other people that they had to love.

Lying in bed at night, eyes tightly closed but not really asleep, he was determined to dream dreams of having a mother, a mother of his very own like his pals had: strangely, a dad seemed less important. If he dreamed hard enough it could come true, of that he was sure. Every night, there was the same hoped-for vision of a mummy, *his* mummy reaching out to hold him, but it didn't happen.

Giving up on the dream came gradually. Realistically, over the years, he came to accept it would not be realised and contented himself with growing up in the happy little group of Gran, and Grandad, and then latterly, Sally.

Then it happened! After thirty years of dreaming, Mom chose to appear and gave him the shock of his life!

The increase in family size didn't stop there; he acquired a sister. She'd been around for twenty-five years or so, but without him knowing; a reciprocal situation shared with his sister, for whom only one person could be criticised – *Mom*. A vast ocean separated them for all those years and if he hadn't started writing about Rabid Revenge, he might never have found out about Angelina.

It wasn't easy for Angie either. She was finding it strange, having a brother. Then she got married, and, with that event, Derek acquired a brother-in-law. He thought of Sam as more of a brother, a younger brother. He had never had a brother, and he liked it; it was nice to be able to talk easily with another close male relation who was young, someone who wasn't Grandad!

Derek often reflected that none of this would have happened if it hadn't been for Anton. It was his memory that sparked the book idea, wasn't it? Recently, he'd been almost like a father to him, and, speaking of fathers...

12

At least Twister was willing to continue a dialogue with Derek – but at a distance and only as long as Derek did not use irritating language in the process of communicating, like saying *father* or *dad* out loud!

For a long time the grudge remained; Twister continued to believe he'd been conned by Derek into a face-to-face with Millie. Derek was actually the innocent party this time, but Twister had difficulty believing that.

It took a while and some much-appreciated help from Mabel to win him over to accept that young Toozlethwaite was not to blame. Eventually Twister softened, and, with her encouragement, the flow of information, via emails and telephone conversations, steadily built the facts and stories that were to lead to Derek's book.

It delighted Mabel to help Derek.

She was in the loop, the conduit, and able to use the manipulative control of her boss that she excelled at. Nothing was being missed by her of what Mr James was declaring to Derek, and she loved it, because, though she'd been with him for years she knew little of the detail of his early background. Sitting in the front office of The Fort Knights Musical Agency, every new communication from the main office, revealed by Mr James Hoist to the young author, was also new and fascinating to her.

Each email was dictated by him for her to type and send to Derek, and with every phone call it had become his habit to walk around the room using the phone on hands-free – she couldn't help listening, so she missed nothing!

Mabel was paying special attention to what she was learning, and proving a staunch ally to Derek.

Derek's perspective was different from Mabel's. Becoming aware of her boss's previous history for her was thrilling, whereas, for Derek the revelations were now more of an anti-climax.

Initially it had been a shock being linked suddenly to a father, a mother, and a sister – but he'd got over it. The fresh detail ought to have had more impact on his feelings, but no, it didn't. He was being surprisingly mature and nonchalant or, at least, trying to be. Detached, accepting this as run-of-the-mill, almost as if his stumbling on long-lost family members, and their history, was an everyday occurrence.

Surprisingly, what affected him most was to be officially acquiring a brother-in-law, and being invited to be best man at Sam's wedding was an important moment. It would not be as important as at his own wedding, of course, but still a big honour ...and he'd never had a younger brother.

13

Inviting Derek to be his best man was really an automatic choice for Sam. They had become good mates in a very short time however, that invitation was about the limit of Sam's involvement in the organisation of the wedding day; that was to be Angelina's privilege.

By no means was it intended to be a grand affair.

For the official part of the ceremony it was to be the Registry Office, the one serving Newingsworth, Slatterfoot and surrounding districts, with attendance by family only – plus Anton. From there it would then be on to the New Farmhouse Hotel for a modest reception, where the family was to be joined by new friends made by Angie while doing the spell of work at Anton's, and a neighbour from Buttercup Avenue. Some of Sam's fellow teachers would be invited, including the headmaster, Mr Brummage – apparently known affectionately, in Derek's days, as 'Beakie', Angie was informed by her future husband... He'd learned that from Derek one day on one of their bicycle jaunts when the beer had engendered nostalgia for Derek's good old schooldays.

A little more controversial was the invitation sent to Twister – Angie's own idea – after a bit of careful thought and, to Angie's mind, the correct thing to do. It was the natural thing, as well, wasn't it? Don't all brides like to have their father in attendance on the special day? She would have preferred Pop Schwarz, the much-loved stepfather she'd grown up with, but, being deceased, he couldn't attend. It would be an opportunity to get to know the man who'd spawned her, she decided, a man whom she had never actually met – and it could also be the chance for her mother and her old lover to get together again and settle differences.

"Mom will really appreciate this," Angie told Sam. "It will show her how much I care."

"Yea...? If you say so, Honey..." was Sam's hesitant comment.

Anyway, she was the bride; it was her day, so if she wanted it, it would have to happen.

Of course, not being consulted beforehand about being brought together again with Mr James Hoist was not appreciated by the older woman at all. Millie abhorred the idea, especially when, to her horror she learned that Twister had accepted the invitation.

Twister *wasn't* there! Maybe it was fortunate that, at the last minute, Mr James Hoist feigned a sudden illness, and sent his apologies. "Oh dear, he won't be coming after all," Angie sadly told her mother, feeling sorry to disappoint her. Millie made no fuss, didn't even pretend to be disappointed. The handsome cheque, which arrived with the apology to the young couple from the real father, who was destined to remain faceless a little longer, tended to soften the disappointment felt by Angie too.

When considering the music that she would like to use for her wedding, Angie remembered a day, in Anton's, shortly before she learned who Derek really was.

Derek had taken the opportunity to drop off a stack of old LPs at Anton's in preparation for use later at the party. She hadn't been speaking to him, possibly because she was lost in the midst of a stack of new tables for the restaurant, but she heard him congratulate Hammy and Anton on the transformation, before shooting off again. She also heard him talking to Hammy.

"Nice to see that you have been working well with the young American girl," he'd said.

Luckily, Angie noticed where he'd left them – the records. Just like a man. There they were dumped on the floor in the middle of the passage. With work still being finalised around them, there was every chance of a breakage, so as a safety precaution she moved them.

For most people nowadays, including Angelina, just seeing old long-play records is a novelty. In this case, their content was also unusual. They were all by the same band and, to her surprise, she recognised the name: *'Rabid Revenge'*. *Why this music? Mum's band?* At the time she thought it to be an incredible coincidence, but said nothing to anyone else – it was none of her business...

If she hadn't moved the stack of albums to a safer place at that moment there might not have been any entertainment that evening, and it was these records that sparked the idea. So, before the wedding, they were borrowed from her brother.

Yes, it sure was a surprise for Sam on the big day, hearing the voice booming out from the Registry Office loudspeakers and then recognising it as being that of the woman who was about to become his mother-in-law. Her recorded voice singing, 'Don't put your foot in it this time, Big Boy', as he and Derek walked into the room, shook him a little.

"Is that who I think it is...?" was said out of the corner of his mouth to his best man.

"Could be," was the non-committal response from Derek who had been just as surprised at hearing his mother's voice.

"You got any more surprises? ...*Buddy?*"

This was not the time to protest his innocence, Derek knew, and he couldn't snitch on his new sister, so he just grinned back

"A *cool* Registrar..." he suggested as the bride appeared.

With a smile, beforehand, the Registrar had agreed to Angie's request of a change from the normal type of music. She wanted to have "something a little different". Sam was not consulted prior to that phone call. Well ...it was *her* special day.

Everyone in the room was smiling, including the Registrar, Sam noted, and even though the joke obviously was at his expense, he went along with it and forced a grin, which to the others almost looked real.

The song he recognised, but he had never really listened to the lyrics, lyrics that were making a very belittling job of males. Today, the opportunity to hear the words clearly was unavoidable; he was grateful that it was only a short time before Angelina appeared at his side and the music was faded out.

Although she could see that Sam's smile appeared a bit strained, Angie was delighted at the beaming grin on Mom's face; being her music, she recognised the unique guitar intro immediately and knew exactly what was to follow. There was a slight tinge of modest embarrassment accompanying Mom's grin.

The public procedure to become officially hitched in front of the invited relatives and friends was relatively brief. The couple then left the room to sign forms. The interim entertainment, selected by Angie, continued with another of her mother's hits that began the moment the side door closed. The music wasn't played at the full volume normally used for Rabid Revenge music but it was loud enough to get the feet and fingers, of those left in the room, tapping along and continued until Sam and Angelina emerged as the newly married couple.

Angelina had been very selective in the choices of music. Being a heavy rock band in the seventies, the choice of words for the songs Millie wrote tended to be a bit rough, tough, and sexist – to the detriment of the male species, so Sam this time had re-entered to Millie singing the final chorus of '*Yea, ah luv ya, Baby*'. The timing was perfect to catch the final verse...

"...No, no, ah don't believe in Cupid. Of course I trust ya, or am ah bein' stoopid? Don't you linger with any other, or ah'll break your every finger, Brother... Yea, ah luv ya, Baby..."

Also included at the reception, in the group of Sam's colleagues, was the High School's Administration Officer, Brenda Bothwell – very familiar from Derek's youth, but now as an adult – trouble! What the trouble had been, and how it had affected Derek, was not part of the reminiscing passed on to Sam because, even though it had happened a while ago, it remained a sensitive issue in the Toozlethwaite household.

The presence there of Ms Bothwell made Derek distinctly uncomfortable. Big Brenda, as she was known during his schooldays, was someone who contributed to his marital problems, and therefore was to be avoided – just in case... She claimed it to have been one big joke, but, being all at his expense he failed to see the funny side. It seemed sensible to have very little contact with Brenda at the reception and he had moderate success. Then he noticed Sally delightedly chatting away with her. Incredible! It was as if nothing had ever happened between them – and yet this was the person who...?

Keeping his distance still seemed sensible. He could only conclude that he would never understand women.

What about Sam's side of the family? How many of them were there, or, to put it another way – how many of them weren't? What was noticeable was the dearth of family members attending to support him. In fact, the total count for the Walters' clan, other than Sam himself, amounted to – zero.

Old Grandad Walters stayed in Newingsworth, but he was living in the Newingsworth Nursing Home, and although he was only ten minutes away, there was no chance of an appearance – he was only just living.

The person who might have attended would have been Sam's dad, Theobald Walters: Sailor, as he was known in the days of Rabid Revenge. Sam had no idea where his father was, other than the probability of it being somewhere in the States, so there was little point in attempting to send an invitation. Being an entertainer, his father always tended to rove about, and anyway, they'd lost contact a long while ago. Over the years, they had just drifted apart.

Before the wedding, for his best-man speech, Derek had considered recounting the moment he and Sam first met at Newingsworth High School. There was also a temptation to show everyone an enlarged copy of Sam's photo – the one taken by Hector in Bisko's – to gain a cheap laugh. It showed Sam's wide-eyed shocked stare – caused by Hector's camera flashlight being inches from his nose; it looked funny and was anything but flattering. Would Sam and Grandad laugh with everyone else? Perhaps not... Derek could visualise Grandad slipping under the table in embarrassment, rightly so, of course, because it was his thoughtlessness caused all the trouble – but, public humiliation, was that deserved? No, too unkind, cruel in fact, because Grandad hadn't realised ...so, thinking more about it, exposing these events was wrong.

When it came to the actual day, an amusing 'Honest ...no matter how we behave ...we do like Americans!' speech was what he presented instead. That way, no one was offended, and by the end of the day everyone had had a great time – even Sam.

14

The phone call from Sophie Clerkenwell-Brown came out of the blue. Thankfully her call was to his mobile. The last time, the call arriving on his home phone gave him palpitations because Sally answered, with Mom sitting listening. He felt the palpitations threatening again during this call. There was no-one else around to hear, but that wasn't the problem – it was what she was proposing. She wanted to have a meeting with him – at the New Farmhouse Hotel.

"Are you crazy?" he responded in sudden panic. "That's two minutes along the road from home, and run by Sally's relatives. Obviously I am well known by everyone there, and they'd probably recognise you, and the word would get back to Sally, and..."

"Derek, you panic too easily – relax... I know what I'm doing. We need to talk in more detail about how we are to present this book of yours. Anyway, you can include what happens when we meet as a chapter in your book, if it all works out ok."

"And if it doesn't?" he said fearfully.

"Then it will have been a bit of fun – and there'll be no book!" she laughed.

He didn't feel like laughing. What was she up to? She had a brazen confidence – he knew that for a fact – but to appear in the hotel, run by Sally's Aunt Thelma and Uncle Hamish, what is she thinking of? These were people who'd met her at Anton's when he'd pre-launched the book, and couldn't possibly fail to recognise her ...or 'him'. They surely couldn't fail to see what was going on, and she couldn't possibly pull off the disguise of being Mr Brown again, surely? That would really be chancing it...

But wait – had anyone actually known that it was Sophie that night at the party? No! The odd comment had been made about his publisher, Mr Brown, being a bit effeminate, but they'd seen her and accepted her as being a man with a moustache so, she did get away with it; why not again?

One person did know what was going on ...that was his father-in-law. Alexander was the only person with that knowledge, and he'd sworn, on that bottle of 8-year-old malt whisky Derek gave him as a bribe, that he would keep it to himself.

Derek knew he could trust his father-in-law – implicitly – or rather he hoped he could. What was unsettling was that he could be a real idiot at times. How a clever bank manager could have landed himself in the back of the wrong car and ended up in London – by mistake! If he could create a blunder as big as that, what else he could get up to – by mistake...?

The intelligence of his publisher was being grossly underestimated by Derek however. Sophie could be considerably smarter than he sometimes gave her credit for; some thought had been given by her to a plan, before calling him...

"I will become 'Ms Clerk', who is dear Mr Brown's dedicated old secretary," Sophie told him, and Derek began to feel a bit more calm and confident as she explained how she saw it unfolding.

As far as the world would be concerned, dear Mr Brown had become seriously ill, and wouldn't be able to cope with his work for a while. He'd caught an unidentified virus that made him highly infectious, and he would be quarantined in a private hospital for many months.

This person, good old Mr Brown – being a man of high principles, a man who had to keep a promise, a man who had committed himself to publishing Derek Tee's not-yet-written book – he could not bear the thought of letting this new young author down, certainly not after Derek Tee had been showing so much promise and working so hard to complete his first book. If he let down this young man, Mr Brown was sure that the guilt he would experience would hinder any recovery. Because, unfortunately, he would not be able to follow it through himself, he was therefore passing all responsibility for the project to his extremely capable and trustworthy old secretary,

Ms Clerk. A maiden lady, dedicated to both the publishing industry and to dear Mr Brown, which meant, as a consequence, Ms Clerk had never married...

Derek was impressed!

"You do make Mr Brown sound real," he said admiringly to her, but, he wondered, can you make the about-to-be-generated dear little Ms Clerk appear to be a real old woman.

It was several hours after the phone call that Derek recollected a comment made weeks ago by Sophie. She'd said that he was the one who could make up the stories – she was just a simple publisher with no brain. She'd been lying!

Now he was curious, rather than apprehensive, which was a much more pleasant feeling for a perpetual worrier, curious as to how she would achieve this fantasy. He sincerely hoped she could pull it off, more for his own sake, than for hers.

Becoming slightly plumper by the minute, though healthy and mobile, Sally was still working. It was her choice to carry on at the Gazette for as long as she could.

"Derek..." she shouted from the bedroom, "could you bring in a few more cushions. I can't get comfortable. My back's a bit painful again."

The cushions were taken in and he stood there, looking proudly at his very own sweet wife. Her shape was gradually changing, and he wondered how whale-like she would be in a few months' time, and should they be purchasing more cushions to cope?

Inside that belly, something was getting bigger, and bigger. Both Sally and Derek referred to the content as 'something' because they didn't know yet if it was a boy or a girl. Sally didn't want to know – yet. Daisy was convinced it was twins. That probably should have been disturbing for Derek, but he cared not – whatever was in there – it was his!

As his wife smiled up at him, his conscience tweaked, ever so slightly, but it tweaked nonetheless, because her demand came to mind: "Your publisher must be male!" The stipulation had needed no detail explanation for Derek. He knew, only too well, the previous circumstances...

Sally must not find out who he really is to meet at the hotel tomorrow – that it is very much a female, even though it is for totally innocent reasons to do with the book. If Sally were to find out it was Sophie, it might not be a boy, or a girl, or twins, his wife would present him with, she would have kittens...

"I'm going up to the Hotel tomorrow," he told her, "...to meet with Ms Clerk. That's going to be her name – I mean, that *is* her name; she's Mr Brown's secretary. You've spoken to her haven't you, a couple of times. I believe she is a really *old* dear. Because Mr Brown is not keeping well, his *old* secretary will be up here to talk about the book on his behalf."

"I hope she knows what she's doing, Derek, having to take over from Mr Brown? That's a big responsibility, and another thing, I'm not happy that this *is* a woman, even though she is old. I haven't forgotten your ridiculous behaviour with that Sophie Clerkenwell-Brown. It's even annoying that I can remember *her* name..."

Derek stood, looking straight at her, feeling guilty about telling the lies, but even worse – worried that she could tell. He was right to worry. Even though he didn't know what the give-away signs were when he was lying, Sally had sussed them out. He knew that she knew what gave him away, and any moment she was going to put him on the spot.

"Our 'something' – it moved," she said excitedly, holding the bulge, and giving a long sigh of contentment.

Phew, he thought ...a lucky distraction, or else pregnancy had affected her skill for detection.

"As I was saying, if she is old, she might not be able to do the job." She was wriggling about rearranging the cushions, "But I suppose all she'll be doing is keeping the whole thing moving, even if it is only slowly."

Too many cushions now, so some were tossed off the bed onto the floor... "And, by the way, Mom is back at the hotel. I forgot to say. She phoned earlier today to the office. Her flight will be late and she won't bother popping in here this evening. She'll go straight to the hotel. You'll probably see her when you go up tomorrow. She might even get the chance to meet Ms Clerk. Oh, and I invited Mom back for a meal with us in the evening. She'll be giving me all the news then. She promised. I can't wait..."

15

The following afternoon, Derek did not know what to expect when he entered the hotel reception and bar area. All day he had been repeating the name 'Ms Clerk' in his head. He didn't want to ask for the wrong person, and he certainly didn't want to mention the name Sophie...

Why did she do it this way – abbreviating her own name? Someone will twig surely, although, to get from either Mr Brown, or Ms Clerk, to Sophie Clerkenwell-Brown would probably take a genius – like his wife!

He looked around. Neither Thelma nor Hammy were about. Ah, but there was Mom, sitting on the settee in the corner, chatting to a little lady, older than her; it seemed that Mom just couldn't resist introducing herself and chatting to people.

He went over. "Hello," he said, "I hope I'm not interrupting." He gave a nod of acknowledgement to the little lady sitting with Mom.

"Oh hello, *Sweaty*," Millie said, turning her cheek towards him in expectation of the obligatory kiss, an identical characteristic of his gran, he realised, and he felt obliged. He smiled down at her, bent over and gave her a welcoming peck on the cheek.

"Sally said you were coming up tonight, Sweaty," Mom said. *I wish she wouldn't insist on calling me Sweaty,* "...to see this lady I believe."

"Oh, no, no..." he immediately responded, shaking his head and smiling apologetically to the little old lady.

"...But Ms Clerk told me you were meeting her here," and she turned to the lady beside her, "...didn't you, dear?" and then looked up at Derek with a quizzical expression. "Don't you know each other?" she enquired. Sometimes, for a son who was hers, he could be pretty dumb, she concluded.

"We've only spoken on the phone," piped up little Ms Clerk, struggling to stand up, but failing and falling back onto the seat.

Surely this little grey-haired, frail, frumpy-looking person could not possibly be...

"I am pleased to meet you, after such a long time, Mr Tee," she said.

Derek stood open-mouthed. This time she'd struggled a little harder and succeeded in standing, and was holding out her hand.

"Would it be very cheeky of me to call you ...Derek? We've spoken so often, I feel I know you so well."

"I ...oh, uhmmm..." *Is this really her...?* His face reddened, he felt so guilty, and exposed as he realised he was standing in front of Mom, shaking Sophie's hand, in public... *I must get out of here...* "No, no, of course it would – no, I mean – it wouldn't," stumbled out of his mouth like the idiot he believed he'd suddenly become.

Sophie smiled sweetly up at the face of this quivering wreck in front of her, from whom she would have expected a more professional response, wondering if he was truly capable of ever completing a book...

"...And ...and ...and what do I call you, eh ...Ms Clerk?" He'd almost forgotten her agreed title, as he was afraid he would... "I don't know your first name," eventually followed.

"Ms Clerk would do nicely, young man," she replied graciously. "I like my dealings with Mr Brown's clients, to be kept on a proper formal business-like basis, especially when it is with a handsome young fellow like you, Derek..."

Accompanying that comment with the fluttering of her eyes caught him completely off guard. God, what is she trying to do to me? Making him burn with embarrassment in front of Mom, who in a very short time would be carrying every single word back to Sally...

He was in it up to his armpits – that was for sure, but, wait, he hadn't recognised her, had he? Therefore, why should anyone else? Not surprisingly, he relaxed very slightly. It was not the normally vivacious young blonde who was standing in front of him. This dear old soul, who had grey hair, make-up that looked as if applied by trowel including blusher on her cheeks, was wearing a tweed skirt, a buttoned-up-to-the-neck blouse, half-glasses, which she was peering over, and flat shoes – and that was only for starters. There was a good chance that the skirt had an elasticised waist, too. The handbag she clutched looked like it was made from an old carpet, and her perfume... (he didn't know a lot about these sorts of things) was it Lavender, or maybe Lily of the Valley? Could it be Californian Poppy? Whatever it was, to Derek's nose, it was the smell of very old age. Boy – was she good... If only Alexander could have been here to see this!

Alexander considered himself to be a bit of an actor, his speciality being female parts. Derek thought how jealous he would have been to see the great job done with this outfit and make-up. He could never compete – but he couldn't tell Alexander, now could he? He'd already found out that she'd played the part of Mr Brown, and promised to keep that a secret, but exposing him to Ms Clerk, no, that would be chancing it...

Incredibly, Sophie looked as old as his gran, although his gran was into modern perfumes nowadays.

"You'll have to excuse us, Mrs Schwarz. We have a lot to do," Sophie said primly, "...so I'll have to tear myself away for a while, and talk with this shy young man. I'm here for a few days, so I do hope we will meet again, later, and continue our chat. I was enjoying it so much."

Derek followed Ms Clerk out of the room, "like a little lap dog," is how Mom would detail the story to Sally later.

16

It had been life-changing for many people that night at Anton's, and led to a giant leap forward for 'Rabid Revenge Revisited'. With contributions now in his filing system: from Millie – a new mother, Twister – a new father, Angelina – a new sister, and Sam – a new 'brother', this book was no longer just a story of rock stars: it was rapidly becoming a family saga. It was also very personal and now all about relationships...

Galling when Derek thought of it now ...all that time ago, having met Sam and failing then to be aware that he was Sailor's boy, the American son of one of the blokes he was attempting to research. There he had been, standing right in front of his nose. Some investigative journalist he was! Derek felt foolish at the missed opportunity, but that's the way it goes sometimes...

"Why didn't you tell me when we first met?" Sam had asked Derek that night at Anton's, as all the hidden relatives came out of the woodwork. This was the first he'd learned of Derek's book being about 'Rabid Revenge'. Help could have been available so much sooner. There was a reason, Derek reminded him. On the day they met they had almost come to blows! The face in Grandad's photo ...it was *his* ...remember?

Currently, Sam's boyhood memories were being added to Derek's rapidly expanding notes. It seemed great at the start when Sam remembered travelling about the country with his dad. It was sad though, when he thought more about it and had to tell Derek that he realised he actually knew very little about his father's young days in Newingsworth.

This was not too surprising for Derek. The pattern for the others was much the same it seemed – as if their 'growing-up' wasn't worth remembering.

Information went both ways, and Sam learned from Derek – of his involvement with Jonathan's parents; how Derek had been the one to tell them that Growler, their son, was no longer of this world. Knocked down by a truck in Minnesota, and killed. Sam had known Growler.

And the grandad ...Sam's, still living in Newingsworth, though hearing the news of a surviving relative was spoiled a little by learning that he was in poor health. Alzheimer's wasn't kind to a person. The poor man, I'll have to meet him, and give him some support, was Sam's immediate thought. Must let him know he has family nearby, someone to turn to, he vowed.

Searching for British relatives had never even occurred to him before. Perhaps he should have checked, he thought guiltily, because, the knowledge of his father going to school in Newingsworth was one of the few things he did have. He could have tried to look for family when he arrived but, at the time, his own survival was of greater concern. Arriving in the country, starting at a new school, and encouraging Angie to leave Detroit to join him, had taken up his early days here. Unknown relations had been the least of his worries.

There was no question – he had to visit the old guy.

Angie went along too, for moral support.

"Hi," said Sam, and gave his grandad a gentle hug.

"Hello again," was the reply from the old fellow. "You haven't been here in ages. It's great that you've come. I missed you."

"Hi. I am Angie. It's nice to meet you," she said and gave him a hug and a peck on the cheek.

"Hello again," he said. "It's nice to see you. You haven't been here in ages. It's great that you've come. I missed you."

It shouldn't really have come as a surprise to anyone, least of all to the two visitors, that it would be a struggle to communicate. Sam could make no sense out of the ramblings, pleasant though they were. The best bit of the visit had been watching the enjoyment on

Grandad's face while holding Angie's hand. They proudly told him about the baby being on the way, and he smiled benignly, giving her hand an affectionate little squeeze, not wanting to let go.

They were both feeling emotional as they left him. Grandad Walters had been so happy during the whole visit and had then waved a cheery goodbye as they left. It was a sad fact, unfortunately, that he had not a Scooby-doo as to who they were – the young man and the young lady, the people who had been kind enough to visit him!

Nevertheless, Sam and Angie remembered their visit and felt good about it.

Grandad Walters forgot...

17

Sam was now standing farther up the hill, his gaze sweeping around the countryside. It looked wonderful in the bright sunlight. Who could wish for a more pleasant place to live? The birds darting around in trees which were so fresh and green; leaves fluttering soothingly in the gentle breeze; the lowing of cattle in a distant field.

The warm comfortable sensation in the pit of his stomach confirmed it all for him, yes, life was wonderful, and he was living in the best country in the world!

The two bicycles were lying dumped, unlocked, on the lower part of the slope at the edge of the trees. Leaving them like that, unlocked, in the middle of Newingsworth, according to Derek, would not be at all wise, but out here in the countryside it was different. Anyway, it was unlikely many people would be passing to see them. Being well out of sight of any road traffic, which was sparse about here anyway, there was less chance of them being pinched, but if that did happen, it would be a long walk home...

Stopping for a leak had been essential for both blokes and, neither being the type who took pleasure in obtaining relief in public they deemed this to be a suitable place. It was not the first time Derek had taken a break here but it was the first time since he and Sam became pals, and it was happening on a bright sunny day. This spot was idyllic and Sam was sure to be impressed, Derek convinced himself before they'd even stopped.

Moments earlier, Derek had been standing with his nose roughly two feet away from the trunk of a large ancient tree – his gaze extending no farther than the rough bark, and the small spiders moving quickly within the crevices – when it occurred to him that this was a good moment to ask himself a very pertinent question. *Why? Was he the only one who acted like this?*

It was not a subject he'd discussed with anyone before but, why, when a guy has to go to the toilet in the open air, is it against a tree? Did it make him at one with nature, or was it simply a pretended desire for privacy? Could it be a male thing, a marking of territory, perhaps – *'this tree is mine'*...? It is amazing how philosophical three pints of bitter can make a cyclist...

Sam joined him on the little hillside, and they sat down, side by side, as good pals should be able to do, saying nothing. Derek was tempted ...but didn't ask Sam's opinion about his tree theory.

It was Derek who spoke first though, when the tranquil silence was broken.

"Don't you find it strange ...all this 'about to be a father' thing, because I do? I think women cope better with that sort of thing than us blokes."

"What, at being a father?" Sam responded – the beer could be blamed again.

"No... Anyway, how's Angie getting on?" asked Derek, still finding it odd to have a sister.

"Seems alright," replied Sam, "but did you know they'd challenged each another to see who'd be first to have a little one?"

"Yea, but Sally didn't tell me until afterwards ...long after," said Derek, "after she'd had it confirmed by the doc, and then when she did decide to tell me, it was to say she was going to win a race. She was more delighted telling me she'd be winning, than about telling me she was pregnant!"

"So I knew before you then, but who'd have believed it – a race? Who in their right mind, other than our two, would have agreed to a race to get pregnant? They decided on the night of your party, I was told, and they laughed about it: the very first time they met as relations. I blame strong drink – incredible!"

Silence reigned once more.

"I've never won a race in my whole goddam life," admitted Sam.

"Who'll win this one, do you think?" asked Derek.

"Dead heat?" replied Sam, laconically.

They fell silent again. Sometimes, life seemed simpler if you didn't speak – or think – something to do with three pints of bitter, perhaps...

The partners of Derek and Sam, being five months down the pregnancy path, were avoiding alcohol altogether, as good girls should.

Although Angie and Sam were at last married, along the way Angelina had blown hot and cold on the marriage date. In fact, at one point Sam was convinced that it was all over and that Angie was about to return to Detroit on her own! That she would marry him had been accepted in public at the party; she'd been overcome with emotion then – but she'd taken cold feet immediately after.

At times, Sam could only be bemused by her.

Even though she'd been about to go negative on marriage, she'd secretly chosen to abandon precautions and become pregnant very soon after the party. Not on her own, of course – Sam was involved, but, for him, it was without realising the removal of preventative care, and therefore, the likely consequences. Under the circumstances, if he'd known, his willingness to proceed might have been reduced, but only a little.

After the party Sam was very worried about his relationship with Angie following a serious falling-out with her. As far as work was concerned, having completed successfully the redesign at Anton's, Angie, at a loose end, seemed determined to vanish into a lonely, dark place again.

It was therefore a great relief to him when she suddenly decided 'yes' and they were married. Sam preferred them to be in the wedded state, for the sake of their unborn child, the little girl. They knew the sex of their baby; Angie insisted on a scan, quite the opposite of Sally – Angie had to know.

Thankfully, marriage changed a great deal for Angie and Sam. No longer did she refer to Newingsworth as 'Deadsville'; this was now her home, and with Sam's temporary post having been made permanent, or as permanent as any job ever can be these days, she at long last stopped pining to be back on the other side of the Atlantic.

It helped considerably that Millie came over more and more. It reassured her, Mom being near. Having discovered grandparents that she really liked, who hadn't known she existed – and also finding both Sally and Derek to be great company was making Newingsworth 'different'. It now exuded, for her, a much more welcoming face. She had become part of it rather than a visitor; in fact, she and Sam were settled.

In the States Sam had had the use of Millie's car when he needed one, but buying a car over here was impossible. More correctly, it was decidedly not the way any money earned would be spent. A new house was the target now, still way out of reach but at least an objective to be aiming for. They agreed that making do with Buttercup Avenue was their only option at the moment; hence, Sam started cycling.

"Use my bike for weekends," Sally had said to him. "I'm certainly not going for long runs with Derek now. You don't mind using a girl's bike, do you?"

Sally was still cycling daily to and from work as the roads were fairly level and required the minimum of effort, but even that would not be for much longer, so her bike was lying unused at weekends and available for Sam to use. So Derek and Sam, roaming around together on bikes on Saturday afternoons, were free to enjoy, secretly, liquid refreshment at the distant village pub.

Sally and Angie were bosom buddies, and that contributed to the freedom gained by their spouses. Birth-dates for both girls having been predicted for the same week, Sally and Angelina were progressing through each new stage of body development at almost the same time, giving confidence and support to each other. No question ever needed be left unanswered either because, in moments of doubt, they had a bigger family support group to call on when their own expertise was unable to cope. This group excluded males. Derek and Sam generated their own special name for them: Newingsworth Mafia (Ladies Section).

It was becoming a regular feature at the New Farmhouse Hotel, each Wednesday evening, for the six females to gather for a weekly natter – Sally, Angelina, Thelma, Muriel, Daisy, and Millie. On those evenings, Thelma was glad to take time off, leaving supervision of the staff and care of the hotel to Hammy. Even though she had never been a mother herself and was unlikely ever to become one, her views were thrown into the pot, with everyone else's.

When they were meeting, Hammy was curious. These females were going into the lounge and closing the doors behind them to make sure he couldn't hear what they were talking about, of that he was pretty sure, and he wasn't the only one who was nosey.

Hector and Alexander also were keen to know what was going on, but were having a distinct lack of success at finding out. Daisy was simply dismissing Hector's enquiries, while the most Alexander was getting out of Muriel, if he asked her anything about it, was a sly smile.

There was something afoot ...definitely!

In reality, the secrecy began by accident on the first evening they got together. Thelma had arranged for tea to be brought through to the little group at eight o'clock, and, because the only other staff member on duty was busy at that time, Hammy stepped into the breach and wheeled in the trolley. As he opened the door to the lounge and entered the room, the previously giggling voices went silent. Hammy felt awkward because the silence continued until he left the room. There was a cursory dismissive, "Thank you," shouted by Thelma as he closed the door again, and the giggling restarted. His ears burned.

Though the silence he experienced was a pure coincidence, their having reached a natural break in the chatter, to Hammy it had not appeared that way at all.

"Whit, in the name o' the wee man, urr they up tae?" That was the question. "Jist a wee quick phone call tae Hector, that'll find oot whit's happenin." That was the answer. "He'll know whit it is, ahm sure. Aye, he'll know." ...But he didn't.

The following week, at the meeting, Daisy happened to say how curious Hector had been when she'd left the house that evening, alone, without him. She suspected he still had memories of the days when the secrecy had been vital surrounding her 'Monday' departures – when she'd been Granny Wisdom – especially as he hadn't known at that time. Looking back, it was funny, though he was quite upset; this time, he would have to get over it and stop being so suspicious.

"Why don't we keep it secret from all of them – have our own little secret society?" suggested Muriel, with a smile, "Keep them on tenterhooks?"

Sally and Angie were all for the idea. Thelma had no objections. Daisy decided to go along with it too but felt a touch of discomfort – obviously, Hector hadn't properly healed from the last time...

So, it was agreed. Whatever happened on these Wednesday evenings would not be divulged. The males might get to know who attended, but no more than that.

Although Daisy was the eldest, a gran, and a mother, when they were all together she wanted to be 'one of the girls', so she insisted on being called Daisy. She was unaware that, to Derek and Sam's fevered imaginations, she was no longer just 'Gran'. They awarded her a much grander title; she was '*Big G*' in their eyes, the 'matriarch' – the hard-nosed, stand-no-nonsense, boss of an active branch of the Newingsworth Mafia: Ladies Section. She would have giggled if she had known!

Without the male partners being told why, these 'Mafia' meetings were changed to a Saturday afternoon. There were no complaints from Derek or Sam. With their wives at the meetings, and no questions likely to be asked, they were free to enjoy cycling together and a visit to the pub each week. The other males were desperately inquisitive about the female's meetings; Derek and Sam didn't give a hoot. They simply appreciated the freedom.

It wasn't long before a seventh member was invited to join the female's group. Being a Saturday, it was a non-working day for her and, although she was a spinster of uncertain age and not able to guarantee to attend quite as regularly as the others, it was destined that she would become a welcome addition to the secret society. They all loved to listen to her, when she was there.

The new member was dear little Ms Josephine Clerk. She had worked her way effectively into this tight-knit female group, and was thoroughly enjoying the experience. When Derek and Sam learned this, they joked about her – did she deserve a nickname? In fact, now that they'd started with Gran, what could they come up with for the others?

Beneath the lighthearted banter, this development had Derek greatly worried, a worry he had to keep to himself. It disturbed him because he feared that Sophie was getting too sure of herself. If the truth came out and the others discovered who she really was, it would be he who'd suffer in the end. That thought he could not share with anyone – and it was not funny.

18

Time was against him – the book... The Book, THE BOOK! Derek was pushing himself harder than ever to finalise the words to be committed to print. If only he didn't have to go to the Gazette office each day he could concentrate full time on the blooming thing – if only...

It wouldn't always be like this. One day he would earn a fortune from the brilliant works he would be presenting to a grateful public; hardbacks, paperbacks, eBooks, audio, extrasensory perception, you name it – whatever manner he would be using to communicate to the world, at that particular time, would be selling by the millions. Then he would be requested to adapt his work for television – no, the big screen; nothing was impossible. He could visualise it so easily; even eBay would be chock-a-block with his words being regurgitated to clamouring fans ...and, he wouldn't have to work!

Now, *that* was the art of positive thinking, when he hadn't had even his first struggling attempt published. Yes, it was a supremely egotistical and totally unrealistic thought, but essential if he was to retain some confidence in his own ability to achieve the near impossible.

Obviously, he had to continue earning real money, and his only obvious source, for which he was extremely grateful, was the Gazette. Sally would stop working eventually. He was soon to be a father. Although she said she wanted to go on as long as she could, she was beginning to look forward to having the baby; there was even a suggestion about becoming a permanent stay-at-home mum, and if so, a valuable source of income was about to dry up. It would be wise if he remained employed.

As for the book! Desperation was setting in and, though many chapters were nearly there, none was completed and, annoyingly, more ideas kept forming, ideas that he wanted to incorporate before editing a final version.

And now – Sophie was demanding a date.

At least he knew where it was all heading, at long last. The vast amount of factual information and his rambling thoughts were now capable of being grouped together to form a nearly-finalised book.

The band's early days obviously gave him an introduction. Though he was lacking firm facts for this, with some inventive and imaginative 'padding', their 'Happy Years at School' had been created. He was quite relaxed about this part. Neither Millie, nor Twister, could remember much about what actually happened back then, and only old Duckett remained of the teaching staff from that period of learning, so Derek gave himself total freedom to invent some novel and hilariously outlandish school-day incidents. Surely the fiction was unlikely to be questioned by anyone, he told himself.

The story would be balanced by highs and lows. It would toy with the emotions of his readers ...*the work of a craftsman*, he told himself modestly.

The tears would be guaranteed to flow in the second section, Derek predicted, because he'd made the most of the 'abandoned baby' theme: the sad dilemma of a mother torn between fame and fortune, and the sobbing child she was leaving in the arms of a forlorn grandmother. He felt a bit sorry for himself as he composed this part, even though he was too young to remember. Daisy didn't care what he actually wrote so he had a fairly free hand there too. "Just get on with it," Gran had said. Though his childhood with his grandparents had not been perfect it was as good as all his pals, but he couldn't write that! With a surge of imagination, all the sufferings he could conjure up were heaped together into one big stack of lies...

Editing of the 'early successful years' of Rabid Revenge required a bit more care than the previous sections; the two main protagonists were feeding him the facts. A conflict was brewing, between what was being fed by Twister, and the memories carried over the intervening period by Millie. Some bitterness was creeping in and some reaction would be inevitable – Derek was fairly sure about that. He would have to cross his fingers that he had struck a balance that could be considered nearly acceptable. Time would tell.

For the next part, Twister being the only person supplying him with stories for the long period after Millie left the band, there was no-one to contradict his version. This made selecting the words to use so much easier. The sarcasm, the bitterness, and the obvious bad feeling that Twister carried from those days, was being reflected in what he was feeding to Derek. Therefore, Derek was forced to tread a careful line – selecting only parts that made the band appear to be a cohesive, happy unit.

Was Twister exaggerating the conflict? It surely couldn't have been so bleak an experience – but, he was the one who'd been there, so how could Derek dispute the facts he'd been given? All he could do was distort them a little – make them more pleasant reading – and hope Twister didn't notice.

For the grand finale, Derek himself was the hero, and this was more enjoyable to manipulate. He was proudly stating that in the process of his search, 'he had pulled the family together'. It was he who would shine in the final section. He wavered in his choice of pictures showing himself. Eventually one from the YouTube video was included: the one where he wore the plastic nose and glasses, but so that there would be no mistake, emphasis was made in the text that 'he was using artificial aids!'

Interspersed throughout the book would be a grand selection of photographs of the band: some from the newspapers, others retrieved from drawers and cupboards by Millie and Twister. Pictures of family members through the ages would also be included.

Derek discovered one that had been taken of him by Grandad, shortly after he'd been misbehaving. Gran had been giving him a telling-off for breaking the window, and he remembered the moment quite clearly. This image, the tear-stained face and the hang-dog demeanour, was perfect to add to the pathos of the second section – his supposed dreadful childhood.

Wisely, the now infamous photo of Sam taken by Hector in Bisko's, was excluded.

Enough was enough. After a highly successful evening's work, it was time to forget all about the book, its end almost in sight – he'd cracked it! He could concentrate now on the final stage of his going-to-bed routine: brushing of teeth. Feeling weary and sleepy...

The phone-call!

How could he have forgotten?

He was wide-awake again (Mabel to be thanked for the inbuilt alarm) because, suddenly remembered, was an earlier conversation today – and her question. It was only a smidgen of an idea admittedly, but it could mean the reconciliation of Mom with his reluctant father.

In the process of a few more Rabid Revenge details being elicited by phone from her, Mabel had asked why he couldn't bring them together again. Wouldn't it be a victory for true love and romance if he succeeded, she'd said? He'd agreed that somewhere deep down they must have feelings for each other, and there could be a bonus if it did work out – another heartfelt chapter to the book – and you can't beat a happy ending, can you? Then another question was asked, simple enough, to a son about his mother.

"Does Millie still sing, Derek?"

He had no idea – but at least, he had a substantial excuse for his ignorance – a gap of over thirty-plus years in the relationship.

An established fact was that Millie had been a very able singer when young, but that was thirty-odd years ago: famous all over USA, singing and performing, and with a renowned reputation as the writer of many of the successful songs the band had used. Derek had never asked the question, could she *still* sing?

Twister demonstrated at the party that he was still a capable all-round entertainer, in fact, he was very competent. On party night, unfortunately, he was cut off in his prime but he had proved he could still perform.

Could Mom do it too? Did she still write songs, he wondered, though styles change? Back then, she'd been young, a girl – a rock singer with a hard edge to her voice, almost brazen in fact. Now older, a mature woman and, Derek realised uncomfortably, she still sounded brazen...

He had become very familiar with his mother's younger recorded voice. All of Rabid Revenge's LPs, the ones he'd been given by Mr and Mrs Jones, had been listened to with rapt attention. The songs she'd sung, and the other hits they'd had after she'd left, had been played so many times that Derek almost knew them all off by heart, but those words would not sound right coming from Mom's mouth now.

Their music was now on his mobile, and on his PC, thanks to the modern equipment they had at the Newingsworth Bowling Club. The original albums, vinyl and in their original covers, donated to him by Jonathan T Jones' parents, sat on the shelf, prized, but now only decoration.

His conscience would not let him forget once having 'borrowed' an album; 'pinched' was nearer the truth. The tracks on that album were played less often, because thinking about what he did made him queasy. Thankfully it was Sadie who was the singer on those, and not Mom, therefore played only rarely.

They really shouldn't have forgiven him; he didn't deserve the way they'd reacted. Though he hadn't seen them since the party, even thinking about Growler's parents made his ears start to burn. It had been one of the darker moments of Derek's life ...but look at the time! At this time of night he shouldn't really be thinking about anything other than completing the book. Actually, he should be thinking only of sleep – but the possibility of bringing Mom and Twister together was intriguing.

What if he succeeded? What if Mom could make a comeback? What if she wrote some new material, and had her ex-lover Twister help with the marketing of the results; he must have contacts in the record industry. What if he was able to pull a few strings – and then they got together to sing a duet? Yes, what if Mom and Twister sang together – a love song?

Perhaps his thoughts were becoming a bit too fanciful... It might have been a promising idea except it was rather obvious that they couldn't stand the sight of each other – but they could still record duets.

In his head Derek was becoming determined to make it work. They wouldn't have to be together if it was organised correctly. It wouldn't be the first time singers have recorded duets without being face to face, or even in the same recording studio. In fact, didn't someone once record something with her long-dead dad? Natalie Cole it was... He remembered his gran at the time saying how wonderful that record was. Nat King Cole had been a favourite of hers. So, on that basis might it be wise to record Twister's tracks first, so that if Millie was successful in bumping him off, like she'd already attempted, the recording as a duet could still be made to work? Think of the publicity from that!

Maybe through time they could be encouraged to get along – with his help. What if they were to start performing together again, build a new band – with young instrumentalists backing them? Twister could play guitar, Millie would do the vocals, and write the material. I suppose I could produce; wouldn't go on tour with them, well not until after Sally has the baby. I could probably write some songs myself...

"Derek!" Sally shouted from the bedroom. "Are you coming to bed?"

What? He looked at his hand. It was still holding his toothbrush with the little morsel of toothpaste waiting, ready for him.

"Do you see the time?"

"Yes, sorry..."

"Are you forgetting I'm pregnant and need my beauty sleep?"

"No, sorry..."

"I'll just be dropping off – then you'll come in and waken me, as usual... DEREK!"

He shook himself. "I mean, yes ...sorry, on my way ...sorry..." The final shout startled him. He'd been drifting off into a dream again, he realised, fantasising and replying on auto-pilot: almost asleep, standing in the bathroom, gazing in the mirror.

Anyway, these were silly ideas. Neither of his parents would be in the least interested in ever seeing each other again. That was pretty clear, but what if...? And he was wide awake again! *Maybe, if I have a word with Curly; he is always interested in new ideas for LITTLE RADIO fm, isn't he? He is a good mate; he listened the last time. I could probably win him over again...*

Something practical was forming in his mind: Granny Wisdom as the narrator could do a radio series about the group, yes... People loved Granny Wisdom, and with Rabid Revenge's roots having been in Newingsworth, it was a programme crying out for local radio. You can't beat the local link...

There would be no sleep tonight – he could tell – he'd have to straighten out his thoughts ...and if Millie and Twister were live, in the studio, on separate weeks, they wouldn't have to meet each other, and all would be well...

And it would be more publicity for the book.

19

The phone call from Sophie was taken at work in the Gazette Office on Monday. Fortunately it was lunchtime, and thankfully, Derek was the only person in the office. She wanted a meeting with him. It would have to be face to face, she insisted, and he would have to present her with all the work that was intended to make up the content of his masterly tome, that is, if they were to be continuing with the project. Her director was putting Sophie under pressure.

So, the big push was on. A final deadline must be set. Meeting on Wednesday!

It is called the *Torrid Hedgehog* Inn, and, for donkey's years outside the entrance, the original hand-painted sign has been swinging and squeaking continuously when there is a breeze. It is an annoying noise if you are hearing it for the first time, but the residents of the pub have become so used to it that it would be missed if the squeak ever stopped!

On the sign is displayed the emblem of the establishment – an angry little hedgehog with, instead of spikes on its back, flames. It is obviously a well-cared-for sign, which will last for many more years; well worth the few free pints the landlord supplies to the local artist who occasionally is called-on to freshen the paintwork.

This pub has low ceilings, and dull lighting, and surfaces that look as if the duster is an unwelcome visitor – except for the bar. There could be no complaint on that score, the bar is spotless, with the pumps gleaming; supplying beers well worth returning for – each week if you come from afar, and daily if you are a local. They serve good pub-grub too.

For many weeks now it had been the habit of Derek and Sam to visit this pub – but only on Saturdays, so, as the meeting is planned for Wednesday lunchtime, he won't be bumping into Sam when he sees Sophie here; Monday to Friday, during the day, Sam will be teaching at the High School.

There can be no chance of being seen by anyone who knows them – it will be safe...

On Tuesday evening, Derek explained to Sally that he would be meeting little old Ms Josephine Clerk for lunch the following day.

"Where are you going to eat?" his wife asked innocently, and the little white lie tripped off his tongue, oh so easily...

"Don't know," he replied. "She said she knew somewhere, and would pick me up in her car at the end of the lane, late morning."

No further comment came from Sally. She wasn't questioning him more? Now that was strange, he thought... Why? Was he becoming more of an expert at telling fibs? Could he be hiding the warning signs more effectively because Sally had actually accepted what he'd said without question? Either he'd stopped displaying the giveaways that she'd been able to see in the past, or pregnancy was having an effect on her sensory capabilities.

In preparation for the following day, he had packed into folders hard copies of the material needed. It was all in draft form, double-spaced and single-sided, amounting to a great deal of paper. The scribbled notes would also be taken, just in case, as well as copies of the various photos that he would like to use. These would be sifted through, he knew, whittled down to an appropriate amount to suit the editorial style, no doubt. He also added a couple of spare packs of paper in case there was a need to rearrange the whole thing. All was then placed in a large cardboard box, a box that he barely managed to carry to the hallway of the cottage. He hoped it wouldn't rain. Meeting Sophie at the main road meant this heavy box would have to be carried for the length of the lane.

The destination of the out-of-the-way country pub was his choice – The *Torrid Hedgehog*, the Saturday cycling venue, of which neither Sally, nor Angelina, was aware; a secret their spouses had somehow successfully kept from them.

However, when Sally said she was ambivalent about going to work tomorrow, wondering whether she would be feeling well enough, Derek had a panicky flutter, very disturbed to hear that. Sadly, the cause was not concern for Sally's pregnant state or that she was feeling out of sorts, oh no, it was because she might spot him with someone who didn't look like a little old lady! Ms Josephine Clerk would be meeting him in 'plain clothes'; that is what had been said and it meant she'd have no disguise for this outing, so, he would be in the company of an easily recognisable Sophie.

After all the panic, Sally was well enough to go to work, so it was a much relieved Derek who cycled back home to the cottage late on Wednesday morning, leaving his wife at her desk in the Gazette Office, far away. He was in a hurry because he wanted to change and have a shower to freshen up before meeting Sophie.

Last night he had hoped that it would be dry when he carried the filled cardboard container the length of the lane. However his initial pleasure at the rain staying away was tempered by the fact it was a sunny day, a very warm, sunny day. He'd freshened up as planned but, by the time he carried the heavy box for the length of the lane in the hot mid-day sunshine, he felt exceedingly clammy and it was obvious the shower had been a waste of time.

Sophie arrived as arranged, in her smart little car – looking absolutely ravishing. On her, plain clothes were anything but plain – tight mini-skirt, tight blouse with plunging front, long fine-gold chain around her neck that tantalisingly vanished into the cleavage, high heels, and full war-paint – although she probably would claim it was make-up. Being an open-topped car, her blonde hair was carefully protected beneath a gent's dog-toothed cloth cap.

It was a low-seated sports car, and he was to sit beside her. He would have to try hard to ignore the legs that were displayed so well when she sat snugly at the wheel in the bucket seat. They would be travelling on the same road to Little Typington that he and Sam used each Saturday. For the two males, once a week, it was a journey that they both appreciated, full of admiration for the delightful scenery surrounding them as they pedalled along.

Today, Derek tried to force himself to look at the same scenery with the same wonderment – but with better things to look at, he failed miserably.

20

To slip into the pub with his cardboard box of paperwork, and have a meal and do some serious work – without being noticed by the landlord, or the locals – was really what Derek was hoping for. Wouldn't it be terrible if any word of this secret meeting with Sophie got out – he would be back here with Sam on Saturday! He struggled through the double swing-doors carrying the large cardboard box, feeling incredibly self-conscious. For the regulars of this pub it was an unusual occurrence: the sort of thing that sticks in people's minds. They would all be curious to know the contents of the box.

He needn't have worried, because, in truth, no-one even glanced in his direction – every eye was on Sophie!

He ordered drinks, with Sophie very sensibly going for the soft stuff. Glad to be a passenger, today he could choose alcohol; he needed something to help him relax a little. Hot food was selected and ordered from the landlord and, while they waited for it, he removed his book from the box section by section, spreading them over the table as Sophie's scrutiny began.

It was a relief to hear her say that she was impressed. Of course, every detail wasn't being considered, but it looked as if it would all be moving forward satisfactorily.

After they'd been working for a while, Derek was able to relax a little and glance around the large room. Surprisingly, to a great extent, the spectacular appearance of Sophie had apparently been forgotten by the regulars. Personal concerns of beer, food, and the day's gossip seemed to have overtaken the earlier interesting entrance, although one person was continuing to throw an admiring glance or two in Sophie's direction: the gentleman at the bar, the landlord.

Coming in with Sam started many weeks ago, on Saturdays, but Derek still felt like a newcomer in a close-knit small community. Both had made a point of speaking to the landlord, but he wasn't the friendliest of persons – towards them anyway – and hadn't chatted freely. Derek was relying on that continuing. Surely, he wouldn't comment about his companion to Sam? Derek realised that an explanation would be needed if he did.

He would have to think of something innocuous, but credible, to tell Sam – but that could come later. There was a lot of work to get through now, so they kept ploughing away, reviewing and selecting the various parts. Sophie used a magic marker extensively, but in a positive manner, rearranging to create more impact. She seemed to know what she was doing.

When the hot food was delivered, space was cleared for the plates to be laid on the table, but having food didn't stop them. With dedication the work went on, shuffling the paper around while trying to avoid too many food stains getting on the valuable work.

The standard of photos, being from newspaper cuttings in some cases, was questionable for reproduction, but there were plenty to choose from, so, in the end, sufficient were deemed suitable. 'Rabid Revenge' would be displayed to their advantage.

By the time they'd eaten, the plates cleared away, and the meal rounded off with coffee, most of the tasks had been completed. Agreement had been reached on the choice of material to tell Derek's tale, though the sequencing of the information and titles for chapters had been revised with many parts reduced and others parts filled out a little. In conclusion, the work he'd done to date, although not yet completed, had reached the stage where a final date could now be considered.

Derek's head was spinning – time for a break! "I'll have to visit the little boy's room," he felt obliged to announce at that point, the tension of the occasion having an effect on his bladder – and two pints of lager with the meal no doubt contributing to his need. Today, the normal routine when with Sam – taking a leak in the woods on the way home – was not an option, so he excused himself and stood up to go the pub's toilet.

That was when he heard the distinctive *phut-phut-phut* of a scooter. It had obviously come to a halt and parked just outside. He smiled to himself. Grandad's sounded just like that, but, of course all scooters sounded the same – pathetic compared to the *vroom-vroom* of Sophie's little sports car.

As he turned, through the dusty window he caught a glimpse of two people dismounting. They were removing their crash helmets, and carefully balancing them on the seat. It was only a casual glance, but then... Oh! No...!

It was Gran's coat he recognised first, then Grandad's balding head. They were about to enter the pub and, not surprisingly, he panicked! He didn't have time to go back to say to Sophie what was happening. He was outside the Gent's and they were about to come in the front door so he hurried into the washroom wondering if he could jam the door shut so that no-one else would get in. Don't come in here! He growled silently but fiercely through gritted teeth at his grandad, He was swithering about saying a prayer as well...

A quick check that the cubicles were empty, then he risked opening the door a crack and peeping out. His grandparents had chosen to sit at the table across from where he'd been, where Sophie was still sitting, and who, as usual, was showing as much leg as was barely decent.

"Oh God..." he whispered to himself, "...will they recognise her?"

Of course not, he quickly realised. They couldn't possibly know her as Sophie. Neither of them had ever met her as herself. The only time they'd all been together was at the party when she was Mr Brown – with a moustache. These factors did little to relax him because he knew very well that his gran was not exactly dumb.

Sophie didn't appear to have noticed them. How will *she* react when she looks up and they see each other – that was the question! Any moment she was bound to. Only last Saturday she would have been sitting chatting to Daisy, face to face at the Ladies Mafia – but then she was little old Ms Josephine Clerk, of course!

Derek could see his grandad quite clearly. The dirty devil – he's eying Sophie up and down. Then he heard his gran's voice say one word, which could be seen to be instantly effective.

"Hector!"

It was all that was needed – Grandad got the message immediately.

"Did you say something, Daisy?" he asked innocently...

Hearing the sharp reprimand from across the narrow passage caused Sophie to look up from the notes she was reading and to glance over at the man at the other table. That was out of habit. Sophie had always been more interested in males. A smile still lingered on the man's face. She wasn't sure, but he seemed familiar.

As she sat waiting for Derek to return she tried to recollect why she might think that she knew him, but no... She'd no idea. She met so many people, sometimes for only a short time, so it was not too unusual for her to fail to get an immediate link. Anyway, where was Derek? And then she glanced at the man's companion...

Hell's Bells! It's Daisy!

Twenty minutes later, Derek was still peering out of the door, with his foot jammed against it in case anyone dared to try and enter, and he could see that Sophie was getting anxious. He had been away a long while.

For all that time Sophie had kept her eyes averted from Daisy, feeling that she was about to be identified at any moment and there was nothing she could do about it. Recognising Daisy had instantly tuned her mind back to the party, the night at Anton's where she'd met Derek's grandad. *Where the hell is Derek, leaving me like this?* There was a sudden realisation of how long he'd been gone. Has something happened to him, she wondered? Does he know who I am sitting beside? She was getting more and more agitated. She'd have to move...

She stood and crossed the room towards the Ladies' Toilet, which was the next door along from the Gent's. As she passed, it gave Derek his one chance.

"Psssssst..."

She turned towards the sound – his nose could just be seen.

"Sophie, could you take the box out to the car," he hissed. "I can't come back out through this door again. I'll have to leave by the window."

"What? But I can't..." she started to hiss back at him, and then noticed the landlord giving her a funny look.

"I'll explain in the car," Derek hissed again, and the door to the Gents' was closed.

She dreaded to think what had caused this. I can't come out, he'd said. Had he had an accident? Selfishly, her thoughts concerned the return journey, and what she could do to protect her good car seats...

Sophie went back to the table. The heavy box, since repacked by her while she patiently waited Derek's return, was sitting on one of the chairs. This box contained all of Derek's valuable paperwork, with the alterations they'd discussed and agreed, all vital for the book.

It was very heavy – she couldn't possibly carry it. Should she just abandon it?

No, it couldn't be left behind – that would be cruel. Derek would never forgive her. So, she started to try and lift it, under her breath cursing Derek – and her tight skirt. As she wriggled it up a little to permit some easier leg movement she heard a name being said once again, behind her at the table opposite.

"Hector...!"

"But it is a h-h-h-h-h-heavy b-b-b-b-box," came the response from Hector to his lady.

"It's not the box you're looking at, is it?"

Those words were spat out in a very caustic manner, Sophie thought. By the tone of Daisy's voice poor Hector must be getting close to a final warning. Please don't recognise me Daisy, was Sophie's silent desire, and please don't look at me as if I am trying to steal your husband!

Earlier she had been almost unaware of the pub clientele sitting around them; the visit had been going so well, until now. She and Derek had been concentrating and totally absorbed in the concerns of his book; now, the clientele was the only thing she could think of, particularly her two closest neighbours.

How the hell had Derek managed to have an accident in the toilet, especially when there was a ruddy big box like this to have to carry out to the...?

"C-c-can I h-h-h-h-h-help you with th-th-th-that?" asked the voice behind her, and it was Hector.

"I'd certainly appreciate it, if you would," she said, and gave him a grateful smile.

She knew she attracted attention almost everywhere she went, but she'd become hardened to it. It was not unusual for a male to want to be the knight in shining armour when she appeared to have any awkward moments, but this knight beside her offering his assistance today was a little past it!

Still, Hector insisted, and she didn't stop him as he took one end of the box and she took the other, and they made their way towards the door. The sweet smile Sophie gave Daisy in passing only managed to elicit a glare in response, but it wasn't of recognition...

"It is v-very h-h-h-h-heavy. I p-p-p-presume someone c-c-c-carried it in f-f-f-for you?"

Save your breath old fellow, she thought, or we'll never make it to the car. Having Derek's grandad collapse in a heap in front of her was not a pleasant thought and could start to make life more complicated.

"Yes," she replied, managing to restrain herself from explaining it had actually been his grandson who'd brought it inwards. The mood she was now in, she was tempted to land Derek in it – how dare he make me look so ridiculous – but instead, she thanked Hector profusely for being such a gentleman.

"Not many about nowadays," she added.

Hector could only give a weak smile at that, as he struggled to straighten. It felt as if he'd done himself an injury. His back – pain! His mind went ahead. What would Daisy say if he mentioned it when he returned to the table? It was clear that to receive sympathy for acquiring a strained muscle in these circumstances was extremely unlikely; in fact, to suffer in silence would be very wise.

Moments before, Derek managed with difficulty to clamber out of the toilet via a very small window. He was hidden round the corner as Sophie and Hector appeared. After his grandad left, he was about to step out and join Sophie who was now opening the car door, when another figure came out from the back door of the inn.

"Oy...! You!"

It was the landlord.

"Are you trying to dodge paying, Missie?" he shouted at Sophie. Derek dodged back around the corner.

When he eventually joined her, it was an extremely embarrassed and irate Sophie sitting at the wheel, revving the engine fiercely, having stumped up the money for the bill.

Derek was lucky to get in!

He had barely closed the door seconds before she accelerated out of the car park. She would have left him behind if he hadn't jumped in quickly – he was almost sure of that, although he hoped he was wrong – but he wasn't...

Sophie drove back in a hostile silence, furious at Derek's behaviour, but also, for the duration of the journey, worrying about what state the seat would be in, after her passenger left!

Derek just sat there, gloomily hoping that the landlord wouldn't remember him.

21

"For heaven's sake, Derek, what are they up to? Do you know? Have they told you?"

This was Alexander. His blustering query was the result of sitting at his desk in the Bank, at a loose end, ruminating during free time caused by the last minute cancellation of an account-holder's appointment. For the previous half-hour he had let unconfirmed suspicions about his wife disturb him until he could handle it no longer, hence this phone call to Derek at the office.

"Alexander, you are tending to ask me some very vague questions, and rather too regularly," was Derek's response, "...and it would help if you were to tell me who we are talking about?"

"My Muriel, of course, and your wife, and your sister, and my sister, and your mother, and your grandmother, and that Josephine ...Thingy ...whatsername? Your doddery publisher woman? Do you want me to go on?"

"Why? What's the problem?"

"It's like a secret society. I can't get any information out of Muriel about what they talk about or what they get up to, and I feel I ought to know. Have you asked Sally?"

"No. I don't want to rock the boat. I am just pleased that she hasn't complained when Sam and I escape on a Saturday afternoon together to have a few..."

Derek stopped.

"A few what's?" asked his father-in-law, suspecting that there was something he was missing out on...

"A few drinks if you must know. We found a great pub, which sells local real ale and we go there on the bikes. It's great. No-one ever bothers us and we can do whatever we like – but Sally and Angelina don't know that."

"That's a bit selfish, just the two of you? Why haven't you invited me? Anyway, it looks as if the girls have formed a secret society, and we are excluded, so I suggest that we males form one of our own."

"Oh, so what you are really saying is – you want to join us on Saturday afternoons." *Trust me and my big mouth,* Derek silently thought.

"But of course, and I'm sure there are others who would be delighted to get some fresh air with us," continued Alexander.

Oh, oh... This was progressing the wrong way.

"...Such as?"

"Well there's Hector and Hammy, then there's your colleague, Spider, he rides a bike doesn't he?"

"Well, Spider – yes, he could do it; he's young and fit, but Grandad and Hammy? It's nearly fifteen miles each way to that pub, you know."

"Well, Hector and Hammy could go on the scooter. Hector would be pleased to do that, I'm sure. He likes to be out and about, and as Daisy will be with the other girls – she won't be there to stop the old guy."

"Oh, I don't know..."

"Just ask them. You'll see. You can let me know later what time we're starting and where we'll be meeting, once you have sorted it all out."

And at that, the call was over.

Rob was having a day off – to look after the children. They were on holiday today, but it clashed with his wife's outing with her old school pals, so Rob had been told yet again, it was his problem...

This was not an unusual occurrence in the life of Rob and Elizabeth Sheldon. He might be the one who earned the pennies in their house, but Elizabeth was the one who manipulated the rules, and in a manner very much to suit herself.

She was a loving mother but, when a school holiday fell on a day that she had arranged for something special (like meeting her friends, or a day out to the big city), having failed to mark the calendar to show the boys at home on that day, their care was always laid in the lap of her husband.

He suspected that for this holiday he *had* marked it – but stupidly used a pencil. His wife had rubbed it out, so, one thing was certain, next time he noted it down, he would use a biro...

Rob wasn't stupid though. In the past, when this sort of unexpected event occurred, there was always someone to save the day for him. The person who had always allowed him to dodge responsibility for his two unruly boys had been the wonderful Sally, but Sally wasn't in the office now – pregnancy. So, for the months ahead and until she returned, he would have no choice but to take the day off and play the doting father to his two unruly monsters.

"I must remember to check the calendar more often," he muttered to himself.

Today, without Rob, there were still three individuals in the Gazette office. Sally's replacement had moved in. Sitting at her desk was the new female. Her name was Christine. She'd previously worked in the building's Main Reception, downstairs, a job she'd held for many years. Standing-in for Sally on a temporary basis had happened on the few occasions when Sally was absent through illness. Short stays previously, but it would be for a bit longer this time. Christine was to be here until Sally's maternity leave ended. In the meantime, someone temporary had been taken on to do her job downstairs.

Derek reckoned Christine was about the same age as Muriel, Sally's mum, so there was a different atmosphere in the office now. She was very capable and picked up her new tasks quickly, but she was excessively motherly in Derek's opinion – and nosy.

From the start, Spider didn't like her much, but she liked Spider. "He's not married is he, Derek?" she asked, with a knowing look in Spider's direction on the day she moved in.

Being a bit older than Derek, Spider was not young, and, so far, a confirmed bachelor. Christine was about twelve years older than him. Derek jokingly told Spider about the interest Christine was showing and how she fancied him, and then with a straight face, that she was targeting him as her toy-boy.

Spider didn't find it funny – he had seen the signals himself and was afraid it could be true.

He would be a big softie and unable to protect himself if she came on to him, Derek suspected, so, to give his friend and colleague some protection Derek suggested that between them they should infer that Spider was 'taken'. If it would help, Derek offered to create a fictitious fiancé for him. Having another female already in the background surely would warn Christine off. Whatever Spider wanted this conjured-up lover to be – he could have. That was Derek's generous offer, and when he added, "I'll put the frills to the story," Spider jumped at the idea...

With his long-term interest in horse racing, it was inevitable that his 'dream girl' would be the daughter of a highly successful racehorse owner. She would live in a mansion in the country, and be much younger than he was, but madly in love with him. Her name would be 'Penelope' – which coincidentally happened to be the name of the horse that he considered to be a cert for the 2.00 o'clock at Kempton Park – and *she* was a beauty. Somehow, the way the thoughts tumbled out of Spider's mouth it didn't seem to Derek that this vision was conjured up on the spur of the moment!

Derek contributed that she also should be insanely jealous, verging on the homicidal, and willing to take on any other female who might dare to threaten the beautiful relationship.

Drip-feeding the story into office gossip would be Derek's task.

For a full week, Spider's secret life, and his deep love of 'Penelope', was fed to Christine in daily instalments by Derek at the tea break. Christine, poor soul, thought she was being very clever wheedling this information out of him...

Derek let her have the full works: how Spider first met sweet little Penelope at nursery school, and how they fought over whose turn it was on the wooden rocking horse, until the beautiful moment – the first time they rode the wooden rocking horse, *together*. That had been followed by their first shared cigarette – aged four and a half ... Then the sad bit: Penelope having been sent to school in Switzerland.

Dreadfully painful for Spider, especially as this occurred at the same time that his parent's had won the Irish Sweepstake – and then split up over a disagreement about the 'winnings'. That's when poor little Spider was abandoned to a life 'In Care'. His good fortune at meeting Penelope again was when she came in to place a bet at 'Saddanbroke's the Bookmakers', where Spider used to work. Finally, the story brought bang up to date: falling madly and passionately in love once again even though her father forbade it and how their love continued to bind them resolutely, together, *forever*.

Of course, he had to be careful to keep Spider informed of the tales he was telling – sometimes inspiration caused him to get carried away. Christine had to swear not to let Spider know that Derek had divulged his carefully guarded secret life, and, that Penelope must never get to know what Christine now had been told, because, who knows how she might react.

Christine left Spider alone after that.

As the week progressed, and due of course to the wafer-thin walls of the office, everything that was told to Christine was overheard by Rob. He was amazed to learn about Spider's background. This was stuff that had never before been mentioned about him. He passed on this information to Elizabeth, his wife, and both treated Spider quite differently from then on.

Rob suspected that this was the reason for his excellent knowledge of the sport of horse racing – insider information for betting was always good for a few pounds. As it was, Spider became appreciated a great deal more, and, as you would expect for an affair of the heart, his love for 'Penelope' remained a secret!

As far as Christine was concerned, romance between her and Spider was to be a non-starter. She would have to settle for remaining motherly towards them all – but it wouldn't stop her being nosy.

"How do you fancy joining us on the bikes at the weekend, Spider?" Derek asked, after the phone call from Alexander. "Are you free to go for a run on Saturday afternoons?"

"Oh – haven't been on the bike for weeks. Might be a bit stiff, but yea, I'll be there."

"I am a bit of a cyclist too..." chipped in Christine.

"That's nice," was all that came back from Derek and Spider.

"There could be a few of us, but I'll have to phone first to check," Derek said to Spider.

"I could be free at the weekend..." offered the once-again-ignored-female voice.

Alexander had suggested Hector would want to come along too, so Derek phoned Blytheton Road, and it was Gran who answered.

"How's Sally doing?" was her first question.

"Fine," Derek replied.

"Did you buy the cot, then?"

"Buy a cot? I didn't know we'd chosen one..."

"Well, you didn't, but we all agreed that the one Bisko's had on special offer, this week, would be perfect – big enough for twins... It was blue, too. Sam will be getting the same instruction – Muriel can get a special arrangement just now on that sort of stuff – ten per cent off."

"Oh..." was all Derek could manage.

He'd already been told by Sally that Daisy informed her, not only that she was carrying twins, but they would both be boys! Muriel had gone along with the 'twins' diagnosis, but was pretty sure it was to be a boy *and* a girl – to do with the shape of the bump apparently!

It sounded as if the Newingsworth Mafia, Ladies Section, was in control of proceedings and that neither he nor Sam would be having much choice in many matters. As Alexander said, it also seemed like things were being discussed by the wrong people, secretly.

Derek had suggested to Sally that it would be wiser for her to go for the scan and find out with a little more technical certainty what the future would be bringing, but that simply elicited a dismissive response, 'Oh no, no, no, Derek, don't be silly...'

"Maybe I wasn't listening when Sally told me, Gran. I didn't know it had all been decided ...but look, I'm at work just now. May I speak to Grandad, please?"

The phone at Blytheton Road was laid on the table as she went to fetch him from the shed. He was cleaning his scooter.

"H-h-h-hello D-D-D-D-D-Derek."

"Hi Grandad, would you like to join us on a bike ride on Saturday afternoon?"

"How f-f-f-f-f-f-far is it?"

"Up to about thirty miles."

"What?" came back loud and clear, with not a trace of a stutter...

"Take it easy, Grandad. Can you tell me, does Hammy have access to a bike?"

"N-n-n-no, I d-d-d-don't th-th-think so. These days, he's always s-s-s-scrounging r-r-r-rides everywhere."

"Well, in that case, would you like to use the scooter, and give Hammy a lift?"

"Yes, I could d-d-d-d-d-do that easy en-n-n-n-n-nough."

"Ok, I'll get back to you with the details, when we've worked out where we're going. Bye."

"B-b-b-b-b-b-bye."

Derek hung up.

Strange not having Sally sitting in the office.

"It must be lovely having friends to go cycling with, on a Saturday afternoon... Must be really great fun... I have a bicycle ...a Raleigh ...a three-speed gear... I love cycling..."

The words came wistfully from the desk where Sally used to be; a pitiful little cry for attention that was ignored by both Derek and Spider as they concentrated on the work in hand.

22

Yes ...two could play the game, or rather, two groups could.

The females had now established their meeting on Saturday afternoons, and if the females could successfully get together without divulging what it was all about, then their male counterparts could do it too, even though the males in question couldn't think of anything to be secretive about.

The 'Newingsworth Mafia, Male Section' was about to have its very first meeting. With no wives or partners at home to nag them, or prevent them doing whatever they wanted, the males had arranged to meet in secret too, on Saturday afternoons at their own venue.

Word was passed around. Anton's would be the starting point at one o'clock. Because the Council did not permit motor vehicles to park outside the restaurant from Mondays to Saturdays, and also because Anton had placed a sign outside the new, large, front windows prohibiting the placement of bicycles against the glass, the big Italian allowed the scooter and four bikes to be parked in the little yard at the back.

Would the meeting remain covert? In the office yesterday, because Christine was aware that something was being planned for Saturday, Derek and Spider had to be careful how they talked about the 'where' in case she overheard and, thankfully, their caution had paid off. There was relief that she had not appeared. It would be embarrassing for them if a female were to turn up for their first male-only secret meeting, wouldn't it?

The ordinary members were sitting around the table together. It was a beautiful sunny day outside but a little chilly if you weren't on the move. For the cyclists, the exercise would certainly keep them warm, but the sedentary pursuit of sitting on the motor scooter might be cooler so Hector and Hammy wisely were wearing fleeces. Spider and Alexander both wore Lycra cycling outfits, being a little more dedicated to the sport than the others, and for Sam and Derek, it was more mundane apparel – jeans and tee-shirts.

The group was very appreciative of Anton, making a table available for them, and for having laid on a light meal. Even though it was Saturday and he had an almost full restaurant, he was kindly letting them use the place as a base camp. Therefore, as a consequence and with only a brief ceremony, Anton was made an honorary member.

He would have been made a full member of the group except for his being incapable of mounting, or balancing on, a bicycle these days. Unfortunately he couldn't go on the scooter either because there were only two places available on it and they were already filled.

Meeting in the restaurant would be only for a short time, because an outdoor activity was the intention, though the destination had not yet been decided by the group. Where they would be going would be voted on – once they had partaken of some refreshing food and drink.

Derek and Sam had the stamina to cope with a thirty-mile journey maximum and, from experience, knew that it could be achieved only provided there was a rest halfway, and a toilet-break. Therefore, it was agreed that today's run should not be too far. In deference to their weak leg muscles, Sam proposed going to a place that he and Derek had visited on their normal Saturday afternoon excursion. It seemed perfect to him.

"It's in Little Typington," he told the others. "It's a great pub, the *Torrid Hedgehog*, isn't it Derek?"

"Hmmmm..." was Derek's hesitant reaction, which received a funny look from Sam, who had expected Derek to be all for it. It had been good last time, hadn't it?

"That's a g-g-g-g-great idea," piped up Hector, "I've b-b-b-b-b-been there."

"I haven't, but it suits me fine," added Spider.

"I haven't either, but I'll go along with the rest of you," said Alexander.

"An' ah'll gang wherever ma good freen, Sinbad, taks me," said the slightly rotund passenger who would be occupying the scooter's rear seat.

"Hmmmmm..." Derek said again.

"That'sa realla nicea place. Gotta special character of itsa owna. I knowa the landlord – Bigga Jeemmy," threw in Anton, "but you makea sure you pay him. Bigga Jeemmy no likea you, if you no pay."

Derek's memory of Bigga Jeemmy was very clear since it was only a few days ago he'd seen him – the man had not been overly happy on that visit. Then again, Sophie wasn't happy either, being chased by an angry landlord; most displeased she was – but at least she'd paid!

He couldn't very well have come out of the toilet door, with his gran and grandad sitting there, guaranteed to see him. Very awkward! Maybe one day he would apologise to the landlord, if he ever got to know him well enough, and perhaps they'd have a good laugh about it. Would Sophie ever laugh with him again, he wondered... For some reason she didn't half go on about her car seat! Sophie would be remembered clearly by the landlord – he couldn't take his eyes off her – but had he noticed who was with her?

After such a short time, it could be embarrassing to go back, particularly if Big Jeemmy had a good memory for faces – Derek's in particular! Was there anywhere else as an alternative – another destination? *No, I'm being silly*, he told himself. *The landlord sees lots of people every day, and to him I'd be only one face in a thousand, so to heck, why not...* "Yes, I'll go along with it too," said Derek more confidently, because that's how decisions were made by men – *real* men ...but!

It turned out to be a slightly longer journey than originally intended, thanks to the fork in the road, and Hector's memory. Derek and Sam knew the correct route and this wasn't it. The older pair on the scooter at the front had joined the wrong road. Shouting, by the other four, was to no avail, so they had little alternative but to follow, trying to catch them. Hector, 'phut-phut-phutting' along with confidence, was failing to see the arm-waving going on behind him and, although he was not very far ahead and going at a slower speed than usual to let the cyclists keep pace, neither of the two on the scooter could hear their shouts. To make it worse they appeared to be attempting, unsuccessfully, to have a conversation with each other. Hector was wearing his own safety helmet, and Hammy's head had been squashed into Daisy's. The cyclists had little choice but to follow rather than lose them.

"What about using the mobile?" Spider suggested, as they raced along.

"They'd never hear that either," retorted Alexander.

Derek and Sam made no comment, other than cursing under their breaths – they were feeling the pace. It was another four miles before they caught up with the scooter, and that was only thanks to Hector's bladder, and the three cups of tea he'd had with his lunch.

They all stopped and had a short rest then returned the way they'd come, surprised that in the race to catch the wayward pair they hadn't noticed how hilly the road was. This time at the junction they took the correct road and two of the cyclists – in particular, the ones in the jeans and tee-shirts – were especially delighted to arrive at the *Torrid Hedgehog* Inn, and to dismount from what had begun to feel like razor-sharp saddles.

In they went, Alexander, Hammy, Sam, Spider, and Hector.

"I'll catch up with you in a minute," Derek shouted. "Just want to adjust something..."

Now he'd arrived, any confidence felt earlier had vanished. He didn't want to go in, but the others wouldn't permit him to remain outside, and after a few moments Alexander popped his head back out.

"Come on, Derek," he shouted. "Last in pays – you are on the bell."

So, in he went. They were lined up at the bar, orders having been placed, and the pints now being pulled very efficiently by Bigga Jeemmy...

"He's paying," said Alexander, carefully pointing out Derek to the landlord. "Watch him though, he doesn't part easily with money, does this one."

"Oh, I know that," said the landlord, looking straight at Derek. "...Is the girlfriend not here today then?"

"What?" Derek exclaimed in a panic. "You must be mixing me up with someone else. I am a happily married..."

"Sir, we've been here before," Sam chipped in. "Him and me. You didn't think I was his girlfriend, now did you?"

It eased the moment for Derek when everybody laughed, including the landlord, but it wasn't over. As he filled the last glass, the one for Hector – half a pint only, Bigga Jeemmy looked straight at Derek and continued, "I'd say you must have a *double* then!"

"That's very generous of you, yes, I'll accept that – a double – if you insist," Derek quickly responded as he turned smirking to the others, successfully causing more laughter, while struggling to appear unconcerned.

"Not what I meant..." said Bigga Jeemmy, who was not amused and moved farther along the bar to serve another gent.

"C-c-c-c-c-crisps..." Hector came out with, once they'd all sat down at a table. "We'll have to have c-c-c-c-c-crisps as w-w-w-well, D-D-D-D-D-Derek."

So, Derek dutifully returned to the bar and asked for a selection of different types of crisps, six packets please.

"Could have sworn it was you, you know?" the landlord continued in a quiet voice.

"Why?" said Derek, becoming alarmed about what might be coming next, and not wanting to know. Anton said this man gets upset if someone doesn't pay the... But Sophie did pay, didn't she? Yes, of course she did, relax...

"A blonde, she was ...a luscious little blonde, in fact. Is your name 'Andy'?"

"No... But I *know* an Andy – he's my friend," replied Derek eagerly, suddenly feeling a little less targeted.

"And he looks like you?"

Derek nodded.

"And he's passionate for 'Sophie'?" continued Bigga Jeemmy.

How did this guy know her name – and Andy's – and that he was passionate? Wow... Wait a minute... Have they been here together? I thought the other day was her first visit...

"A right pillock he was, leaving her to pay the bill, while he scarpered out of the toilet window. He behaved like a proper Muppet! I felt sorry for her. She would give him hell afterwards, no doubt – and he would have deserved it!"

"How do you know all this?" Derek asked tentatively, attempting to look concerned for his mate, rather than himself.

"The embroidered hankie: 'My undying love, from Andy to Sophie.' it said on it – all hand-done... Obviously a keep-sake and not the sort of handkerchief she'd use for her nose. She dropped it on the way out. Do you know her, as well?"

"Uhmmm..." Remaining non-committal seemed wise at this moment.

"Maybe you could give it back to this 'Sophie', although I doubt that she'd want it now, unless they've patched it up. You could always give it back to the twit who made it, your doppelganger, Passionate Andy. I kept it because I thought they might come in again, but they haven't, and I want rid of it now. Anyway, Andy will be a brave man to show his face in here again. He'll be paying in advance if he does!"

"I'll take it off your hands then," said Derek, grabbing the handkerchief as if he was a really obliging bloke.

What a relief to get away from the bar without the others getting involved. It could only have become worse if they had. As he went back over to the table with the crisps, it occurred to him – the words on the handkerchief – he hadn't been aware that Sophie and Andy were so close. Another thing: he hadn't realised how good Andy was – at needlework!

23

The deadline arrived and he'd done it! The job was completed. It was in a finished and edited state. "Rabid Revenge Revisited" was ready to be passed to Sophie. The grand finale had arrived. Yes, a book now existed – *his* book.

Phew...

He'd worked like a mad-skull on it, much to Sally's gradually increasing annoyance because, as the weeks were progressing, she was getting plumper, less enthusiastic, and less able to be doing all the housekeeping routines on her own.

"That's it – complete!" he proclaimed proudly, but all he received from Sally was a tired little smile of acknowledgement. "Sorry sweetheart. I'll make it up to you," he said with a sadly-deflated-anti-climactic comprehension. "I'll do the housework all on my own for the next two weeks – after I've got rid of this to Ssss..." He almost said Sophie! "s ...someone who can take it on to the final stage, that being your friend Josephine of course, little old Ms Clerk."

"Oh, goody, goody," said Sally, with as much enthusiasm as a blancmange. "I'm going to lie down."

The compulsion Sophie had to continue her role as little old Ms Clerk was beyond Derek's comprehension. As far as he was concerned, by meeting with Sally and the rest of the female Mafia every Saturday afternoon, she was sailing mighty close to the wind. Strangely, it was almost as if she were enjoying being in their company and it was no longer just a way to help him get the book completed.

How in the name of heaven was it all going to end? Would she go on forever, or just vanish and never return to the group? If she vanished, how would he be able to get future books published? She'd been his lifeline and made the process so easy for him. Very easy indeed, that was, other than the mind-blowing struggle he'd had preventing Sally realising the truth!

If Sophie went, he'd have to find another publisher and how would he manage that? It could take ages – and it would have to be a male, or Sally would be on her high horse again! To think, he had been convinced that when he finished this first book, he would be feeling euphoric, able to relax, and go on to enjoy writing another – and have it published too.

He had dreamed of this moment, imagined it for so long – the exhilaration! ...So why, instead, did he feel uneasy?

24

As part of her daily routine, Angelina walked over to join Sally for lunch in the cottage. The countryside around the cottage was so much more pleasant than Buttercup Avenue. Although living in a rented house in a town street was fine for the moment it could not compare to having the countryside on your doorstep, as Sally had, so she and Sam were saving for their own house in the future. It was a fairly long walk across town, but she was fit, and saw no problem in that.

It was now only one more week before their due dates. Supportive of each other, enjoying each other's company, they shared ideas and thoughts and, having come from different backgrounds and different countries, many varied subjects could be, and were, discussed: almost endless chatter every time they met. Before lunch, being a beautiful morning today, they decided to go out with the dog: Sally, Angie and Jilly, a long walk across the fields. Angie liked dogs, especially Sally's little poodle, Jilly, and Jilly liked Angie. Jilly only disliked Derek!

After lunch, what could possibly be more natural for a couple of very heavily pregnant young females to do than deciding to paint the kitchen walls? What a good use of their time – and of the emulsion. The paint was just lying there.

When he'd placed the tin of paint in the kitchen – the one bought out of the kindness of his heart a few weeks ago – Derek had said to Sally, "It is just in case my pregnant wife wants something to do in her idle moments." Perhaps he could have made it clearer that he had been joking!

Neither Sally, nor Angelina, had any special plans for this Friday afternoon, and, to be honest, neither gave this 'activity of the day' a lot of thought. As they both felt fit and healthy, and as it would be giving them something 'different' to do, rather than lolling around feeling plump, they decided – why not paint the kitchen? It had seemed a fun idea at the time, and, it would be a big surprise for Derek when he got back...

Being Friday, it was the final day of Sam's school week, and other than a little blip along the way, he had not regretted his decision to leave Detroit and the thankless task he'd faced with the kids in the classes back there. His job in Newingsworth High School was now permanent and hard work, but by comparison, teaching in the UK seemed like a holiday.

Here, coupled with enjoyment, he was finding daily challenges presented by the schoolchildren more confrontational – difficult pupils are never hard to find in a classroom – but he could certainly claim to be better than he used to be at coping. It also helped that he was liked as a teacher. All things considered, particularly with Angie happy and pregnant, his life now seemed much more pleasant. He looked forward to the special arrangements planned for the next few days.

Derek wouldn't be at home over the weekend so Sam and Angelina would be staying at Toozlethwaite Manor, as company for Sally, until he returned. This pleased Angie. Sam would be joining them after school, bringing with him her case and all the essentials for a relaxing weekend. As Angie was walking over anyway she had wanted to carry the case herself, but Sam insisted that it would tire her out; just take things easy, he told her...

So, what about Derek, where was he? Far away – and for that Derek could be indebted to Curly. Curly had manipulated the deal, organising the trip for him, all expenses paid.

Curly's agreement had been reached with a colleague in another studio, a distant studio. For Derek's book it meant more valuable publicity, which he couldn't really refuse and, obviously, would eventually be to his financial benefit. Curly wasn't doing it just for the sake of friendship. The rub-off for Graham Stockman was that although the other organisation would be doing the recording and editing etcetera, for their own local transmission, the deal he'd made was giving Graham an option, at a later date, to charge them for the privilege of broadcasting their programme on 'LITTLE RADIO fm', his own station, serving Newingsworth, Slatterfoot and surrounding districts.

Derek had travelled by train, his destination being Inverness. It was a long way from Newingsworth, especially at a time like this with Sally pregnant, but he was comforted by the knowledge that his sister and Sam would be with Sally over the weekend. That would allow him to relax a bit.

The timing was the unfortunate part of the deal – the recording had to be done now, and, being just before the baby was due, he had been reluctant to leave his wife at home on her own. He departed this morning before Angie appeared, but with the knowledge that she would be arriving shortly. It was very considerate of her to come over, bearing in mind that she was at the same stage of pregnancy as Sally.

He'd be travelling back on the Sunday morning train. Sally would be fine until then...

It was fortunate, Thelma calling in for a cuppa ...she was well aware of the plan for the weekend, details of the special circumstances having been discussed during last Saturday's Mafia Meeting. The two girls were to be together and Derek would be away, so she decided to nip down to see them. They would be sitting back, feet up, sipping cups of tea, and she could join them and chat...

The reality horrified her!

To find the two of them cleaning the paintbrushes, having only just finished painting walls, was most unexpected. "Only passing the time," they'd explained and Thelma just knew... Even though the kitchen now looked so much brighter, she told them that thinking they could achieve something so physical without adverse effect had been delusional, and events proved her correct.

It was quite an amazing coincidence for both to be expecting their babies in the same week but, "Oh no, it won't actually happen like that," everyone agreed. It was most unlikely to happen on the given date; "A well-known fact," everyone declared. So, two very pregnant shapes laughed off Thelma's comments.

"I don't feel any effect," said Angelina, although she did feel slightly unsure.

"...And neither do I," said Sally.

Two hours later, they did feel the effects and it didn't take long to establish that they had both started...

Definitely no more painting! Anyway, one coat would do fine, both girls decided – it had been done carefully and covered well – certainly worth the effort. So, what the heck? If something was about to happen, let it happen, and, the race is on!

The question then became, who will be first?

Many months ago when they'd been told, Derek and Sam both said they were horrified. The lads were not complaining about Sally and Angelina having challenged each other to be the first to have a baby, but that they hadn't been party to the plot beforehand. They had been *used*, they said – like sex-objects – which didn't feel at all manly ...but they had only been joking. They'd enjoyed it!

"Have we cheated?" the two young mothers-to-be asked each other. They felt guilty because they'd caused it – a bit like match fixing – but, they concluded, both cheating at the same time must balance out.

It was still a race!

The regularity of the pains, for each, was checked, and Thelma was correct – they shouldn't have been painting. She stayed with them, and phoned Hammy to bring the vehicle round now.

"You are going to be a Good Samaritan and take two young ladies to hospital, Mr Macintosh," her husband was told on the phone, "and if you don't hurry, you will finish up playing midwife while getting there. By the way, have you ever delivered a baby?"

The chances of that happening were slim, Thelma knew, but Hammy didn't. He was round at the front door of the cottage with vehicle doors open and ready to go in no time at all. The notorious lane and the terrible surface had been negotiated at breakneck speed, without going over the edge for a change... This was urgent!

Thelma stayed behind to lock up, promising to communicate with Derek and Sam, as Hammy helped the girls into the car making sure they were comfortable and safely belted-up. He was urging them on; to his mind they seemed to be moving so slowly – and then they were off, at speed, back down the lane.

It was Sam who was phoned first.

"Hello," he said, as he walked casually home from school, just about to reach Buttercup Avenue to collect the case and looking forward to joining his wife soon at the cottage.

"Hello," said Thelma "I'm phoning to tell you of a slight change of arrangements. Angelina has decided not to spend the weekend at the cottage after all. You can, of course, if you wish. You can collect the key from the hotel, if you need it – when you get back."

"Get back? Why, where am I going?"

"...To Marsdonfield General Hospital – with Angie's packed case. You are about to become a daddy..."

"Wow..." said Sam.

There wasn't much point in phoning Derek. He would probably just be arriving at Inverness Rail Station, and not be able to talk comfortably. Anyway, being so far away, there was little he could do. A text to him, asking him to contact her at a suitable moment – that seemed the more practical idea. She could explain what had happened much more easily afterwards on the phone. What do I say on the text, she pondered – I'm not very good at this? She wouldn't want to scare him by sending the wrong message, and must be brief, so...

'PLEASE PHONE – KITCHEN SHOULDN'T HAVE BEEN PAINTED BLUE – BOTH NOW IN LABOUR – THELMA XXX.' She sent it.

He received it. What the heck's this about? Blue? Whose kitchen is she talking about? Derek read it again: Labour ...that's strange? Sally and I have always voted Lib Dem? Has Thelma sent this text to the wrong person?

Having attempted to do a cryptic crossword during his long train journey but having failed to solve most of the clues, Derek left the train feeling utterly incompetent; he was not thinking straight at all, and now reading this text, he was totally flummoxed ...until he phoned Thelma!

25

He had promised to take her into town for some personal items – he was going in anyway, he said, and would drop her off – but he hadn't appeared, so Millie was at reception to ask where Hamish was. He left only moments ago in the car, she was informed by the girl at reception, and in a rush, but didn't say where he was going.

It must have been something very important to make him forget about me, Millie concluded modestly. A movement at the hotel entrance caught her eye. A white poodle on an extending lead was pawing at the glass but failing to move the swing-doors.

Eventually, at the other end of the lead, Thelma appeared, pushing open the door, cheeks flushed and slightly out of breath. She had just walked at a rapid pace along the lane, pulled most of the way by Jilly, quite happy at having another walk with someone she liked.

"Ah, Millie ...the very person... Must get a seat first," Thelma barely managed to speak, as she hurried across and plonked herself on the settee beside Millie. Jilly jumped up, tail wagging, pleased to see Millie. "Your daughter, Angie ...and Sally..." Thelma was gasping. "...Gone!" Millie had to wait... "...With Hammy ...to the hospital ...they've started!"

The young girl on reception was beckoned over and wordlessly, with a few waves of the hand, a nod, and a shooing motion towards the poodle, Thelma conveyed the need for Jilly to be taken off her hands. The poodle went away happily with the girl to enjoy a biscuit and a bowl of water.

"I need a drink too!" Thelma croaked.

Millie went into the kitchen. No doubt Thelma's wish was for something stronger but a glass of water was all that appeared. It helped. The rest of the story was recounted with a bit more fluidity, and Millie learned why Hammy had rushed off. It had been more important than me, she conceded to herself.

"Have you told Derek and Sam yet?" Millie asked.

"Yes. Sam is going to the hospital right away, but Derek – he's in Inverness."

"Where's that, honey? Is it far?"

Thelma gave Millie a quick reminder of the geography of the United Kingdom, and it was accepted that though it might not be a great distance by American standards, in the UK it could be considered to be 'far'.

"So Sally has no one with her? Angie will have Sam. I must go – right away..." Millie declared.

"Why don't you collect Daisy?" suggested Thelma.

"Yes, you are right. Sally would appreciate her being there too, I'm sure."

A taxi was arranged and arrived promptly. Millie had just left when the phone rang at Reception.

"Mrs Macintosh, it's for you. It's Mr Toozlethwaite," called out the girl.

When he spoke, Thelma was surprised at how calm he sounded.

"Oh Derek – isn't it wonderful?" she cooed.

She expected him to be at least as excited as she was. She was only going to be an aunt, but he was about to become a father. Surely he should be excited? However, from the text message, to get excited about the colour of someone's kitchen and their voting habits certainly hadn't occurred to Derek.

"Derek, you are about to become a *dad*..." she told him, and gave him a swift resume of the events as they'd occurred so far.

There was a silence...

"Derek... Derek... Are you still there...?"

"But I'm... I can't..."

"Don't worry. Millie and Daisy are off to keep her company, and anyway, there's not a lot you would be doing if you were here anyway, is there?"

Standing in the station, in a foreign land, made a depressed Derek just a little more so; so far away, and being told he would be useless anyway – even if he were any closer...

"...And we'll keep you informed of developments," said Thelma.

"I'll get back home as soon as I can. Maybe I could speak to Sally herself – at the hospital... at a suitable moment. I'm going straight to the studio now to start work, but another thing, Thelma – is the kitchen really blue?"

Is it always wet in Scotland, wondered Derek? He was pretty sure that it started raining the moment he crossed over the border. England dry – Scotland wet, sounded like a football score when he thought of it like that.

He'd had a miserable journey on the train, people using mobiles almost continuously, the windows steamed up, babies crying, and his attempt at the crossword disastrous. To help pass the time he would have tried dozing but, the fat chap opposite who had beaten him to it, with the drool at his gaping mouth, put him off that idea.

Thelma's message coming through, as he was leaving the train, about poor Sally and Angie had taken him by surprise. It wasn't supposed to be happening yet! Imagine though, his wife and his sister, both about to have a baby at the same time... and they could both be disappointed! Their race – it might be a draw, but they should never have challenged each other in the first place, even if it had been an unusual night at the party.

Travelling across town to the recording studio in a taxi, with the rain pelting down and in the dusk, everything looked dismal. Any bright lights only emphasised the angle of the rainfall in the wind. It was the first time he'd been here – his first time in Scotland, as a matter of fact. What a welcome!

As he went over the bridge, he could just about make out that the Ness seemed a fast flowing river – there was certainly a lot of water about tonight – and through the droplets on the taxi's windows he could see, reflected, the lights of the riverbank buildings. He could imagine that on a clear starry night it would look delightful – tonight, the place looked ominous.

Sally would be alright, he told himself. Help was at hand for them both, and they were together. Here he was, feeling sorry for himself, sitting in this taxi, alone – well almost alone – somebody had to drive it.

Why did it have to be this weekend, me being up here – when she needs me? But, as Thelma kindly pointed out, if I had been there, at the hospital, I'd be just like the proverbial spare-whatever at a wedding ...and why did they paint the kitchen? I bought the emulsion for the spare room – blue, for our little boy.

He remembered the comment he'd made at the time. It was meant as a joke! It was bought for me to use. I didn't expect somebody else to be using it – especially not my wife and my sister and in their very advanced stages of pregnancy...

Derek gave an involuntary shudder when he thought of it – a blue kitchen – must look horrible...

And the rain continued...

26

It was difficult to tell who was most exhausted after the two babies arrived, but obviously, being the ones who'd actual done the physical having-the-baby bits, Sally and Angelina, should probably be given the credit – but they weren't alone in claiming fatigue.

Others suffered too...

Over many hours, being the mother of Angie and the mother-in-law of Sally, Millie was continuously darting back and forth from room to room. She'd been determined to keep bang-up-to-date with any changes in their situations. It *had* to be a perfect birth for both of them. Her conscience drove her to ensure that she'd be there for them, whatever the emergency – if there was one.

The ever-present feeling of guilt, now, at abandoning her own little baby nearly thirty-three years ago, was having a continuing effect and it annoyed her. She'd suffered little remorse in all that time, deliberately avoiding the fact for years but, subconsciously the regrets had remained. Feeling them pour down on her head on this occasion was both surprising and unnerving. It still hurt...

Daisy, as the grandmother of Angie, and Sally's gran-in-law and having developed a deep affection for them both, had also been scurrying between them. Now, after the event, she was, as Hector would have put it so aptly, "...kn-n-n-n-nackered!"

Muriel, being Sally's mum, was obviously concerned more with her daughter than she was with Angie, and more so because of the absence of Derek. She spent time with Angie as well, but would not leave Sally on her own. Opportunities to visit Angie were taken when Millie and Daisy coincided in Sally's room and she *had* to get out. There were moments, Muriel felt, when it would have been nice to have seen Daisy and Millie far enough – they were such fusspots, especially Millie, having to make up for lost time, it seemed... Oh, she did go on!

Sally is *my* daughter, Muriel fretted, and needs *me* more than anyone else. She is my flesh and blood, and today I am her only really close family support. At least Angie had her husband with her. He hadn't shot off to the wilds of Scotland, abandoning his pregnant wife when she needed him desperately! How could Derek have been so thoughtless?

Sam just sat there. He had not recovered.

"He's like a zombie..." Daisy whispered to Millie, in a stage whisper that Muriel also heard clearly and agreed with.

Sam heard nothing...

He sat, as if in a trance, unable to believe that it was all over and that he was now a daddy. He'd never liked hospitals. They scared him. Angie having a baby scared him. Cutting his finger scared him. Having to be in the building for the very essential purpose of being at Angie's side because she wanted and needed him had helped him slightly to overcome his fear of all things medical. Even though it was all over, and he had held his little daughter for a moment, he still felt uncomfortable. Then there was the smell; the antiseptic smell; he hated it. To a certain extent Sam envied Derek – being far away – he'd successfully avoided it all. Derek was smart!

Technically Sally could claim victory but, for the family records, the result of the competition would be declared a draw. Edwin was the first to have been introduced to the big wide world, but Annabel was only about an hour and a bit later. Anyway, both infants would have the same birth date.

The two girls hadn't yet had the chance to speak to each other or to see each other's newly born infant, but Millie and Daisy did such good job of communication, that the young mothers felt that they were in the same room.

Hector was a bit peeved at being left behind when Millie and Daisy shot off in the taxi to the hospital.

"Poppa, you'd just be a nuisance at the hospital," his daughter said to him, annoyingly.

He did not like this name she was using since returning to Newingsworth: 'Poppa'. She stays away for thirty years and then she comes back and ...but he supposed, he could learn to live with it as long as he didn't have to say it! He'd have great difficulty with p-p-p-p-p-p...

"Better if you stayed here, and slept in the chair – as you normally do, Poppa."

There, she said it again, but she was right, and he did just that!

The phone was ringing out in the hallway for some time before he woke up, and realised what had disturbed him, and it was good news. He was pleased to be informed by his wife that both mothers, and both babies, were doing well and he was delighted to be invited to visit as soon as he liked, because both babies were looking forward to meeting their great-grandad Hector Smith.

Exhilaration was what he felt being called 'great-grandad', and was then a bit deflated when he realised how that only happens to old men ...but he wasn't going to let that stop him meeting the two newly-born members of the family. He had a scooter and he knew how to use it, so in no time at all, he was there beside them.

Alexander was not in attendance either.

For some, the prospect of becoming a grandad was great, but for Alexander? No ...and it was all because suddenly he'd be joining the ranks of 'ancients', which to his mind did not seem correct for a man of his tender years. Last night, Muriel said she would let him know the instant the 'grandad moment' occurred.

"I can't wait," he'd said to her as she left the house, but she knew he meant not one word!

Looking in the mirror before going to bed worsened his depressed mood, probably due to the darned reading spectacles, rather than just the impending birth of a grandchild.

Reading glasses meant greater definition; there was no problem for distances, thank goodness, but for close-up he could see clearly nowadays – too clearly when looking in a mirror. His eyesight had allowed him to ignore the infernal worry lines that would only worsen when he became a grandad, of that he was absolutely certain.

Thicker make-up might be required for stage performances in future. Oh dear me, he thought, at the Dramatic Society next month, will I be asked to audition for the part of one of the *old* people? Although ...what if it is to play the old mad biddy, the central female character in 'She Was Born To Kill...'? He could settle for that. In fact, he would have to add some worry lines for her... Yes... Now what sort of finery would I wear for that? Silk, next to the skin, preferably...

An anxious father, far away in Inverness, was beginning to feel the effect of fatigue setting in. Nervousness, and working with this small recently-met team in a strange environment, was getting the better of him. Not only were they strangers but most of them spoke a bit like Hammy, which meant that he regularly reacted wrongly to misunderstood instructions: a language thing...

Perhaps starting work immediately after such a long journey hadn't been smart, and not knowing if everything was going well for Sally at the hospital was churning away at the back of his mind. Another irritating, disturbing factor, hindering his concentration was, deep down, the fear that his absence in Sally's time of need would be held against him for the rest of their married life.

Right now, he wanted to get on with it and complete the recording session quickly so that he could hurry south again, back to Sally's side. That's where he was really needed...

They slogged on, working hard in the studio, recording the hour-long feature and making good progress. It was coming together although it was tiring and frustrating going over the same thing time and time again.

No one on the radio programme production team was aware of the other things currently filling Derek's head. He hadn't told them he was about to become a father. They were strangers; they wouldn't want to be burdened with his worries. He was there to work. He didn't want anyone to realise that his mind was elsewhere. There was a job to be done, so together they got stuck into it with concentrated effort –

until the moment he checked his phone during a break and found the text message:

'Come home soon, Daddy. I want to introduce myself, love from your little son, Edwin.'

He read it and let out a whoop of joy. Obviously Thelma could learn a thing or two about texting from this lad... He couldn't contain himself after that, and proudly told his new colleagues that he had become the father of a bouncing baby boy. Perfect timing: a rest break was called and they left him in peace to get on the phone right away, "Cause we ken whit wimmen urr like!"

There were tears in his eyes when he managed to get through to speak to Sally. Not only was he a new father, he was told, but little Annabel had also popped-out to make him an uncle!

Learning of the double birth stopped everything – this was not the time to be working – it would have to be longer than a 'jist a wee break'. He was slapped on the back and shaken by the hand, but chided for being so secretive about the nearness of the event.

"Ye're in Sco'land, remember!" he was told in no uncertain way. "Ye canny keep somethin' like that tae yersel', mon! Share an' share alike! Whit sort o' folk d'ye think we urr, eh? At a time like this, the only thing tae dae is tae get blootered – the gither!"

So, they immediately sent out for a six-pack of beer for each of them, and of course, "We couldnae drink the beer withoot huvvin the fish suppers in oor hauns. An' mak sure ye get them smothered wi' plenty sa't and vinegar," the one who would fetch them was instructed....

Yes, in Inverness they were well practiced at getting blootered!

27

A little bit of understanding should be shown for new fathers like him – well, Derek thought so anyway! A lot of sympathy was not expected, but he reckoned he deserved some. Why should it be reserved solely for women? Sad that the medical profession did not seem to recognise an obvious one, that the poor dad could be affected by Post-Natal Stress! It happens to mothers, doesn't it, so, why not dads?

Since the arrival of two additional mouths to feed – ET and Jilly, and with Sally giving up her job – who could possibly deny that being the family's sole breadwinner, carried extra burdens and heavy responsibility for the father?

He had to accept though, in the eyes of others, the effect on him could be considered slightly less traumatic than the actual process of giving birth. To many, his having not even been present at his wife's bedside to hold her hand when it all happened, the amazing event could not possibly have affected him at all. To his mind, that comment was way off...

He continued reading his book but couldn't concentrate... He knew differently and it was galling, Sally thinking she was the only one suffering. He was thinking too... *I wish she would sit still!*

Having children, does it make a mummy's brain go mushy? This was the big question currently fighting to take up semi-permanent occupancy of her head. Oh dear, I've done it again, she chided herself silently. I am obviously losing control. Is it worse than yesterday? Yattering away either to no-one, or everyone, seemed to be happening more often...

It began several days ago – or at least that was when she noticed it. It was only occasionally, as far as she could tell, but was it becoming a habit? Was it worsening? Talking out loud as thoughts occurred was both annoying and embarrassing – particularly since she became aware of doing it, especially in public places. Of course, the moment she realised – she stopped, but then there were the funny looks...

She couldn't recall this sort of thing running in the family – *apart from that time when Aunt Thelma...?* She stopped in mid-thought, *but that was for different reasons* ...and here I am doing it again, in my own living room, and in front of...

Wait a moment... Did I actually speak aloud just now, or not?

There was uncertainty on this occasion. If he didn't answer her question, was it because she hadn't been speaking out loud, or because he was becoming so self-centred these days that he was not hearing her or, worse still, deliberately ignoring her? So, why didn't he reply? He, for one, should know it is very rude to ignore his wife talking to him – even if his wife doesn't know she is doing it.

As she was thinking this through, her eyes were on her husband sitting opposite. He glanced up, with a questioning look on his face when he realised she was looking at him.

"What...?" was all he came out with. He waited, and then wriggled uncomfortably, and tried to smile at the staring face. The stare continued; then she gave an almost imperceptible shake of her head, as if she pitied him. He gave her an odd look, turning away, then a further rapid furtive glance, before returning to reading his most favourite book ever – his own.

Ah well, she thought feeling a touch happier, at least that proved it. If her look could gain his attention and make him feel guilty, he wouldn't dare ignore her words – therefore, it had been a silent thought! Is it possible then to go mad ...silently? Another thing, would this feeling have lasted so long if it were only temporary ...because now it was impossible to think without every thought causing agitation!

She sat fidgeting on the edge of her seat. Thankfully, all was peaceful in the bedroom next door – ET's feeding having been successfully completed. At least his eating and sleeping was no trouble. It was his crying that seemed to bring on her little problem.

In here, sitting at the other side of the room on the settee, Derek was infuriatingly normal, totally relaxed, not a care in the world had he, lying sprawled out with one leg up on the cushions, engrossed yet again in reading his own book, while she sat just waiting for her head to go ...POP!

Stop! This is ridiculous! Things mustn't continue this way, she told herself – making sure her thoughts remained silent; an answer must be found! It was a pity that, this evening, her only close contact was Derek. He was her husband, yes, and he was nice fellow, yes, but it would be of little use asking him for help. She knew that for certain.

There was no urge either for her to discuss it over the phone with anyone, too embarrassing, and anyway, who could she discuss going bonkers with? Nonetheless, if her mind was to be set at ease, the question would have to be asked and an answer found.

Suddenly she realised, it was not impossible for her to find one herself, and although it was obviously a temptation that she knew she should resist – it would have to be done... Drastic measures were called for; she would Google it.

Now it was morning, and she felt no better, in fact probably worse with a new question bouncing around her pounding brain and fast becoming the over-riding one. It was about last night's search... Had it been worth the effort? She had found facts, opinions, conjecture, old wives tales, cross references, and recommendations, but had the answer been found...? Decidedly unlikely!

In truth, her brain now seemed woolly, really no better than mushy and, overall, in no way calmed – and, here she was, about to face yet another day.

However, confronted with the vast accumulation of detail from numerous websites about birthing babies, she was close to concluding that her condition could not be attributed truly to the birth process. It was now six weeks since that most traumatic moment of her life, when she had brought ET into the world – a fairly recent event. It seemed longer ago, but from what she'd picked up on the internet trawl, it might not be the cause of her problem. Still, she was not totally convinced one way or the other...

Taking a positive step last night, to discover something about it, had helped. Although, the cause of her problematic symptoms was as yet unresolved, she now knew that it did not have to remain a mystery. The answer was somewhere in there, sitting on the table in front of her, the result of last evening's search – very likely searching for her and, if it wasn't, there was still the internet! Not a task she relished. It was guaranteed to be long and painstaking

Crammed on one piece of paper alone was a list of sixty-three strangely named afflictions and, unfortunately, if she needed greater knowledge, each one would require further 'Googling'! Printing them in larger type would have helped. Peering at the names with screwed-up eyes made not a whit of difference, but it did help her make the decision. She'd remain in ignorance! Easier not to know...

"Give up," she said out loud, deliberately and to no-one, other than the other two small inhabitants of the room, who ignored her. Crossing to the waste bin, she tore the sheet into little pieces, opened the container with her foot, and they were gone!

It didn't help.

It was difficult even thinking straight these days. Beyond her control unfortunately, was the timing and duration of ET's crying, which would almost certainly recommence at any moment and did not make the situation any easier.

Whatever the cause, Sally Toozlethwaite's self-confidence had zeroed. She was feeling closer and closer to the edge, dreadfully close: just waiting. Apprehensive, indecisive and decidedly stressed this morning, she was sitting in the cottage staring vacantly out over the fields, thankful for the temporary silence.

Before he left the cottage earlier, when she'd told him the way she was feeling, Derek had laughed. Not only that, he cruelly threw words of wisdom at her – her words, he'd reminded her, words that so often since they'd met she had thrown at him: her words, he emphasised once more, "Remember?" She'd done it to help and her words had worked for him...

As one who experienced confidence swings, going from the

supreme to the abysmal with monotonous regularity, here he was actually admitting that sometimes what she'd said had helped, harsh though it had always felt at the time.

This morning she hadn't wanted to hear them being said out loud: not back to her. She knew what they were... "So ...and I mean this sincerely," he'd continued, putting his hands on her shoulders and looking straight at her. "Pull yourself together!" Hearing her own words said sharply, shocked her! "Now it might seem unsympathetic," he added dramatically, "but those very words have pulled me back from the brink on many occasions." Was he smirking?

Having said his goodbyes to all, he kissed her on the cheek, and left. "Have a nice day," he shouted back, as he cycled off to work, waving cheerily, without a care in the world.

Why don't men suffer the way women do? Sally asked herself; if they did, they would be more sympathetic; but he was probably right. If only he had not said it in such a self-righteous way; it was the tone of his voice! It was all right for her to say things like that to him, and for her to be self-righteous, but...

"Pull yourself together..." His comments jarred in her head, but now here she was repeating them aloud again, as she sat fidgeting, and there was another thing ...in repeating her wise words, was he really being a supportive, loving and caring husband, or was he simply being sarcastic? He would be given the benefit of the doubt this time but...

It was certainly true that he had often lacked self-confidence and decisiveness and she'd pushed him a bit; morale boosters. However, and it was worth noting as it occurred to her, that when he'd been feeling low it had never been associated with giving birth, had it?

Whoa!

She thought that through again, slowly... It is therefore possible to feel low without giving birth! Now that sudden inspiration had a remarkable effect on her. If giving birth hadn't been the problem with him, why should it be a problem with her? (To someone not actually suffering the way Sally was, this may appear to be slightly skewed logic, but she grasped it gratefully, as a convincing reason, and held onto it).

Yes, both suffering the same condition – and why? Because it is contagious! It was suddenly so obvious; she had fathomed it out at last... "I've simply caught his bug. Of course, it could be marriage as well – now, that is stressful, especially marriage to Derek. Hmmm, yes, *Derek, it could be because of you. In fact, it is because of you* ...and, dear husband, now I am experiencing it, I know exactly how it feels and you have my sympathy!"

28

The wide grin on his face said it all, and due entirely to the object sitting on the table in front of him. A warm glow of self-satisfaction surrounded Derek, rather like the advert for a well-known brand of porridge oats that sends you out, ready to face the winter's cold.

At one point he'd given up the hope of ever finishing it, and then suddenly it was done! The book was on the shelves, and on the internet, and on the move – his book. People were actually buying it – his book... At last, the target of completing it successfully achieved, it was now published and, more difficult to believe, it was selling extremely well. Advance publicity helped a lot and they'd achieved that between them.

Sophie deserved a very big thank you – she'd pushed him, she'd had the contacts, she made it happen for him – but Sally must not find that out. To Sally, it was all due to Josephine, the dear diminutive, prim, little old Ms Clerk; she was the one who'd helped him, Sally's little friend, Josephine...

ET will be proud of me, he thought, and that is a certainty. Not yet, of course, because he is only a baby, but when he grows up he will approach me, admiringly, for fatherly advice, probably about the time he reaches his fifteenth year – a difficult time in a young man's life when decisions have to be made... My God, I'll be nearly forty-seven then! What a frightening thought! "Dad, tell me please..." and Derek was able to imagine the manly voice his son would have, "...should I follow in your footsteps and become a world-famous, loved-by-the-public writer, like yourself, or not?"

"I am glad you asked me that, ET..." Derek visualised himself replying, wisely... *ET! No, that's not right! Don't want him saddled, like me, with a silly nickname all his life! Have to get out of the habit...* "Edwin ...my dear boy, you must understand it has not been an easy path I have had to follow," he would explain modestly. "I have had to make many major decisions in my life, decisions which may not have seemed justified at the time, but..."

Derek thought about some of these decisions. Like when he gave up working for the Slatterfoot Evening News – hmm? Or like his questionable choices of subjects to write about – both failures? Hmmm ...yes. Like keeping it a secret from Sally that his female publisher was Sophie ...hmmm?

"Are you alright, Derek?" asked Sally, "You look as if you are on another planet."

Suddenly he was back, realising that three pairs of eyes were staring in his direction. It was surprisingly discomfiting to be stared at by your wife, your young child, and the dog.

"ET wants Daddy to change his nappy – whether Daddy wants to or not!" the young child's mother told the father, as she smilingly handed him the slightly pongy infant.

"But..." was the extent of his objection as Sally turned on her heel and left him to it. ET began to cry: to have ET was another decision that had been slightly beyond his control.

It was all history; the decisions: right or wrong, part of the learning experience, but it was all working out correctly now, wasn't it? And his luck would continue as long as Sally didn't find out that his publisher was a female called Sophie.

No matter, looking and seeing his book sitting there filled him with unusual confidence. He felt as if he could tackle anything at that moment – except changing ET's nappy!

There he was, with a very large grin on his face, in Bisko's Book Department – now a popular published author. Who would have believed it? It was a big bookshop, one of the best and incredibly busy – unfortunately now the only bookseller in Newingsworth – and he was on the premises to sign copies of his new book, the one that made it for him: 'Rabid Revenge Revisited' – his only one, so far, he reminded himself.

Derek was returning to sit back down at the table in the corner of the book department ready to continue, glad to have had a break, giving his signing hand time to recover.

The queue had begun forming at ten o'clock with only a few lonely souls to begin with, including Hammy and Hector. They stood there patiently, each clutching the free copy he'd given them, waiting to have them signed by the author. When they left the store, they told him they intended wandering along to the Newingsworth Old Folk's Club. When he next saw them Derek would check that they still had their copies; he suspected that they would be raffling them off in the club.

The next book was laid down in front of him, opened, ready for his signature. "Would you like it dedicated to anyone?" he asked the man standing waiting.

"Yes please – to my wife, Grace," he answered, "and now you've completed this book, what will you write about next?"

Derek stopped in mid-signature in a panic, the wrong question to be asked. A chilling thought. He'd have to start something else: but what? He felt the hairs on the back of his neck rise in fear; what was he going to do now? He'd have to face it sometime... He pulled his mind back to the present when he realised that the person standing in front of him was giving him a funny look.

"I wish I knew," he answered honestly. The signature was completed and a personal message added. Derek smiled weakly as he handed it back, feeling that by not having a good answer he'd disappointed this fan, but he seemed satisfied, as had all the others today. Avoid thinking about it now, he told himself, there will be plenty quieter moments. Looking up with a smile for the next person, he was about to ask her reason for buying his book, but the question rapidly re-formed as it was leaving his mouth.

"Oh! No! Why? ...What are you doing here? What if Sally were to see you?" he hissed at Sophie, standing in front of him holding the book open.

Sophie was not supposed to be here. She should certainly not be standing in front of him like this, certainly not looking as drop-dead gorgeous as she was. They mustn't be seen together!

"Sally is my friend – are you forgetting that, Derek?" smiled back a confident Sophie.

"Not if she finds out that you are not really Josephine," he whispered desperately.

"Oh, but I am..." she smiled back. "Who else could possibly be her? ...And anyway I had to see how you were coping with your new-found fame? Oh, and I also thought you might want to show gratitude to your publisher. Maybe take her out to lunch, for example?"

Derek turned slightly as he realised someone else had appeared at his side. "Hello, Derek. Oh, sorry... I'm not interrupting am I?" His grandmother was suddenly there at his elbow. "I was just doing some shopping and I remembered that you'd be here," Daisy said, and turning to Sophie, "You are a fan are you? It's a good book, isn't it?"

"Worth every penny, I'd say. He's my favourite author," Sophie smiled back.

"And he's my favourite grandson," Daisy said proudly.

Derek was sitting, wanting the upper floor of Bisko's to open up, and let him fall through without anyone noticing he'd gone... Surely Daisy had to recognise this person; for months they'd been speaking to each other, every time they sat together at the Mafia Meetings...

Derek looked at his grandmother, feeling panic welling in his chest. How long had she been standing there? Had she heard any of what he and Sophie had said?

"Haven't we met before?" Daisy asked Sophie, giving her the once-over.

"Where would that have been?" bluffed Sophie.

"Can't quite remember," replied Daisy.

"My memory is not so good either. It must be an age thing," replied this lithe little blonde, who couldn't possibly be a day over thirty.

She calmly lifted the book, which had now been signed, saying, "Thank you so much," in an exaggerated manner, and with another big smile, firstly to Daisy, then to Derek, she turned on her heel, and sashayed off, jiggling her well-proportioned derriere. Derek was still sitting frozen in his chair, gazing hypnotically as the mini-skirted figure merged with Bisko's motley customers and was gone.

"Derek, you have others waiting, and don't become mesmerised by all the good looking ones, or I'll have to tell Sally and she will get upset. Now, I must finish the shopping."

So Derek forced a smile for his grandma, thanked her and said it was nice that she'd popped over to see him, and she said it was time to go. Unfortunately, thanks to her slightly threatening words, for him a little of the shine had gone from the morning. She stood up straight, looking at the others in the queue, "My grandson," she repeated to make sure they all knew, then turned on her heel, fetched her part-filled trolley and toddled off.

Derek was greatly relieved. There could be repercussions if she mentioned this to Sally. As the next person in the queue stepped up to the table, he reminded himself to behave like a successful author, and forced himself to relax again.

The next person didn't have his full attention immediately though. Derek continued idly watching his grandma walk off, and somehow he couldn't help but notice Grandma's rear – it didn't wiggle in quite the same way as Sophie's.

29

Bisko's was busy, permitting Derek's delightfully-shaped publisher to merge easily into the crowd, but it was unfortunate that co-incidentally Mrs Masterton also happened to be mingling with the store's customers today.

The next door neighbour of Muriel and Alexander Donaldson was, now and then and privately of course, partial to a little tipple. She had a reputation to maintain of being prim and proper, but she had two vices, bingo and sherry, both kept very secret from her neighbours in Cloverton.

Another bottle of sherry was the very necessary reason for Mrs Masterton's being here today. To have such an excellent store in the area to visit, when the sherry bottle was suddenly empty again, was much appreciated. She'd found they sold a reasonable quality, "Without feeling one is being charged an inordinate sum for the pleasure," although she suspected her previous bargain had been a smaller bottle. Before purchasing today, she checked. Surprisingly, it was the same as the empty at home – standard size; strange though, the sherry wasn't lasting as long as it used to.

As she wheeled a trolley around the store her glances were being directed everywhere, living up to the reputation gained over many years at Cloverton as 'the eyes and ears of the neighbourhood'. Mrs Violet Masterton had honed her observational skills to a standard higher than that demanded by many of the world's foremost spying organisations. Her memory bank for faces and incidents was remarkably receptive, and surprisingly effective, for someone of her age.

It was the shapely figure of the pert little blonde she first noticed, making her way over to where crowds seemed to be queuing to purchase a book. She had to give credit to that youngster's figure. The wiggle was something incredible to behold, she admitted to herself. I was like that at one time, she thought, only a little taller. The female was familiar, but the memory this time didn't perform to its usual level and the link didn't come to mind as quickly as it should.

I have had dealings with her but who is she again? Why do I know her?

Of course ...I remember now ...that time with Thelma Donaldson, when that bitch had the audacity to challenge my writing abilities: this was the one who was with her; claimed to be a publisher, didn't she. I remember now, the shrubbery. That little blonde was nearly flattened by fat Thelma. Hee-hee-hee! Funny, until she called the police! It took a few weeks to live that down ...but what is she doing here in Newingsworth? I thought she lived in London. What is the book anyway?

The big poster said 'Rabid Revenge Revisited – by Derek Tee.' Another one told her, 'Meet the author in store today – buy a copy and have it signed now!'

Derek Tee? Never heard of him ...but she had! The person at the table doing the signing – she knew him. He'd caused trouble next door, in the Donaldson's house – about the time of the fuss with Muriel. A rogue! He had something to do with it. She'd been certain at the time; didn't know why he wasn't thrown in prison then... Derek Tee is not his real name, she knew. What was it then? A stupid name... Toozlethwaite... Yes, got married eventually to the daughter, poor girl. Imagine being called Toozlethwaite, Sally Toozlethwaite!

Mrs Violet Masterton used to consider herself to be a very close friend of Mrs Donaldson next door, but that was before 'Thelma' arrived on the scene. *That woman, Thelma, she was brazen; worked in the Bingo Hall for a time – my Bingo Hall! She nearly let everyone in Cloverton know about that. I'd have killed her if that had happened... Now, where's little Miss Wiggle gone? Ah, there she is, chatting up Toozlethwaite. Bet she does a lot of that. I wonder if his wife knows about her – she looks the type to cause trouble. You can't have a wiggle like that and not cause trouble...*

Toozlethwaite looks a bit worried talking to her. It's a guilty look if you ask me, wants her to go away obviously, and now there's another one joined in. He looks even guiltier now...

She is leaving him, the young one; going towards Electrical Goods. I think I'll head her off.

Sophie had a wide grin on her face. Here she was in the middle of a large superstore with hundreds of people milling around, doing their Saturday shopping, and who should she bump into but Daisy. Wasn't that incredible – and while she was talking to Derek! One of the very few people she knew in Newingsworth had happened to catch her and Derek together. She hoped this wasn't going to cause trouble for him and thanked goodness that Daisy didn't recognise her. The 'Josephine' disguise must be doing the trick.

Sophie was one of the few people, walking about the store today, who was not carrying a wire basket or pushing a trolley, but that wasn't making it any easier to get about. Shoppers could be so inconsiderate towards each other, like leaving a trolley in the middle of the aisle, so other trolleys couldn't pass, or having it straddling the space – like this one...

"Excuse me," she said to the older woman.

"What?" was the insolent response directed back at Sophie.

"Could you possibly let me pass, please?" Sophie tried again, keeping cool. It was obviously with great reluctance and apparent difficulty that the trolley was moved, though it couldn't possibly be heavy with only one bottle of sherry rolling about. Sophie managed to squeeze through the small space she was given. "Thank you," she mouthed with a hint of sarcasm, as she looked at the woman who seemed familiar for some unknown reason.

At least she'd reached the section for the beans, peas, and assorted other tinned vegetables, but was still having to squash her way through the crowded aisles towards the exit. That's when a trolley hit her gently in the back. She ignored it. Some idiots can't control a trolley... Then it happened again.

She glanced round behind her, and who should it be? It was the older woman, again, the one with the sherry. Has she been drinking it already, wondered Sophie? *Ignore her; just make for the way out* ...until she was pushed in the back once more, this time with a little more force!

"Please, stop doing that ...or I'll... Do I know you?" she demanded of the woman.

"You don't remember me then."

"Should I?"

"You and your friend Thelma made a laughing stock of me a while ago. Have you forgotten?" and, as she asked, the trolley was pushed against Sophie's stomach, causing her to gasp. "The last time I didn't get the chance to say how much I disliked you," spat out the little old trolley pusher.

"I remember you now," said Sophie keeping her cool with great effort. "I've no idea what your real name is, but you were the one who tried to steal someone else's story. Oh yes indeed, I remember you now!"

"Oh how I laughed when big fat Thelma fell on top of you," snarled Mrs Masterton. "That was really funny..."

"But not as funny as this!" smiled Sophie, as she leaned forward and pushed the trolley, suddenly!

At a certain age, although the mind may be perfectly sharp and capable, it is often the case that the body's balance is not. Taking advantage of that, plus the element of surprise, can be deadly!

The Store's security man was not at all happy, having to come to the aid of a little old lady who had fallen against the high stack of baked-bean tins. She had done a great job, scattering them all over the main aisle and then, in a very public display of bad temper, she proceeded to berate him for taking so long to get there, and blamed it all on the stupid trolley! The one purchase that this person had in her trolley was carried for her by the Security Man to the check-out and on the way he did a careful check. Yes, the seal over the top of this bottle of sherry was still intact.

"You can never be too careful with apparently innocent old ladies," the Security Man reported later...

30

Jilly was definitely her dog. At least there was no problem with the name. From the start, no doubt or question existed about what she would be called, and that was mainly because Sally chose the name herself without Derek's involvement. She was quite proud of that. This dog would not be called nicknames – like ET.

When Sally stopped working, not long before ET was born, she decided a dog would be good company. They lived just clear of the edge of the town, actually in the countryside, so it seemed reasonable to her that a dog should enjoy the surroundings too. She would grow up with the baby, and be the perfect completion of a happy family. Sally loved Jilly; not in the way she loved ET of course, but who could resist her little darling Jilly? Look, she's smiling...

"Oh, my little pet, who could possibly not like you?"

Well, Derek for one and he had good reason, though he tried hard to avoid saying it out loud: sweet little Jilly did not like him, a fact recognised on the very first meeting when he tried to pat her head and she almost sank her sharp little teeth into his hand. He pulled back quickly enough on that occasion and avoided any painful injury, but was considerably more wary from then on.

It was not up for discussion, he knew, but Derek wondered if Sally ever regretted having the dog, although, he also knew that if she did have regrets she would never admit it! Why he had given in, heaven only knows. As if one pesky little screamer was not enough to contend with – ET, at least, was satisfied simply to suck daddy's finger. Neither did Derek mind going out with the pram, he was, in fact, rather proud to be doing that with ET, but he hated taking Jilly. He was happy pushing the pram, because that's what new daddy's were supposed to do, but the dog always spoiled things, wanting to get into it as well.

Derek felt perfectly justified in how he thought of the poodle – mark you, this thought he kept to himself – but 'a little bitch' described her perfectly. A pesky, miniature, white bitch of a poodle! That wasn't a dog any man should be seen with.

"You surely can't refuse your pregnant wife," Sally had said, displaying a pet-lip at his hesitation to agree when a dog was suggested. That was over two months ago. At the time, Derek counted to ten, realised there was no choice but to submit, and Sally had her way.

"When baby arrives, won't he be jealous of your little darling doggy?" he asked sarcastically at the time, but Sally ignored him...

It was difficult to hear the background music emanating from 'Classic FM Morning Selection'; it was being almost drowned out by ET's screams for more nourishment. *He is a greedy little...* Sally thought, but she was feeling better, with at least some confidence restored. It was great, even if she couldn't think particularly well due to the noise in the kitchen.

She liked listening to the radio now that she was at home with ET, and Jilly around the cottage for most of the day; she was alone with them for a lot of the weekend too, Derek still having to go out and about. He was continuing to publicise the book – him and little old Ms Clerk, the publisher's secretary – *my friend, dear Josephine – it's amazing how she copes at her age...*

The weather would have to be wet again today, she sighed, especially as there was a pile of nappies awaiting attention. A pile of Derek's shirts also waited to be put into the washing machine; probably unwise to put them both in the same wash, she decided, so even though there was a bit of an aroma they might have to sit there another day.

The jury was out in Toozlethwaite Manor on the usage of good old-fashioned nappies. Cloth or paper, which was really better? Cotton was currently in use but she had to keep convincing herself it was the right thing to do. It was supposed to be more 'green' to re-use these cotton everlasting baby-poo-catchers, rather than their use-once-and-throw-away paper counterparts. The big disadvantage of using cotton 'diapers', as Millie and Angie called them, was Derek's stomach, because that organ of his couldn't cope with emptying them after ET had done his duty by filling them. So, guess who was doing the rinsing-out?

The house hadn't yet been cleaned. That could wait until after the daily walk. She had to take ET out in the pram for some essential fresh air – just the two of them. It was wet, so Jilly wouldn't want to go. She'd be at home on her own for a while. She was never pleased being alone in the house though and Sally crossed her fingers that the cushions wouldn't be torn to shreds again. It would mean a special doggy-walk for Jilly later, when the rain stopped. Dear little Jilly didn't like getting wet – she would far rather piddle on the floor than go out in the rain, much to Derek's annoyance.

Sally was falling behind with the housework and odd jobs around the house. She would be first to admit that she had never been wonderful at that sort of thing but, since having ET, she was worse. There was always a grand plan, but where her days went she could not understand. By the end of each one, yet another grand plan had failed to be achieved.

When she stopped and gave up her job, four weeks before having ET, Derek predicted that she would get bored very quickly, sitting on her own doing nothing, particularly after working full-time at the Gazette for so long. She'd had four weeks to fill, doing something productive before the baby was due. For example, that's why he'd bought the emulsion paint, *she* thought – for the kitchen, *she* thought – for her to use, *she* thought – wrongly!

Painting the kitchen with Angie had been fun, the two of them had really enjoyed that Friday afternoon, even if it did cause a bit of a panic later. The kitchen was done in one day, a beautiful pale blue, which Derek hated. He'd had to go out and buy more for the baby's room. He still grumped about it, saying the kitchen would have to be painted again, a better colour.

"Get on with it then!" Sally had suggested, but it was still blue...

That's Derek for you.

Sally had important things to do at the moment – like feeding the constantly hungry baby. She was very relieved to have chosen to go for bottle feeding: the rate he was consuming milk: what if she hadn't? She gave a shudder.

When at work, she had always considered herself to be the most efficient and capable one in the office. It was she who had maintained office routines, processing information back and forth between the other three, but now... How things change, these days her brain was barely coping with one thing at a time.

"I'm just coming, ET darling, do not fret," she shouted in the direction of the demanding wail. "You'd think you'd never been fed before. Give over!"

It could have been her imagination, but didn't the volume of his wail only increase at that comment? She was glad the next door neighbours were miles away. At least, she was the only one being regularly driven to distraction.

Her next door neighbours were not exactly next door. Thelma and Hammy, Mr and Mrs Macintosh, or Uncle Hamish and Aunt Thelma as she now thought of them, were along at the New Farmhouse Hotel. A lot had happened for them in the ten months since the hotel had been opened; for starters, their wedding.

Hammy had insisted that they get married really quickly, something to do with his age, he said; for him life seemed to be passing much too quickly. Thelma had accepted a fairly simple affair at Slatterfoot Registry Office, followed by a reception back at the hotel for the family and a few of their close friends. That had been more than four months ago.

Being a little more mature than normal for matrimony, both had become fairly set in their ways, but something had to give and it was Thelma who tended to comply with her new husband's ways. She was finding wedded bliss to be not quite so 'blissed' as she had hoped. She was the flexible and tolerant one, even though she'd been single all her life, with more reason to be self-centred.

She'd never settled down: affairs, yes – but marriage, never.

Hammy had been married before, for a long time, and that was

Thelma's problem. He seemed to expect her to be a reincarnation of Sybil, his previous wife. When he'd returned at the end of a hard day's work on the farm, which he'd never avoided, he'd been waited on hand and foot. Although his Sybil laboured in many other ways, she'd enjoyed doing most things for him when they were at home, even his paperwork, at which he was useless. Then she died. Life careered downhill for Hammy after that, including the business. His basic problem was that he was a *doer* rather than a thinker and he wasn't properly house trained.

It was time-consuming, but Thelma was forcing herself to be patient – gradually introducing necessary changes without her new husband realising that he was being manipulated: sometimes frustrating for Thelma but, overall, it was paying off.

Hamish was the Manager of the hotel, but still very reliant on wifely support. Thelma would tell him what was required, and he'd be on to it like a shot. Although a bit awkward at times, they'd managed so far and she was determined to make it succeed; she had no intention of giving up on Hammy, or the marriage, or the Hotel, so there...

The hotel was actually her brother's, so Alexander should be more involved but, although he had financed the whole business set-up, he appeared to have little interest in their activities. Thelma therefore had free reign and was the driving force in the Mr and Mrs Macintosh team. As she and Hammy were far too old to have any natural family of their own, she looked on this project as her baby.

The website set up by Thelma to advertise the hotel was surprisingly successful at pulling in clientele. Business, though not brilliant, had been moderately good. They had extended the building to create a larger dining area and the new chef they had taken on was a real find. Even locals were being enticed in, to sample the food. Word of mouth was proving its worth and evening meals were becoming very popular. Thankfully, this was having only a minor effect on Anton's place.

A link from Newingsworth Bowling Club contributed to some of the success. A national competition was held during the summer, and the Secretary had recommended the Hotel to distant visitors and competitors. Many heeded his advice, and it was a very busy period. As a consequence, the Secretary received a free meal every Saturday evening for the four-week duration of the event, as a little thank you. Being a bachelor who hated cooking, he really appreciated that.

The power of the internet amazed Hammy. In addition to the bowling competitors, and a particular local who'd made this his secret venue for meeting his next-door-neighbour's wife, they had been getting random overseas customers too. People from far off, who'd seen the website and been sufficiently impressed to give it a go. They'd come from Japan, France, Germany, and Australia, and a young couple from Oban, up north, hoping for some nice English summer weather. Unfortunately it rained that week at Newingsworth – as it did, as usual, back home in Oban. They enjoyed themselves nonetheless, especially as there had been no midges!

In one respect, it had been disheartening for the foreign visitors. Most had arrived thinking it would be a good opportunity to try out, or improve their knowledge of the English language but it hadn't worked too well for them in the hotel because Hammy, insisting on playing 'mine host', wanted to make them feel cared for, and took every chance to talk with them.

For most of these visitors, the confidence they'd acquired in speaking English was rapidly shattered in these chats with Hammy. His Scottish accent totally floored them. Even though they had no notion at all of what he was on about, they went along with him, but they should have realised that by nodding in a wise and intelligent way, he had seen that as an encouragement. Luckily, Hammy laughed at his own jokes, which was a help for them in timing their laughter.

The family of Australians fared a little better, but even they considered themselves failures in comprehending the host, and they felt really bad about it – they were of Scottish descent – this was the language of their ancestors and they couldn't understand a word!

Thelma had a smattering of German, and French, and was able to pass herself in conversations with all nationalities, which was some compensation.

Oh, something else arrived at the hotel three months ago, a lollopy, sandy-coloured, big, daft Labrador pup. They called it Cornelius.

Quite unlike Jilly, Cornelius *liked* Derek...

31

"Weel then, we'll huvv tae get started wi' the golf course, lass," said Hammy "Noo that we're gettin' some guests. We'll hae tae mak it happen soon."

"Will we now? You realise it won't just happen overnight. Anyway how much do you know about designing a golf course?" Thelma asked her husband. Hammy could reply with confidence to that one.

"Weel, me, ah've been tae St Andrews – furr ma holidays, 'The home of golf', one year, when ah wis younger..."

"And you played on the Old Course, then?"

"No, no, dinna be silly, lass – jist the sand. It's a braw beach furr the paddlin'. Oh, an' it's rare furr san'castles as weel, ye ken!"

"You've never played golf at all, have you? You knew fine well that Alexander wanted a golf course next to the hotel. You told him you could do it, didn't you?"

"Och weel, no' quite. Ah told him ah couldnae dae it! An' he said, dinna worry, man, ma sister Thelma wiss a rare golfer at High School when she wiss young, and she'll dae it furr ye – an' these wurr his very ain wurrds. Did Alexander no' say tae you yersel?"

"No, my dear brother did not. So it looks like we're going have to call on the services of a professional designer. That will cost a fortune!"

"Oh we canny dae that noo," said Hammy panicking. "Ah said we'd manage it – the gether."

His wife gave him a hard stare. "And how, exactly, do you propose we do that?"

"Och, come on noo, it canny be that hard, lass. Huvv ye no seen the Open – an' the Masters, on telly. Aw ye need are some big holes in the grun' wi' some saund in them, an' some wee holes wi' flags in them, an' a wheen o' space in atween thum aw; some trees an' boulders an' a wee hut tae hae a cuppa tea on the way roon. Ye've played on thae courses yersel', surely?"

"Very succinctly put," she said sarcastically, "...but I'd suggest there might be a little more to it than that."

"Ah've goat some drawings, somewhere, that'll gie us the boundaries o' the fairm. They show the contoors o' the land, as weel, if ah remember right, wi' aw the wee hillocks."

The drawings that already existed were from the days when this had been worked farmland, and owned by him; nearly one hundred acres of land used, in the early days, by his father for the cattle. Latterly, a lot less acreage was put to use when it became all Hammy's. His business was Macintosh's Chooky Hens, supplying eggs to Bisko's, and any other stores wanting them. A vast area of the land had been left uncultivated.

The likelihood that he'd have a need for these drawings ever again was not really his reason for retaining them. When he'd had to leave the old farmhouse he'd kept them only as a keepsake. Yes, he'd had dreams of returning one day, but never believed that it would happen, and yet it had, even though not to the same old farmhouse.

The premises were very different now. The greatly enlarged building became both the hotel and their home. In consequence, there were numerous places to lose stuff. *If only he could remember where he put the damn things...* "Would ah maybe huvv pitt them in one o' thae?" he murmured to himself as he searched in yet another chest of drawers. As luck would have it, they were; in the back of one where he'd put Sybil's wee treasures; her jewellery, and bookmarks, and other bits and pieces, the things he couldn't possibly discard. That's where the drawings were found and he'd remembered correctly; the land details were shown.

"Look at that, then. At least, we've goat a stairt, huvv we no'? Look ye can see whaur the woods urr, an' the wee hills. The hills we huvv here are nuthin' compared tae the mountains and hills back up north. This grund's no' totally flat, but it's no' far off it. An' look, it shows the stream tae, an' still runnin' the same wey. We could dae somethin' wi' that, ah'm sure"

Some ideas of his own, had started forming in Hammy's mind already, but he didn't want to be too pushy ...not yet!

"Of course, we will be limited to a nine-hole course, you realise, on the area we are going to use. For a full game you have play the circuit twice," his expert wife explained.

"Oh, is that so now? Does tha' no' make ye dizzy then?"

"Hamish – please, be sensible. If we are going to succeed with this, you'll have to behave."

Was it Hamish then? If she's going to be using my Sunday name, it must be serious... He nodded wisely, but with a grin on his face.

"One thing we can decide is that the first hole and the last hole will be near the hotel. That way we won't need a special building for changing facilities," she said, slipping easily into the role of chief designer right away.

"No' too close, mind you. We dinna want the windaes broken wi' a' thae duff gowfers we'll be huvven."

"Agreed," said Thelma, which surprised him.

The plan was laid out on the large table so that all the land could be seen. It showed patches of woodland, and a reasonably sized copse beyond the stream. The stream formed the border of the land for part of the way, and then traversed the middle of the fields almost diagonally. It then ran on the far side of the old farm cottage, now called Toozlethwaite Manor by Derek, and along the access lane until it reached the main road. It continued as part of the local council's responsibility after that, as it wended its way southwards.

"Ah've always thought a golf course was laid oot like bein' oan a ghost train, goin' back and forard, in a wee area that feels much bigger. Oan the Ghost Train, ye jist huvv tae worry aboot kiddyon spider's webs, an' silly lookin' skeletons, an wohoo noises, an' it bein' pitch black, an' that. Oan a golf course, it's much worse – it can be dangerous if ye're no' lookin' – thae golf balls could kill ye..."

Thelma was well used to ignoring most of what Hammy wittered on about, and was studying the information laid out on the table, intrigued by the detail shown.

"It's right what you said earlier though, there are some hillocks, but overall, the ground is really very flat. We'll have to make it more varied." She was warming to the subject. This could become very interesting, a challenge in fact, but, she reminded herself – the hotel still has to function properly. "We could leave the trees – go round on either side of them, and yes, we could do with creating more character on the land," she continued.

"Whit aboot a big puddle in the middle? The water from the burn – we could dig a hole an' form a wee lake, an' use the soil furr some wee undulations. It's gey clayie stuff so ah could jist dig it oot an' flatten it doon, an' it would make a smashin' big puddle in nae time. Ah could sit in the bedroom upstairs an' watch a' the baws droppin' in it. Ah'd come oot later, an' fish them oot, and sell them back tae the lousy golfers..."

"Hammy – that is brilliant – a water-hazard for recycling golf balls – and they'd be clean then too! What more could we ask for? When can we start?"

He suspected that there was a touch of sarcasm in his wife's words.

32

Copying the original drawing was easy – Hammy passed the task to Derek and he obliged very quickly by supplying some prints. They hadn't wanted to spoil the master copy by scribbling ideas all over it, especially as it was one of the few things retained from his past.

So, spread out on the table in front of them was one of the prints, and the design process was about to start, being undertaken by an ex-champion amateur, and an almost clueless novice. The project was about to get underway officially.

Earlier in the day Thelma had walked around the fields, pacing out possibilities for tee and green positions and trying to decide the best lengths for each hole. Visualising, standing on an imaginary tee and assessing the view of the countryside that the golfer would have, spurred her on with the task. Remembering some of the difficult holes she'd tackled as a young player, it occurred to her that a view might be a waste of time! Does a golfer ever look beyond the hazards?

There was certainly more than sufficient area already suitable for rough, the difficult task would be creating fairways. The fact that cattle had been not been grazing all over this land for many years had permitted the grass to grow long in many places.

The positioning of bunkers would have to be considered too. The trick would be in making a course difficult enough to be challenging, without being so awkward that poorer ball-hitters were demoralised. Her mind went back to her younger days. She'd been School Champion for three years. What had she found daunting back then? She remembered various difficult holes, and some bunkers that were formidable.

The physical work would be Hammy's responsibility. Already he had talked to some of his contacts, eager to hire equipment to excavate the pond. He would be ready to make a start the moment Thelma made up her mind on the shape. She had many ideas, but the final decision wasn't clear yet.

"Remember where Sally and Derek's home is," Thelma advised her enthusiastic husband. "They have no idea that they are going to have a golf course on their doorstep, so wouldn't it be better if they were consulted?"

Hammy agreed. Before starting any physical stuff, he'd better warn Derek and Sally of all the work that was about to begin at their back door. He hoped there wouldn't be objections; that could cause delay, but he'd understand if there were. He would be making a great deal of noise with machinery and probably disturbing little ET. Sally would not be thanking Uncle Hammy if she couldn't get the little one to sleep because of him. He'd speak to them tomorrow...

Soil would be a bi-product of digging a large hole for the pond. That could be used to level off some of the fairway surfaces, and the remainder would be used to create some artificial hillocks; then the hole in the ground? Just add the water, as it would have said if it were a baking recipe. The natural supply from the stream would do that, but a small dam would probably be required to prevent the pond drying out in mid-summer. That would mean a reduction of water further downstream while the pond was filling. Would anyone complain if the stream dried up – Derek for instance?

By pumping water from the stream, Derek had created a water feature in his garden: a stream with a little waterfall, which went into another stream which burbled into a small pond with water plants– all thank to plastic DIY kits... He had even introduced goldfish.

"An' it looks smashin' tae..." Hammy commented to his wife.

Thelma suddenly got on her high horse, and retorted that it would be a good thing if there wasn't any water for it anyway. A pond, or a water feature, wasn't a good thing to have with a youngster in the family.

"Och, awaw ye go... The wee yin isnae even walkin' yet," Hammy retorted, "An' it's the *only* thing in the gairden that Derek has tried t' dae, an' succeeded wae!"

Thelma stormed off at that. Hammy could be so pig-headed at times, she muttered to herself.

Some of the shrubs that had self-seeded would need to be removed, and good-quality turf for the greens and tees would have to be obtained, and the greens would take a great deal of work to get right – yes, there would be plenty to do. A big fence would probably be required to prevent stray balls affecting Sally and Derek; balls drifting into their windows, or worse still, injuring someone in their back garden, particularly baby ET, would be a disaster. Although that would not be acceptable, a golf course with people hitting balls was still a good way off, and it would be a long time before any balls were sliced or hooked, or even hit straight down the middle. A fence would be needed, but not yet. There were more pressing tasks to be completed.

These random thoughts were all added to the master layout, which was now in pride of place on the wall in their private sitting room. Arrows showed the direction of play, the circles indicated the rough positions of tees and greens. Bunkers could be left until some of the permanent features became a little clearer in Thelma's head, and would then be established.

Though Thelma had doubted her own capabilities at the beginning, she was accepting it now as a challenge, and was starting to enjoy it. With the correct frame of mind, each little set-back was proving to be only that; she was getting used to having to rethink.

Hammy annoyed her by commenting that all they were creating "wid be a guid walk in the fresh air, that wid be ruined if ye loast the stupid wee ba'..." She suspected that to be something he'd heard on television, from one of these Smart-Alec commentators – although surely said by them in a more sophisticated way – so she ignored him.

Then there was the finance. What they were about to embark on would require big money, and bank loans could not be plucked off trees. Should they have to worry about that though? Of course not! It was Alexander's land, it was Alexander's desire to have the golf course – Alexander was a bank manager!

All they would have to do, she and Hammy, would be to make it happen, she was the brains, and he was the brawn. Very importantly, they must not become down-hearted – bearing in mind it wouldn't be easy. They weren't young; in fact, to be honest, Hammy was positively old! It could take years to complete if they designed and co-ordinated the project as they were hoping to, on the cheap.

Hammy suggested that to do it quicker they might consider *robbing* the bank? Thelma put that on the back burner – but who knows – it might turn out to be a good idea...

33

Hammy had always found it useful to have a 'friend' on the local council, especially when it came to land development, or planning permission, or suchlike, and the current talk he'd had with his 'friend' had been good. He'd been given the nod, and the wink. If they were planning to have a golf course development as part of the hotel complex, then don't worry, if there were any 'difficulties' they could be 'taken care of', he had been informed

Doing favours in the past for some influential people had always paid dividends in the long run, Hammy had found. It was just unfortunate that a lot of the folk he'd helped over the many years he'd been in Newingsworth, and who 'owed him', hadn't lasted the pace like he had.

"Ah can only talk tae those yins tha' urr still livin'," he confided sadly to Thelma.

He was eager to make a start. The shape of the pond had been pegged out in accordance with Thelma's instructions, and the loan of a digger had been obtained. It was sitting in the field at the back of the premises just waiting for him to jump into the driving seat. He had the key, but he'd never driven one of these things before. This disturbed Thelma.

"Nae bother, dinna fech yersell, Hen," he told his slightly anxious wife. "It'll be jist like drivin' a bus..."

He didn't mention he hadn't done that either!

The safety of this planned pond had been discussed at length by Thelma and Hammy.

The land was well beyond the town boundary, but Hammy could

visualise that the local kids, on learning of it, would fancy a paddle or a swim – he would have, if he'd had the chance when he was young, he told her. A large expanse of water was always an attraction – and a hazard – particularly for youngsters, so it would not be deep, about three feet was the plan, and it would be sloped all around the edges, and the water would feed in and out of the diverted stream.

There was some uncertainty in the plan. The stream had never dried up totally at any time when the land was being worked by either his father before him, or Hammy himself. It had actually run very low on occasions during the rare, hot summers, so there would be a need to block the outlet to ensure that water always filled the pond, or at least made it controllable.

It had been a good team he'd had working for him, building the hotel, and they would be the ones he would call on to build a barrier, when he'd made the hole. Once that was done there was a lot of other work they could help with to get things moving. Aye, there would be plenty to do...

Hammy talked to Sally and Derek. They would be able to see the pond easily from the back of the cottage – that's why it was to be called Toozlethwaite Lake. That pleased them. They were also promised reduced rates if they wanted to play on the course in the future. Afterwards, Derek suggested to Sally that he should have had it in writing, because when the course eventually opened Hammy would probably deny he'd said it; Derek knew Hammy...

Incidentally, it wasn't just Derek that little Jilly disliked. Hammy got the same treatment when it suited her. The annoying yap of a white poodle, barking, and snapping away at his ankles while he discussed what was being planned, made him a great deal more appreciative of how docile and friendly his big Cornelius was. Docile, but slobbery, was how Thelma described him – Cornelius, not Hammy.

Hammy couldn't believe that ET was sleeping through the racket the dog was making, but her baby, Sally assured him, although he had been a bit fretful a few weeks ago, was now behaving perfectly and would sleep through any noise, a bit like his father.

While the discussion was taking place, Derek had been trying to get Sally's little darling Jilly to stop barking and, over the weeks, the only way he'd found to be effective with any consistency was to feed her dog biscuits. It worked only for the time it took her to chew and swallow; it also put Derek's fingers in great danger.

Hammy explained how eager he was to get the work underway, and that he was about to begin using the mechanical digger. It might seem a bit noisy, but he'd only be doing it during the day, and be trying his best not to disturb Sally and the baby.

"Ah wis goin' tae try tae begin tomorrow, efter breakfast – urr you awrigh' wi' tha'?" he asked Sally.

"No problem Hammy. You can see how well he sleeps – he's a perfect little darling."

Next day, when Derek went off to the office, and Hammy turned the engine on to start digging, take a guess – who wakened, and yelled all day?

Yes, you are right...

34

The inspiration came to Sally literally moments after ET emptied his mid-day bottle: The females-only nights! They had all enjoyed themselves getting together, so, why not restart the meetings?

The train of thought was triggered in her mind by little Edwin. Basically it was the manner in which ET showed his appreciation of the food – by disposing of excess air in a gigantic burp.

With the 'burp', she thought of 'Hammy'. He'd stayed with them for many months eating meals she had cooked. They were obviously much appreciated, and were celebrated in the same time-honoured medieval manner as did ET, claiming that he was being complimentary to the cook! Unlike ET, he did proffer a mannerly, "*Pardon...*"

Hammy made her think of the 'Hotel', and then 'Thelma', which in turn sparked nice memories of the help from the 'girls'. They'd given lots of guidance and reassurance to her and Angie in the months leading to the births. The wise words they all contributed then had been very much appreciated by two mothers-to-be ...and remembered.

Angie and Sally had been seeing each other regularly ever since they left the hospital with their respective little bundles. They'd been seeing the others too, but never all at the same time.

Wouldn't it be nice to share the pleasure of motherhood, with everyone involved once more, thought Sally? Each one in the group would have a chance to contribute in establishing growing-up rules for ET and Annabel – and there was another thing. Instead of having to look after two babies themselves, all the time, they'd have a break on Saturday afternoons because everyone would be desperate to have a hold!

Before the babies arrived, the meetings were held on Wednesday's at the hotel, which suited Thelma down to the ground; delighted, from the word go that it was on her doorstep. It meant she was always on site for any emergencies and to give advice to Hammy. He was allowed to be in charge on his own when the group met. The evening being fairly quiet in mid-week she had trusted Hammy to cope, and he had.

Eventually, it was changed to Saturday afternoons, but still at the Hotel. This was a little less simple because Saturday was busier, and although Thelma was still on the premises, she did not have any confidence in Hammy being able to manage alone. She continued to leave him solely responsible, but she never fully relaxed when he was, expecting the inevitable to happen. In reality, each Saturday, Hammy coped perfectly...

That's the way it went, right up to one week before the births; each week 'The Female Mafia' got together and shared 'secrets'. It would have continued longer, except for the fact that on the following Saturday Sally and Angelina decided to paint the kitchen, and gave birth.

So, why not get together again? All that homely advice coming each week could do no harm. Little Edwin and Annabel, could surely only benefit in the future from the wise collective decisions of this maternal group. Sally was proud of the idea. All that was needed was a few phone calls and it could be starting again next week.

What should happen about the special birthday surprise for Derek, she wondered? She was still no further forward in deciding what to give him. Whatever it turned out to be, it would have to be as big a thrill as he was currently enjoying with his book's success, but what the form of his present could be was still not obvious. Then it occurred to her, there could be a way – a problem shared... That was the way to move it forward – she could ask the others! "It could be a TEAM decision!" she told the kitchen, talking out loud again, but it didn't seem to matter so much now; she'd got over that problem and could laugh at herself.

Bouncing thoughts around on Saturday afternoons would bring an answer surely, and someone was bound to propose a brilliant idea. Seven female brains working together! Something brilliant would surely to come up...

Perfect!

At that moment little ET decided he had been quiet for long enough, and a wail began. After all the deliberations, uncertainties, and indecision, Sally could cope with this. At least with ET, she didn't have to think – she now knew exactly what was required there...

35

In such a large field, had he been searching for them, they would never have been located, but by pure chance Hammy came across oil drums he'd dumped in the ground many years before. A guilty secret of his youth – remembered only after they'd been effectively punctured. He'd put them in a hole and buried them when he was working with his dad a very long time ago and without his father knowing; a lazy approach to a disposal problem one day, back when he was younger. Now he was having the chance to regret it.

It was most unfortunate that they had not been totally emptied. As dusk approached, all he could do was watch as oil spread over the bottom of the intended pond and, thanks to the clay soil, was unlikely to soak away quickly.

It hadn't been a good day – no, that's not true. The day had been productive, and he had been making reasonable progress – until he'd found the drums. Yes, almost a good day, right up to the moment he heard the clang, and then it became bad – very bad!

The stopping point should have been when he heard metal to metal, but he hadn't realised at first what he'd hit. It was metal, yes, but it could have been any old bit of metal. It would never have occurred to him that that's where he'd put the ruddy things. It was only when he'd mangled them enough to cause them to leak that he successfully made two and two add up correctly, and only then stopped trying to dislodge them with the digger bucket.

Earlier, he had been uncomfortable about the noise made by this mechanical leviathan he was driving, feeling that it would be causing a disturbance to Sally, but now he was hoping it had been loud enough to prevent his ripe curses reaching her ears. It would be even worse if

ET had heard him and one day used the same curses – he'd get the blame...

He couldn't do any more that night. Tomorrow was another day. He would come back out in the morning, fresh and eager, and perhaps by then would have thought of a way of clearing up the oil, although that might not be necessary if it soaked away. Confidence was not great on that score.

"Hammy has been working a bit later than usual," Sally told Derek when he arrived back home later that evening.

The whole day had been a bit noisy but, she was pleased to be able to say, it had not been enough to disturb ET. He'd actually slept right through, and wakened only for his meals. The one upset had been Jilly. She began barking at the door the minute the digging started. Sally had been unable to judge if it was poo-time or a display of doggy bad temper? As a precaution she opened the door to the back garden, and it *had* been bad temper. The screeching and squealing noise made by the tracks of the digger obviously got to her, and in a frenzy of barking, she dived at the fence. She obviously had it in for the driver. She wanted to attack him. If she had been a bigger dog, there was likely that she would have leapt over the fence and gone straight for Hammy's throat so quickly that he would have known no pain.

As it was, Jilly was little. All she could do was yap, and yap, and yap at the fence, until Sally decided it was a yap too many. A mad chase and scramble around the back garden culminated in Sally grabbing her, and bundling her back inside, where she was given a severe talking to. The tone of Sally's voice must have been just perfect to penetrate the dog's brain because Jilly went back into her basket – in a huff – with her stubby little tail refusing to wag for the rest of the day.

Initially, Sally felt guilty at being so nasty to her darling little pet. Interestingly however, that tone of voice had worked. Maybe next time ET misbehaved she could try it on him!

"Oh dear, that must have been upsetting for poor Jilly," Derek said casually, as he sat down at the dinner table, thinking that making conversation was the correct response at that moment.

Wrong!

He was told that the comment he had just made was flippantly lacking in warmth and compassion. In fact he was being cruelly sarcastic and he had never loved, or cared for that dog, *her* dog, "Which is most unfair," Sally accused, "especially when she gives you nothing but unconditional love and affection."

Sally and Derek saw Jilly through different eyes. Sally saw Jilly smile at her, affectionately; when Jilly looked the same way at Derek, Derek saw teeth!

Nowadays Jilly was less inclined to be wetting the kitchen floor, which Derek appreciated, but Jilly's final widdle for the night had to be just before she was tucked up in her bed, and always seemed to be just as Derek had relaxed and settled comfortably into his easy chair. He usually had to be reminded that Sally's little doggy friend required a chance to go for a last widdle.

Their relationship would be so much better if the dog liked him, but then again, for that to work, he would have to like her too.

This final duty of the day was an annoyance but he told himself it was good for doggy discipline, however, she had a mind of her own. Depending on her mood, she either didn't want to go out – and Derek had to get physical, endangering fingers in the process, or she did and went of her own accord – going wild, chasing imaginary rabbits around the garden. Standing at the back door, shouting commands, failed. These, Jilly chose to ignore so Derek got smart. He took to using the extending lead at nights, so that some control was possible. He liked to be the boss occasionally.

As usual, Derek forced himself out of his chair to go outside – he knew he had to, but Jilly was in a 'not moving' mood. She just remained where she was, in her basket, having stayed there since Sally's telling-off, probably still in a huff! Jilly knew her rights. She didn't have to move if she didn't want to, and her body language clearly displayed the signs. As Derek approached her basket, the little face snarled "*Make me...*"

He put on his leather gloves, a routine safety precaution when dealing with this pet, and carefully attached the end of the extending lead to Jilly's collar, trying to ignore the growling, and wary of the sharp teeth displayed. The back door was opened and Derek led the way out.

Fitting an external floodlight was something he'd been meaning to get round to but, being 'well-meaning' didn't make it happen. It would be good to go out on a dark night and not have to peer into inky blackness. However, she was a white dog and as long as she remained in the garden, Jilly could be seen.

Tonight, Derek went out first with the lead extending as he progressed, but with no dog appearing; a 'reluctant' night obviously. Jilly was still in her basket and Derek was alone in the garden, a long piece of cord stretched between them through the kitchen door.

The gate into the field wasn't properly closed, he noticed; that could lead to trouble. He certainly didn't want the dog escaping from the garden. He'd never get her back and that would not please Sally, so he went over to close it properly. As he did so, something moved in the darkness, just beyond the gate. He stepped through and went closer and saw that it was only a large piece of polythene sheet, probably some of Hammy's stuff that had blown loose. It should be picked up before it blew elsewhere.

The end of the lead was still in his hand but now was extended to maximum, and the polythene was out of reach. Should he go back inside and lift Jilly out of the basket; not something to look forward to, or grab the polythene? She could wait...

Leaving the handle of the lead on the ground, through the gate he went to catch the plastic sheet. There was enough light to show a partially oily surface, so he had to be careful how he folded it. Getting oil on his hands he could do without, thank you. Avoiding the messy bits carefully, it was lifted, wrapped smaller and carried to the gate – just as a flash of white passed him!

That damn bitch was loose! The handle for the lead was being pulled along and he'd have to grab it. Seeing the handle hurtling towards the gate, about to pass him, he turned, threw the polythene over the fence into the garden, made a dive for it, and...

Missed! Damn!

"Jilly!" he shouted. "Come here! Don't... run... awaaaaay..."

He expected no response and he got what he expected! Now he'd have to go and find her. Returning to the house without the precious pet would mean a long argument about why he'd let the blooming animal escape, and then he'd be back out to continue searching – but surely she wouldn't get far. The long lead would snag on something and... Oh, but it could get worse – what if she choked?

Sally appeared at the back door, in her dressing gown. "What's wrong Derek? Why are you in the field?"

"No problem darling, just fetching Jilly."

"But why...?" she started; then decided to leave it. "Alright, don't be long..."

He thought he saw a flash of white going towards the silhouette of the parked truck. He could just make out the mounds of earth where work was progressing.

"Jilly!"

He probably should have at least returned for a torch, but there was a small amount of light permeated into the fields from the cottage and it was a white dog he was looking for, so he considered he would manage once his eyes became accustomed to the darkness. Was that a flash of white, again? He hurried towards it, and stumbled on the rough ground, almost falling, but regained his balance, and continued moving forward.

On a downwards slope he could see very little and almost slipped. He nearly tripped again, this time – over a wire on the ground – or was it a dog's lead! He lifted the cord and pulled gently. Success... The retractable end came towards him easily. Jilly would be at the other end. All he had to do was wind her in – like a fish...

There was a yelp as he tightened the cord but he kept pulling. Obviously she was enjoying her freedom and didn't want to come back to him. So he walked backwards, and kept pulling – until he could pull no more; the cord was fully wound back, but, where was she?

In the dark, he reached down towards the end of the lead, and for his trouble, was almost nipped on his gloved hand. He heard the snap of her jaws, rather than feeling them, thank goodness. His eyes had become more accustomed, but all he could see were two eyes, two white ears and a white tail. Was it the poor light? At least she was still attached.

He started to move towards the cottage – she whimpered. He had to drag her along a little, obviously reluctant to move, but that wasn't unusual when Derek was in control, and she whimpered again... He dragged her, a little closer to the cottage gate, where the light was now a bit better, but he still couldn't see her properly, and she whimpered once more...

"Quit moaning, you pesky mutt" he muttered.

She whimpered yet again. He was standing at the gate now, and so was she – and Derek got a whiff. She was covered in diesel oil.

Now she was whimpering and whining alternately, and obviously shivering too.

"You poor dog," he said looking down at her, actually starting to feel sorry for little Jilly, that was until it occurred to him – I am the one who will have to clean the ruddy stuff off...

36

For a hundred and one reasons, organising the female get-together took longer to get off the ground than she thought it would. Having it coinciding with Millie's being in the country was the main difficulty; she was still shooting backwards and forwards across the Atlantic, making sure the restaurant had been continuing to run smoothly without her..

"...And don't forget Josephine," said Millie, from the States.

"Of course not..." was the response at the other end of the line in Newingsworth.

At last they were to be meeting, at the hotel, as before – this time, nine of them, because two babies would be there too, and with both young mothers anticipating the freedom of being bystanders while the other five eager females jostled for the opportunity to be cuddling the little ones.

For Angelina, the previous night had been great. Sam rose dutifully at four a.m. to give their little darling a feed, and just as every well-behaved little Annabel should do, she went back to sleep immediately, allowing Sam to return to his bed – and all happened without Mummy being disturbed.

Not so for Sally. With Derek due to leave early for another promotional, she was the one who rose when ET wanted his feed. Wind, which he normally discharged with enthusiasm, refused to budge for ages ...and, incidentally, Derek slept on!

"Oh Angie, isn't she a perfect little darling," said Thelma, who had been given the privilege of first turn and was holding Annabel close to her. "You are so lucky..."

"Can I take her from you," asked an eager Millie, deciding to takeover, having judged Thelma to have held her long enough. "My dear little grand-daughter... Come to Gran, my little pet."

That's when Sally arrived.

Edwin had been awake for much of the night and, as a result, he was unsettled and cross almost all of the morning. Thankfully, he had fallen asleep in his pram as they left the cottage. Sally attempted to dodge the potholes as she pushed him along the lane but with only limited success and she was grateful that, even being bounced along the pathway, his much-needed sleep was continuing.

The hotel was reached.

Wheeling the pram in, she was greeted by beaming, welcoming smiles from the waiting group, all eager to share another little bundle of joy, as they were doing with Annabel.

Sally was hardly through the door when her mother was over beside her. "Let me take him, please," pleaded Muriel, "...my little grand-son..." and before Sally could even comment, her mother had reached into the pram and lifted Edwin out. He was suddenly awake and everyone knew it! "Oh my goodness..." said a perturbed Nana Donaldson. In a suitable soppy baby-voice, as she gazed at the red-faced, screaming bundle she was holding at arm's length, she added, "...What's wrong today then, little fellow? Tell Nana all about it..." And he did! She tried consoling him but he was having none of it.

"Let me try," offered Daisy. "Derek was much the same if he was wakened suddenly."

The screaming child was handed over willingly.

Sally stood back and watched. Serves them right, she was thinking; they caused the problem, let them solve it. It was obvious that no matter how much Daisy patted and shushed him, she was having no more success than Muriel.

Millie was watching too, trying not to gloat because she was holding a silent and happy Annabel. Millie would not be letting anyone else hold the quiet one, without a fight!

Thelma was at Daisy's elbow and offered to help. Daisy wasn't overly happy about that – she would have managed fine, eventually, but Thelma was clutching at him, and soon had control.

"Maybe if I took him Thelma..." suggested Sally diplomatically, but as Thelma had only just acquired him she was not giving him up, even to his mother.

"It's all right, Sally. He has a little wind, that's all..." she replied confidently, placing his head over her shoulder ...and regurgitated milk went down her back!

"I have a cloth in the pram," said Sally, as another gurgle promised more mess.

Thelma was a tad less eager now and when Josephine offered to take him, he was handed over without a great deal of fuss.

"There, there now," was all Josephine needed to say and, in her arms ET dropped off happily to sleep again, and silence returned.

"Wow..." was the collective comment...

Although the meeting was quite unlike their previous gatherings, having babies in the room beside them, both were at last in their respective prams fast asleep, so it allowed them to chat as they had in the old days.

Sally had been looking forward to it because it was a while since she been 'out', but it wasn't turning out to be fun for her. The babies being with them hadn't brought the magical feeling she had been hoping for. It was obvious that Thelma's mind was on the hotel, and having ET and Annabel with them made it difficult to concentrate on the chatter and all they ever drank at meetings was coffee. It was not working.

Next time will have to be different, she thought. Why not have an 'Away Day', leave normality behind; make the get-together a bit different, and we could all relax: go somewhere to let our hair down and have a drink.

She suggested it to the others.

"But the babies..." complained the relatives and the pretend aunt, "They couldn't come with us... Who would be giving them cuddles? Who will look after the little darlings if we don't?"

"That's what fathers are for," threw in Angie.

"Here, here!" agreed Sally and pointed out it would only be for one week, and that the following weeks they could have them again if they really wanted. At that they all became more enthusiastic.

"So, where to?" was the next question.

It was Daisy who knew a place – just perfect for letting-down hair... "And how do we get there?" asked Millie.

"Leave it to me," said Thelma, abandoning the others to look for her husband. To have a day out together would mean transporting seven females and called for a biggish car. The hotel Range Rover would probably be perfect.

When asked, Hammy proved awkward. He said that it had to be available in case needed to transport guests. Thelma turned on the charm to have her way, and almost succeeded. As usual, he was about to give in to her demand, under pressure, until he asked casually where they would be going in the vehicle.

"Sorry, Hammy – not for your ears, I'm afraid, ladies only..." Thelma replied. The wrong answer, so Thelma had to report to the ladies that the transport she'd hoped for was not available after all. That's when little Ms Josephine Clerk stepped in.

"I'm sure if I asked Mr Brown very nicely, he'd give us a loan of his saloon. He won't be using it if he is ill, will he? It would be big enough," she said. "I'll phone and ask!"

There were moments when Sophie actually believed she had become Ms Josephine Clerk and this was one of them. She was with her newest, and probably her closest friends other than Andy and was enjoying the female companionship. So, she went outside, pretended to make a call on her mobile, then came back with a smile, and a nod.

"He said yes," and with those words, Ms Josephine Clerk became even more popular.

If either Derek or Sam had been at that gathering, they would have appreciated Josephine's entitlement to a step up in the hierarchy – Newingsworth Mafia: Ladies Section: Transport Executive – and they would have promoted her immediately...

37

On the day, 'Josephine' was on her way round, collecting each of them individually – the first stop, 40 Cloverton Drive, for Muriel. Bravely, she had left the safety of the large car and walked up the driveway, looking to her right and, as expected, saw the curtains twitch.

Mrs Masterton, the eyes and ears of Cloverton, was obviously still alive and watching all the comings and goings in the neighbourhood, as usual. Being assaulted in the adjacent driveway on a previous visit had been a humbling experience for Sophie – mini skirt, shoes, and tights – all ruined on that occasion. She had her own back at the Bisko confrontation and came out of that more favourably; the opposition suffering a bruised rear – and bashed baked beans.

Sophie ought to have been pleased to see the old dear surviving, but remembered too well their previous encounters. This should be considered a war zone; she must be wary of further retaliation and be prepared to run if the old woman appeared at the front door.

Walking up the driveway as Ms Josephine Clerk, spinster of a distant parish, she shouldn't have been perturbed. With no chance of being recognised she could have made a funny face at Mrs Masterton and got away with it – but she didn't.

Muriel was *almost* ready.

"Come in a moment, dear, I'll just be another few moments," she said, as she opened her door and Sophie stepped inside. "Come into the front room and have a seat. Oh, Alexander, this is Ms Josephine Clerk, I told you about her. She's been working with Derek – his book!"

Sophie's heart stopped beating, but thankfully restarted, a little faster. She hadn't expected to see Alexander again. Last time she had looked very different.

"You haven't met my husband, have you?" said Muriel.

As they shook hands, and Sophie tried to make it appear convincing that it was their first meeting ever, she noticed the look in Alexander's eyes. It was different this time. The cheeky devil... He was appraising her as an older woman, a friend of his wife's, and one who didn't interest him much. Sophie remembered the other, when, admittedly she'd been wearing different clothes – and a lot less of them. Back then, the look had been lecherous. It wasn't there at the moment and she missed it.

They made the usual small talk, the weather, how sales for Derek's book were doing, where she was staying, etc.

"...And where are you going off to today, then?" he asked, but received no answer. Ms Josephine Clerk went silent, and looked at the floor. "What's all the secrecy? Are you up to something naughty?" he asked her, and a glint appeared in his eyes.

"Oh, that would be telling, wouldn't it?" she said, losing the slight crackle she'd created for Josephine. In her normal Sophie flirting-voice she asked, "Would you like to be there if it was?"

"Oh yes," he replied, sitting forward on his chair, and now much more interested.

"Well, tough – you can't," she retorted, then softened her tone, back to Josephine's, "...because, sadly, there aren't enough seats."

"Have we met somewhere before?" he asked her suspiciously, looking at the old woman a little more carefully.

"Oh, maybe. Which school did you go to – but you'd be few years ahead of me," she said innocently, struggling not to laugh.

Luckily, Muriel appeared, ready at last, and they left Alexander, none the wiser of the destination but desperately trying to remember that voice...

The next collection stop was for Angelina, Buttercup Avenue, and she was standing at the gate waiting for them. She was obviously determined to leave all her troubles behind.

"No pram, no baby, no Sam, no worries... Yeehaw! Let's go guys!" were her first words as she climbed cheerfully into the car.

"Hmm..." was next, as she settled back into the soft rear seat, closing her eyes with a contented smile on her face.

Onwards, to Blytheton Road and, unsurprisingly, Daisy was ready and waiting on the doorstep. "I'm off now, Hector" she called into the house, and made for the car.

"W-w-w-w-wait..." shouted Hector, appearing at the door. "Wh-wh-wh-where are you g-g-g-going? Are you still not t-t-t-telling me? What if there is an em-m-m-m-m-mergency?"

"You'll manage," she replied condescendingly, and, as she climbed aboard, called out, "Have a nice day..." and the car moved off. Smiling at her husband, Daisy waved cheerfully.

Hector glowered back.

Three down, three to go. Sophie was relieved that she would not have to negotiate the lane to collect Sally; she would be waiting at the hotel with the others.

Sophie would never forget that lane... Derek lying exhausted on a roadside verge; he wasn't up to marathon running... Derek was such a pet ...but his silly wife... *Careful, concentrate on the driving!* If Sally ever recognises me in this get-up she'll scratch my eyes out.

Sally had left Derek at the cottage and walked to the hotel. Derek had not been told where they were going. His instructions were to take ET to Blytheton Road. Sam would take Annabel there too and Grandad would be looking forward to them all visiting.

Sally and Angelina had agreed that three men, collectively, would obviously be able to cope with two babies. Surely mothers shouldn't be under pressure all the time?

Millie and Thelma were ready and waiting, sitting at Reception. Sally joined them on the sofa, looking forward to a day away from the baby routine.

Millie was back from Detroit, and in the same hotel room again. More of her time was likely to be spent in the UK both her grand-children being a big attraction. Hammy was considering changing the room name from the 'Chestnut Room' to simply 'Millicent's'.

The room now was permanently booked. Millie's clothing

remained hanging in the wardrobes while she was in the States. This was to save packing and unpacking but, no matter, each time she returned, it was always with another full case.

When the car with its occupants arrived at the New Farmhouse Hotel, and all seven were about ready to go, they decided a little alcohol before leaving would get them warmed up. The day out had begun, and the little drink would make everyone more comfortable – except for Josephine, the Transport Executive. She was generously permitted a soft drink of her choice.

Hammy served them, and hung about. They were bound to mention where they were going – they were women, after all, but it transpired that they were women who could keep a secret – at least from him.

38

'B-b-b-b-b-bemused' would be the word chosen reluctantly by Hector to describe his current state. He was having difficulty in accepting how easily he'd been duped into baby-sitting for his two great-grand-children, Edwin and Annabel. There was no denying that he was incredibly proud of them and loved them being around, but the fact that he had been left in sole charge was a wee bit disturbing. He felt uncomfortable; about to be tested and able to do nothing but fail.

It began just after lunch. Daisy was preening herself to go out. He'd noticed that she hadn't ordered him to get ready, nor had she changed into the clothes she used for the scooter. So he guessed correctly that he was about to be left behind. Just before she walked to the door to leave, she got round to talking to him, her mind obviously occupied by something much more important than him.

"You won't be alone for long," she said as a last minute reassurance. "Derek and Sam will probably pop over to keep you company while I'm out."

"Oh, and wh-wh-wh-where are you g-g-g-g-going then?"

He'd asked it innocently enough, he thought, but she gave him the brush-off.

"I'd love to be able to tell you, but I can't," she replied, rubbing the side of her nose with her forefinger as she said it, and smiling secretly.

"Are you going all al-l-l-l-lone, or with s-s-s-s-s-s-somebody else?" That seemed a reasonable follow-up enquiry, he thought.

"Ah... that would be telling," was her response.

Don't give up, he told himself.

"S-S-S-S-S-Sam and D-D-D-D-D-Derek are coming over – wh-

wh-wh-why?"

"I'm sure they'll let you know when they get here..."

And that was all he succeeded in eliciting from that source of information. He was wary and just getting over all the nonsense with the Granny Wisdom thing. That started as a big secret too! It still unsettled him so he decided to stop thinking about it and, instead, looked forward to the boys coming over. The three of them would probably go out for a drink. They would insist on treating him, wouldn't they? Yes, of course, they would.

It was well over a year since Hector's known family had increased in size, but it was still a novelty to him. Millie coming home had been surprising enough. Finding, he had a grand-daughter, in addition to the grand-son that he knew so well, had been wonderful – and she looked like her mother. Everybody had to admit that. Even Angelina, herself, understood why he'd stared at her in Bisko's many times... *many, many,* times...

He was pleased they'd married, she and Sam, before Annabel was born. It was the right thing to do; both parents getting married when there was a baby; not running away from the problem like Millie had done. Funny, on the day they were married, with Sally being the bridesmaid, there hadn't been much room in the Registry Office for the rest of them to get in. They were both very big girls by then, Hector fondly remembered.

He had felt sorry for Sam. He had needed a lot of persuading but Angie was a determined young lady. Angelina was so like her mother in that respect ...and her grandmother ...all very determined women!

When Derek and Sam arrived together in the taxi Hector was surprised, and even more surprised to see, with them, the babies in carry-cots. The babies were unexpected. Didn't the girls take them with them the last time? This could make a hostelry visit less likely.

It softened the blow when the six-pack was brought out – but they'd borrowed his scooter and gone out, the two of them, leaving him, and the beer – yes – but also the babies! They wouldn't be long, they promised, and would return shortly with Chinese carry-outs to see them all into the evening.

"Why d-d-d-didn't the g-g-g-girls take the b-b-b-b-babies?" Hector had asked, but was met with blank looks from Derek and Sam. "C-c-c-c-come on g-g-g-guys, p-p-p-please... l-l-l-let me into the s-s-s-s-s-s-s-secret..."

Unlike Daisy, the two lads would have told him, if they'd known themselves. They were as much in the dark as he was, so their best guess was that Daisy, Sally, and Angelina, had gone out together without telling any of them where!

Sam and Derek had been gone for an hour, and so far Hector had restricted himself to consuming only one can of beer. The babies had been bottle fed by their respective fathers before they left, so Edwin and Annabel were silent, snoozing away. Hector sat uncomfortably, in his favourite chair, looking across at the cots, keeping very quiet, hoping that nothing would wake them.

He wasn't programmed to cope with babies...

Hurry back, lads, please...

39

Sophie drove the noisy, chattering car-load safely to the destination, guided by Daisy, the only one of the group who admitted to knowing its location.

While Hector sat at home on tenter hooks, the Newingsworth Mafia, Ladies Section, were utterly relaxed and happily enjoying their specially arranged, secret away-day. This venue should make a nice change from the New Farmhouse Hotel, pleasant though that was, because this afternoon they would be relaxing together in the *Torrid Hedgehog*, Little Typington, with no babies to bother them.

Seven of them, ready to begin a 'females only' afternoon and evening, in this old village pub; mobiles switched off and no-one knowing where they were. Pub grub was planned following a few drinks, and at the moment no-one cared about who, or what, they had left behind. Normal life was forgotten in a collective day-out euphoria they succeeded in generating.

Like any village-pub landlord, this one was delighted to have this group suddenly appearing. It meant extra cash in the tills for him as long as he made them feel welcome, so they were given immediate attention at their table, even though the large sign stated 'Bar Service Only – Please'.

The venue was Daisy's brainchild. Having been brought here on the scooter by Hector, a few months ago, had sparked the thought. Getting out of Newingsworth, Slatterfoot and surrounding District meant none of them would be known by the locals. No stories were likely to be carried back to their respective neighbourhoods if anything were to occur, because today they certainly intended to enjoy themselves!

None of the group had divulged this destination to the males so, as long as only Hector knew about this place but remained at home, they'd be safe from any prying eyes or gossiping tongues. However, when it came to gossiping tongues, they were already assembled in the form of Daisy, Millie, Sally, Thelma, Angelina, Muriel and Josephine – who couldn't wait to start telling stories generally to the detriment of the male sex.

Daisy just had to tell all about her previous visit. It started off the giggles as she recounted how 'her Hector' on that day had been beguiled by a blonde floozy in a very short skirt – "And at his age too!" she emphasised... Hector's gawping at the opposite table, the over-exposed posterior, and the enormous box that the blonde dolly-dimple had been struggling with. "He couldn't stop himself," she declared. "There he was, jumping up and offering to become this young blonde bombshell's white knight."

Daisy didn't hold anything back, and whenever it occurred to her, she embellished it for comic effect, but Sophie immediately recognised whose exposed posterior was being discussed, and felt a slight unease. On the other hand, she had difficulty in recognising a lot of what was being recounted. Sophie had to give credit to Daisy – her story was much better than the actual event.

"Oh how he grumbled for the next three days about back pain," Daisy continued. "And not realising why he was being given no sympathy. Dirty old devil – at a bad age... And I'm sure she wasn't even a real blonde."

Being described by Daisy, as an artificial blonde floozy and a dolly-dimple, didn't amuse Sophie as much as it did the others, but today, she was Josephine, so she forced herself to laugh along. At least it softened the blow to her personal esteem to remember that she'd been called considerably worse than that. On previous occasions, it had been by wives who'd objected to what she and their husbands had been getting up to – but that was before Andy came along.

Muriel helped to keep the stories flowing. She just had to mention the slight detour her spouse had taken after the launch party for Derek's book. Not many husbands had gone home that night via

London. It certainly wasn't the shortest way home to Cloverton, Newingsworth – especially when he'd started out in Newingsworth...

Muriel hesitated. "Maybe I should have said it was a pre-book-launch party," she added, "because there wasn't any book at all back then, was there Sally?"

Sally agreed with a laugh. "Made up for it now though, hasn't he? They are already reprinting it. It's selling like hot cakes!" she added.

"They should have printed more than ten in the first place," threw in a laughing Thelma. This was the first time since returning to Newingsworth and her abstaining from alcohol, that she'd let her hair down. A few drinks; just a matter of pacing out the alcohol, she'd said. *I can control myself...*

"Poor Alexander," continued Muriel, "told me he slept on a park bench that night, and a policeman kept wakening him up."

No, that's not true – didn't you know he slept at my place? Sophie wanted to say out loud – telling them it wasn't true – but there had been a policeman, Andy was there. Well done Alexander. Funny how all men are story-tellers and have little secrets that they keep from wives.

"That photo Gramps took of Sam in Bisko's," said Angelina, "That was stupendous, I think, and I want to have it blown up to a large portrait to hang in the front room, but for some reason Sam doesn't like the idea. Did you see it, Mom?"

She turned to Millie.

"I did honey, and I can sure see his point. It makes him look hideous, and it'd give little Annabel nightmares – that's for certain!"

Millie turned to Daisy, "Pop, sure has a lot to answer for, Mom," she declared. "Glad they're friends now..."

"At least Sam speaks English – if only my Hamish could!" Thelma said. She went on to explain how the Japanese tourists who stayed with them recently had struggled with Hammy's version of the language. It wasn't entirely his fault though. He had difficulty understanding them too, but when a question was asked he was determined to help. Eventually, after much bowing, the guests left the grinning Hammy delighted to have improved international relations. Soon afterwards, the visitors appeared at the Reception Desk.

"'*We speaka Tellma prease?*' they said. That's when the receptionist called me," Thelma told them. These poor guests said to '*thank the honoulable gent, but expranation for cullent wolld banking clisis – totarry insclutable!*' They'd only asked for directions to the nearest bank to withdraw cash, so I gave them a map. They were delighted to be able to understand what I was saying. When I said thanks later, on their behalf, to Hamish, his face lit up. He really thought they had been admiring his intelligence!"

Josephine was smiling and laughing along with the rest, but hadn't contributed. She knew something would be expected of her – what could she say? She was a prim elderly spinster who had been concentrating on work for most of her life, so what could she possibly know about men and how silly they could be? At least, that's what Sophie presumed the others considered her life to have been as Josephine, but she decided to go for it...

"Oh, I must tell you about one of my colleagues, a young lady who works for my dear boss, Mr Brown. He almost had to fire her again months ago. My goodness, but she is naughty."

And that caught everyone's attention. How did little Ms Josephine Clerk discover this, they wondered? If it's juicy gossip, this was the time to tell.

"She was a blonde, and you know what they say – that blondes are the worst – calls herself Sophie. I said at the time to Mr Brown when she first applied to join us and he asked my opinion, as he always does, I think it unwise to take her aboard, Sir Arthur. I have a feeling she'll cause you nothing but trouble, but this time he did not listen. No, he did not ...and I was proved correct in no time at all."

"What happened, Josephine?" asked Angelina, as they all leaned forward.

Sophie lowered her voice, and they all leaned in closer still.

"Can I get you ladies any more drinks?" asked the landlord as he passed.

"Go away..." was the rude reaction from the group.

"...She couldn't keep her clothes on." Josephine told them.

"Oh, we know," came from Sally, Thelma and Muriel, in unison.

"I was the one who had to take phone calls from angry wives, and lovers of budding authors whose careers and current love lives were in the process of being shattered. It was painful for me to have to listen to their sobbing – lives ruined by the stupid behaviour of this woman – our employee."

"And did Mr Brown get rid of her? Was she dismissed?" asked Daisy.

"Oh, yes... But that was after..."

"After *what*...?" came from the female chorus.

"After Mrs Brown and I saw what happened in the office..." Sophie stopped, lifted her glass of now flat lemonade, and took a little sip, replacing it carefully on the beer mat, before continuing... "Mr Brown asked me to arrange to have Ms Clerkenwell-Brown attend his office for a disciplinary meeting. I said he should dismiss her, but he said he'd have to let her explain herself. He wasn't sure what she'd really been up to, he said, and anyway how did we know what was being said was true? He saw my disapproving look, I'm sure..."

"And...?" they all said.

"When Mrs Brown came in to see her husband that afternoon, it was unexpected and happened to coincide with Sophie's interview. She asked if her husband would be long, because she was in a hurry. I said I didn't know, and that he'd asked me not to disturb him. I suggested that if I peeped in the keyhole I might be able to judge if the meeting was nearly finished or not. So, I did that – and, I couldn't help myself, I said, *Oh*..."

"Why, what had happened...? What was it, Honey...?" and this time it was Millie who was desperate for more.

"Mrs Brown pushed me aside, and bent down and looked for herself. She made a strange noise then stood up, gave me a glowering look, and threw open the door..." Sophie lifted the glass of flat lemonade again, wishing for something stronger, and took another sip. There was a rapt silence, and only then did she realise that everyone else in the room, including the landlord, was hanging on her every word... "And there she was, the blonde, standing naked – well almost, and Mr Brown with his jacket *and* his tie, lying on the floor – and he *never* takes off his jacket or his tie during working hours... She divorced him after that, and he was never the same man again, hence him lying ill just now... And as for that strumpet – Sophie Clerkenwell-Brown – the one with a compulsion to strip – she was kicked out immediately, but the silly man hired her again the moment his divorce came through. You have to watch out for her – she causes trouble everywhere – she could even be in this room..."

Sophie stopped and looked around, with no break in the attention she was receiving. "But she can't be here today because we all have our clothes on!" Everyone burst out laughing at that, and the general conversation began again around the room.

"That's just how I remember her..." said Sally wistfully, reaching over to gently touch Josephine's hand, "...and to think I blamed poor innocent Derek..."

Isn't life strange, thought Sophie. As 'Sophie' I'm reviled by Sally, as 'Josephine', now a best friend, and yet it's still me? Yes, life is strange.

"That reminds me of when Hammy..." and, as Thelma started into more revelations to make Hammy seem like a really feckless Scotsman, the giggling began again ...and no exaggeration was necessary!

40

Sophie was in her own little world watching the happenings around her. It was only an observation but being sober and feeling slightly out of it, she could see the others now giggling away at the least thing; a little more intoxicated with each new drink, and likely to be less than capable of mobility when it came to time-up...

There were considerable comings and goings in the *Torrid Hedgehog* by the regulars. Though it would not be fair to single out this establishment as being any worse than any other public place, she noticed that their bottoms remained on seats only for as long as it took the memory of the previous cigarette smoke to clear from their brains. They were constantly rising and stepping outside to the fresh air, to pollute it and their lungs once more with cigarette fumes.

No-one smoked in the female group she'd brought – unusual nowadays but nice, she thought, however, it didn't prevent them having just as much exercise as their smoker companions because, with the amount they were drinking there had, eventually, to be regular disposal trips to the 'Ladies'.

Sophie observed that if seven females actually sat together at one time it was for a few moments only. It was lucky that the regulars were mainly males, otherwise there would have been a very long queue all evening! Sophie's liquid retention was coping so much better than the others, because she'd tried a little orange, she'd tried a little lemonade, she'd gone wild and had one half-pint beer shandy and loved the taste but drank it very slowly to make it last. So, she hadn't reached capacity yet.

Late in the afternoon, during a gap in the hilarity, Sally remembered the other reason she'd wanted the outing. Each one of them had been asked, when she'd phoned to arrange the day, to think about what sort of event might be the perfect birthday surprise for Derek. With everyone relaxed, today could be the sort of day when really good ideas could be aired. Maybe one of them would be practical. As she, herself, was feeling a little tiddly, Sally hoped that the others would be able to remember whatever thoughts they'd had before the drinks began to be consumed.

Now was the moment then, while she could still speak, and think straight.

With noise everywhere, simply saying 'listen!' wouldn't work, she knew, so she took off her high-heeled shoe, and banged the table to grab the attention of the other six.

The pub went silent... All eyes were on this female hooligan...

"Shorry, it'sh not for you," Sally told the room. "Thish ish private – sho *you* ...can carry on with the noishe."

The buzz around them began again, and she was able to speak to the girls. "Sho, who remebersh the reashon we're heah? To deshide Derek'sh shurprishe." She was delighted. She'd managed to explain, in only a few words and ever-so clearly, exactly what she'd intended.

Sophie thought a little help might be required with the communication, and reminded all of them, that they had promised to bring an idea along, so, had they? There was a rush for handbags, dumped in a pile on the window sill next to where they were sitting, and an assortment of pieces of paper were found, removed and unfolded.

"So, who's first?" asked Sophie, and then, "Maybe a better idea before we do this, would be to have some food... Who's for that?"

"*Yessssss...*" was the group response.

Something to absorb the liquid seemed sensible to Sophie. She would be the only one extricating them from this drinking hole at the end of the evening, she realised with foreboding, so she would have to try and prevent them losing it altogether.

Unfortunately, being seven of them, the bar staff struggled to supply the chosen food. It appeared, one or two dishes at a time, and so a few more drinks filled the time span. The food service was slow... Sophie suspected that if they carried on at this rate, later, none of them would even be able to move – never mind think and speak.

At least after consuming food, speech returned closer to normal...

"Right, who has the first suggestion?" Sophie asked, taking on the task of chairperson. "I'll write them down as we go along."

Muriel was first. "I thought of a parachute jump," she said, "...not that I'd ever want to do something like that. I get flutters just going down in the lift."

"Abseiling – down a cliff, or maybe even down the side of a high building, or off a bridge. I think they do that in many places about the country," offered Thelma.

"He could do bungee jumping off a bridge too," added Muriel.

"No chance of him jumping – he'd have to be pushed, if I know Derek," offered Sally.

"I thought he might like to drive a battle tank, or a racing car," said Angelina.

"...Can't drive – Derek has never driven a motor vehicle in his sweet little life," said Sally.

"Of course, shucks... I'm so stoopid at times," Angelina said.

"Skiing lessons, or Hang-Gliding, was what I thought," Daisy chipped in.

"Or there's maybe a Hot-Air Balloon journey – they're good too," said Sally.

"Nobody's mentioned a Stripper yet..." Millie threw in. "Any hot-blooded male would go for that... Is he hot-blooded, Honey?" she asked Sally, who just giggled.

"I could do that..." said Josephine, and they all began singing the stripper's music.

Josephine gamely struggled to her feet and started going through the motions of pretending to do a striptease, at which the rest of the inhabitants of the bar joined in, singing and clapping along.

Josephine was doing fine until Millie intervened!

"Give over, Josie, your knickers are far too thick," she yelled. "Don't call us – we'll call you".

Josephine sat down again with a pretend glum look on her face, which drew a sympathetic "Awwww..." from all the watchers, followed by their applause.

"Got to agree there, Josephine," said Sally, "... but sorry, I don't think you'd get Derek excited, either."

How little you know, Sophie thought to herself and smiled, remembering how Derek had enjoyed their first meeting – but she had been covered in mud then...

"Anyway, I can't imagine you naked, Josephine," Sally said, in a kindly but slurred way.

You shouldn't have to imagine dear, thought Sophie, you saw me! Don't you remember? With that thought she hoped Sally wasn't into mind reading...

"What about him going up in the air in a plane? Or a glider?" asked Thelma.

"I like that idea," said Sally. "He once said to me, it must be great to be a pilot. We could book a flying lesson. And if we're all clubbing together, as we said, it shouldn't cost too much for each, would it?"

"Does anyone disagree with what Sally says?" asked Sophie. "No? So that's it. Well then Derek, you are about to get the flight of your life..."

With that decided, the giggling restarted, the glasses were refilled, and everyone made merry. Well, almost everyone – Sophie was still drinking lemonade...

41

It went on for hours. Not a thought was spared for husbands waiting at home anxiously, or babies crying and feeling abandoned by their mothers, or the trouble that these same babies were probably causing their spouses – but why should they give a jot? For Sally and Angelina, it was a chance to let the hair down, to relax totally – it was their night out for a change.

When closing time for the Inn came, the locals began to wend their merry way home to their abodes, these being barely a stone's throw away. It was obvious to the landlord that the ladies, who'd appeared mid-afternoon and partaken of his pub-grub and a large quantity of his alcohol, were going to require carrying-off the premises.

He began to drop the usual hints – the empties gathered from the table under their noses, followed by the blatant noisy washing of the glassware, while giving them disapproving glances; the polishing of these self-same glasses, and then storing them away, with more withering looks in their direction.

What should have been the obvious grand finale – the lights progressively switched off by him, then on, then off and on, and again, off and on – was all to no avail.

They sat there cheering each throw of the switch!

Seven female guests around that one large table – six of whom were well and truly sozzled, and the seventh looking decidedly bored. Boredom is what happens when you are the driver, Sophie told herself, remembering that she'd foolishly volunteered for the noble task. Sophie, the only one whose eyes could see properly, and who still had a functioning brain, could recognise the agitation of the landlord, and his eagerness to be rid of them, so, she took it upon herself to take control.

"Right girls," she called, "...three cheers for the landlord before we go. Hip, hip..."

"Hoor-umph..." was the nearest they got.

Sophie didn't push the 'thank-you' any further but the muffled giggly sort of noises, which the landlord took to be complimentary to him, forced him to smile awkwardly. He then went crimson, and felt bad for wishing them out, but he had to get up early in the morning.

Instructed by Sophie, the other six gathered their things together, "...and get to the toilet now, if you have to, because there will be no stops on the way back." She went outside, unlocked the vehicle, and opened one of the back passenger doors.

She settled for transferring them one at a time, from inside to out.

Daisy was the first to be moved, and although the eldest Mafia Member, she was probably the most capable of the six who'd imbibed. With only a little help, she walked to the car. She was happy to be put into the rear seat and have the belt attached by Sophie.

Thelma was next, requiring a bit more support, and insisting that her dear sister-in-law come at the same time, so Sophie was in the middle with the two inebriates stepping daintily but in opposing directions. She was surprised to get to the car without actually falling over.

Angelina was next. She wanted to go with Sally, but Sophie had already proved to herself that one was sufficient. Angie insisted on telling Sophie what a *won'erful* person she was to be helping Sally and her like this, "an' all the others, Honey," in their hour of need. Her tears started flowing as she kissed Sophie's cheek and explained how happy she was, and how *won'erful* this country was, and that she'd found a *won'erful* Gramps since she'd come here, and that she'd had a really *won'erful*...

"Yea, yea..."

So, four down, two to go...

Millie had been the only one to take advantage of the toilet facilities when Sophie had made the suggestion, but hadn't reappeared yet which Sophie took as a bad sign. Someone was sobbing as she entered the ladies toilet, and as only one cubicle was occupied, it had to be Millie.

"Are you alright Millie? What's wrong? Are you getting homesick again?"

The sobbing stopped. "Oh, Josephine, honey ...I thought you'd left me behind because I'd said something crass... (hic) ...and the friggin' door's jammed."

With a little bit of nudging and rattling from Sophie's side, the door opened, and Millie was guided out to join the others in the vehicle.

In the corner of the room, at the table, Sally had fallen asleep.

"Sally... *Sally*... Time to go..."

"Josephine... I love you (hic)."

You wouldn't be saying that, thought Sophie, if you really knew ...and Sally was the most awkward, between dozing off in the short distance between the Inn and the car, and arms that flayed about every so often. Sophie struggled on, and into the front passenger seat went the floppy body.

Sophie leaned across Sally to attach the seat belt, which she hoped would secure her in an upright position at least, but as she moved her head back, her hair caught in Sally's bracelet, and wakened her. It had happened so suddenly that Sophie couldn't stop – *the wig came off*...

"Aaaaah...!" exclaimed Sally. Her arm was all hairy! A furry creature is attacking me!

The others were suddenly awake too, but there was a deathly hush...

Five mouths hung open, as they saw...

"*Ohhhh...*" said Sally, as she looked directly at the person standing beside her in the poor light of the pub's car park.

Oh, my God, here it comes, thought Sophie, and closed her eyes waiting for the inevitable eruption from Sally as she recognised her hated enemy... but it didn't come?

"Oh, sorry, Josephine... I didn't know..." was all Sally said.

Sophie reached forward and unhooked the hair piece from the bracelet and calmly replaced it on her head once more.

Now it could have been the poor night lighting, it could have been the excess drink. Of course, the fact that Sophie's blonde hair was tucked neatly under a skin-coloured stretchy-vinyl skull cap may have influenced what each individual thought they saw. It was uncomfortable wearing the skin coloured cap under the wig, but maybe very fortunate...

It was a reverential and sombre mood inside the vehicle on the return drive, with none of the ribald humour and raucous behaviour of the earlier journey, and when each was dropped off at the appropriate destination, Sophie was thanked very sincerely for all the trouble they'd put her to this evening – under the circumstances...

"That woman is a *Saint*" she said wistfully.

Hector was being told by Daisy immediately she came in, while he was lying in bed trying to get some sleep, exhausted. He'd been looking after two crying babies, and hadn't been brought the promised Chinese meal until well after eight, because that's when the two lads had deigned to return.

"So willing to talk, and help us with all our troubles, but keeping all her problems to herself," she'd told him.

"S-s-s-s-s-sure..." Hector murmured, dozily, but s-s-s-sympathetically.

Later, Muriel said to Alexander, "Poor Josephine, how sad... she's obviously been having the treatment: what a lovely woman too."

"Hmmm, not so good, eh?" he'd replied, philosophically it appeared, although he hadn't really been listening...

It was the next morning before Hammy was to learn it from Thelma. "She stood there – unflinching, and proud to be a woman – what a *brave* person..." she told him dramatically.

"Ma wee Sybil wiss jist like tha' – righ' tae the end."

Thelma did not consider Hamish's reference to his first wife to have been absolutely necessary just at this moment and walked off.

Millie's comment to Thelma shortly afterwards, was simply that if she had been choosing the wig, she would have selected one for Josephine that would have made her look younger. "The skin she's got is as good as a woman's half her age..." and that was said admiringly.

In Buttercup Road, Angelina was reflecting on the previous night and wondering why her head should be feeling woozy...

"Sam... I'm sure glad I kissed her cheek last night. That woman needs love..."

Sam just gave his wife a funny look, because he had to concentrate on the task in hand. Dealing with a well-filled disposable diaper was not easy, but he was thankful that Angie wasn't demanding of him what Sally demanded of Derek; Sally had stated that only re-usable cotton diapers were permissible to be used for ET, and had to be cleaned out, and washed immediately afterwards – by Derek. (Sam had been told this confidentially – by Derek.) What a tough life that guy has, thought Sam.

It had obviously been a good night out for the girls, but to have his wife staggering into the cottage was a surprise to Derek. Next time he returned a little worse for wear, would this moment be remembered, he asked himself.

"Isn't it sad," Sally had said to Derek as he helped his intoxicated wife to climb into bed, "...about Josephine?"

"What about Josephine?" he'd replied, suspecting that he might be implicated, and hoping there wasn't about to be a row because that would wake up ET again.

"The treatment," she intoned sadly. "Oh dear me, how it has affected her – she's bald."

Derek was puzzled, but thought it wiser to offer no comment...

42

To:derektee123@iamaspecialone.co.uk

From: walters424@rabrev.co.uk

Two days ago, I stumbled across a copy of your recently published massive best seller 'Rabid Revenge Revisited' in what appeared to be the only bookshop remaining in Dundee. After reading the book carefully, hoping to feel uplifted by what has proved in a mass market to be a very popular read about a highly successful rock group, I found myself severely disappointed and depressed.

I perceived your email address, emblazoned brazenly in large type all over the back cover, as being obviously intended for the sole purpose of conveying praise directly to you from a mass audience; well, not in this case.

I'm sorry to disappoint you matey, but I consider it my duty to inform you, the author, of the many inaccuracies in the stories relating particularly to the character nicknamed 'Sailor'. He, I might add was a perfect gentleman, as well as a remarkable guitar player, but you portray him as quite the opposite!

Some of the tales you have manufactured verge on being slanderous, but rather than list your errors in this email, I will firstly await your response and confirmation of your receipt of this.

Respectfully yours forever,

A deeply disenchanted reader.

Coming out of the blue, as this email did, gave Derek rather a shock; especially arriving at a time when our author hero thought he was riding the crest of the wave with everyone in the world loving him.

'Slander' it said...

Impossible, he initially told himself with some indignation; the cheek of this person. With most of the stories mentioning Sailor, all he had done was use the information supplied by Twister, almost verbatim in fact. He'd been there, hadn't he, so he should know? Some of the tales were juicy yes, but nowadays anything goes, doesn't it? How could something I've written possibly be considered slanderous? This was certainly not something to worry about.

Then Derek's mind went back to the self-centred way the other band members had been referred to in early conversations with his 'father' and the touches of bitterness that seemed to creep in occasionally as the tales were recounted. He became a little uneasy. The way James Hoist told it was as if there was little love or loyalty between a group of individuals who had remained together as very popular musicians, and for many years earned a fortune as a result of their collective talents.

Surely there must have been respect for each other and a group bonding, considering the time they'd lasted as a band. Derek had thought that at the time, but hadn't pushed it. The very opposite was the impression given – appearing to dislike each other intensely. As personal evidence had shown, there was little warmth between Millie and Twister certainly, so maybe none of the relationships had been rosy.

Anyway, James Hoist would not have told his son lies about Sailor, would he? Or had he become bitter and twisted over the years? Had Twister gone too far with *his* version of the truth? Worse still, had his son been stupid enough to accept everything he'd been told?

Just a moment... Why, for heaven's sake, Derek asked himself, am I getting upset about a single bolt out of the blue? Who is the guy who has written the email? What do I know of him? Why should I get uptight, or even consider that a reply is necessary? This bloke could be anyone. Maybe a roadie, or perhaps a fan, but he is more probably just a nutter, or a chancer looking for a moment of glory, or some sort of pay-off. He could be anywhere in the world and know nothing of the band and just be trying to make a fast buck. This isn't the first scam to be sent on the internet...

Whoa!

He was maybe not *anywhere* in the world; that was wrong. There were clues. He bought the book, he says, in Dundee ...now where's that again? Oh yea, Scotland. It was purchased in Dundee but it looks as if he could have been a visitor and didn't know the place too well. He says, 'in what *appeared* to be the only bookshop remaining in Dundee'.

This was unsettling. It could turn out to be a Scotsman on the move, one with a grumble! Derek knows a Scotsman... Hammy is a Scotsman. What if he turned out to be like Hammy...? Now that could be bad ...really bad...

Advice was required. Would Sophie be the one to turn to? As a publisher she would be aware of this sort of pitfall, probably faced it many times before. She will know what should be done... Slander, libel, all run of the mill stuff for her...

When he phoned her, Sophie did not react in the confident self-assured way he expected.

"Surely you double-checked your facts, Derek, before you gave the book to us, and anyway you approved the final proofs too, didn't you? You did re-read them I hope?"

"Yes – but..." he tentatively replied, trying to avoid admitting how very hurriedly it was done because he'd fallen so far behind – a deadline yelling at him!

"If it goes to court it is a very expensive business you realise," she added.

"Defended and paid for by the publisher – at least the author is safe," he chipped in.

"Oh no... Haven't you read the small print in your contract? Unfortunately, when this sort of thing occurs, it is the total responsibility of the author, who often finishes up requiring a team of lawyers to deal with it."

"Just a minute... What contract? We had a verbal agreement. You would be looking after everything. All I asked was that Sally wouldn't discover that it was you I was working with – or find out that you are sometimes somebody other than Sophie..."

"That's a pity isn't it, but I've kept my side of the bargain. Sally did think I was a man for a time, but in her eyes now, I'm a little old woman who is becoming a very close friend, whom she probably trusts more than her husband! We'll just have to hope it doesn't come to the crunch then, *won't you* Derek. You'll have to talk this person out of any action or, if you are really stuck, buy him off!"

43

Walking Jilly, after work, became a regular thing for Derek and after ET's arrival his life was even more demanding. To a great extent, he had ignored these demands. Being honest with himself, he admitted that all the paraphernalia and routines generally associated with having a young baby in the house had been absorbed by the dedicated mother of the baby. The book had always come first! He contributed very little in the way of assistance.

'Walking the dog' sort-of salved his conscience, but only slightly, because he hated the task, and he hated the dog, and not too surprisingly, the dog still hated him...

He'd taken to walking it in the fields, still using the extending lead, because, if he released the little bitch he did not trust her to listen to him! He was beginning to meet Hammy quite regularly on these strolls – Hammy and Cornelius.

Derek still had a grudge against Hammy for the oily mess he'd left behind that night when he'd been constructing the pond, but it was now cleaned and improved. It could be seen easily from the cottage and, as a water feature, was obviously beginning to look more like the intended finished attraction.

Credit was due to Hammy for his attention to 'Safety'; it wasn't a deep pond but there were posts holding safety belts already in position. Thelma had struck terror in his heart in case any youngsters should have an accident. Sally had already chased away a couple of young townies; they had been about to have a paddle. Derek smiled as he thought of his young days; exactly what my gang would have been doing...

Jilly gradually accepted walking in wet weather, but only when

Derek insisted and dragged her along with him. It had taken a while and gave him a perverse satisfaction. Then one day she changed. Whether it was wet or dry, instead of being dragged, she chose to become the dragger, running ahead all the time, as if trying to escape from a cruel master. Derek wasn't sure which was better, but he suspected that annoying him, being back in charge, so to speak, gave the dog a way to get her own back...

The doggy-walk routine usually began in the lane. They would leave the house and walk along its length until joining the more substantial track to the hotel, which they followed. Unless the hotel was overly busy and Thelma instructed Hammy remain available on the premises, they linked-up with him and Cornelius, of course. The two men and two dogs would continue walking long enough to need a strong flashlight as the evenings grew darker. There was no street lighting, so, like an insurance policy, Derek always carried a torch. Having Hammy alongside as they continued clockwise through the fields, meant that there was less chance of the pair of them tumbling into a hole if he had created any new bunkers during the day,

They always walked back towards the cottage, where Hammy would, "Pop in furr a wee meenit – jist to say hello tae the wean," although he allowed himself, quite often, to be persuaded to stay a little while longer, and have a refresher.

Jilly was terrified of Cornelius. The only time that poodle displayed any affinity towards Derek was when she used him to shield her from the slobbering, lumbering, bigger Labrador dog, who liked everybody.

It was not raining. The meal was over; ET had been bathed and fed and was now fast asleep, and Sally was sitting in her chair to have another attempt at knitting. Jilly was sitting at the side of Sally's chair, as usual, glaring across at Derek in the other one, daring him to attach a lead to her collar. It was time for the walk...

Now that the weather was a bit colder, the gloves Derek wore to handle the snarling little poodle appeared less of an affectation. They felt uncomfortable only a matter of weeks ago in the warmer weather, uncomfortable, but essential to minimise the effect of the sharp teeth.

Man and dog walked the lane and entered the hotel. Derek sat in the Reception Area, with Jilly sitting reluctantly beside by his chair, giving him ugly looks and growling whenever the mood took her. The awkwardness Derek experienced at the first visit, by bringing Jilly inside, had gone. Bringing a dog into the hotel seemed wrong, but Hammy said if Cornelius was allowed inside, other dogs couldn't be barred.

As a matter of interest, some people had turned down a booking on finding that dogs were permitted inside the hotel, even though it was only in the public spaces and not where food was served, or in the bedrooms. Then again, some people decided not to visit because it was totally 'non-smoking', so Thelma accepted that you can't please everyone. They weren't missed, because the hotel was becoming quite popular.

As usual, Derek was unprepared to cope with the onslaught from Cornelius. He came charging into the hall, straight for the seated Derek. One simple fact that Derek never remembered, was that when sitting down, he was at a perfect level for the paws on his chest and the doggy tongue that lashed about trying to lick his face. He always reminded himself not to do that again, as he struggled to stand. Meanwhile, Jilly had slunk behind the settee, but that just meant that Cornelius had to go and look for her. The chase then began – the two dogs circling around Derek and the settee, with the smaller one keeping ahead, but only just, and Derek desperately trying to avoid tangling the lead.

"Right, Cornelius, ya silly big dugg, c'mon," shouted Hammy at the doorway, and off they all went.

Having dragged Derek all the way from the cottage, the poodle now trotted gingerly behind him, carefully watching the antics of her big doggy friend. Hammy was happy to allow Cornelius to run freely. Lolloping around seemed to the best way to tire him out and Hammy was certainly not willing, or able, to run around with him on the lead.

"Why no' let yer wee freen aff the lead, Derek, an' she can play wi' Cornelius, an' it'll tire them baith oot at the same time?" said Hammy this evening.

"Oh, no... I couldn't do that. I can't trust her. She'd run off..."

said a fearful Derek.

"No she'll no'. Ye huvv tae huvv confidence in yer dug. They'll play the gether. Jist go furr it, man. If she does go, she'll no' go far onywey."

Anyway, now they were out in the open, Jilly was straining and pulling at the fully extended lead, appearing jealous of big Cornelius lolloping around freely. So, Derek made the fatal decision. He wound her in and struggled to unclip the lead without being nipped. She showed little gratitude when he reached down to release her – and the gloves proved their worth once again. Then, she was off!

His flashlight beam was on her for part of the time, and being white, she was easier to see in the dark than Cornelius, but the torch was required also to show Derek where he was walking so, inevitably, he lost sight of her.

Hammy was proud of what he'd achieved so far with his digger. There was now a variety of levels. Some eventually would become putting surfaces, and others were destined to be the future tees. These were safe areas. The dangers were the bunkers: big holes in the ground, oh, and the water feature. Incidentally, some of the bunkers were to be repositioned on Thelma's instructions. Misinterpreting coffee stains that he'd managed to splash on the layout drawings, he had dug a few bunkers in the stupidest of places. To Hammy's acute embarrassment, they would have to be filled in again.

The pond was roughly halfway along the course, and not far away from Toozlethwaite Manor. In daylight from the rear window, Derek's view had been recently transformed from an oily-bottomed excavation to a pleasant-looking pond surrounded by reeds and vegetation. At each end of the pond were footbridges over the stream that flowed through it, and the two males headed for one of them.

The dogs decided to take a different route, a new one for them, the direct one, straight across the pond. There was a splash as Cornelius hit the surface of the water first, followed by another, as Jilly charged in too. Derek and Hammy turned the light towards the sound of splashing.

"At least it's just water this time," said Derek sarcastically to Hammy. "Do you know how long it took me to remove all the oil from Jilly that last time?"

"Onywey, she's a fine wee sweemer," said Hammy ignoring Derek's comment.

She'd never been in the water swimming before, Derek suddenly realised, and hoped she would manage all the way across. The pond was only three feet deep at the most, but he didn't fancy having to wade in to save the stupid poodle.

"So, whit d'ye think o' it then?" asked Hammy as they stopped on the bridge, shining the torchlight around it, and Derek was complimentary as they stood chatting about the various other requirements. Hammy wasn't doing all the development of the golf course himself. The team that had rebuilt the hotel were happy to have work in a fairly slack building spell, so it was progressing reasonably quickly with their assistance.

"It'll no be fit for playin' oan furr a lang time yet, though," Hammy said.

Then they heard squeals, a dog's squeal: a *poodle* dog's squeal.

What had happened? They shone the light all around the pond. The water was now still again – no dog in trouble in the water and Derek was relieved at not having to get wet. The squeals had stopped, but they could hear a dog panting, a big dog panting... It was over towards the wooded area. Had the dogs come across another animal in the dark, they wondered, a fox or a badger, maybe? The trees were sprawled about the course at this part, and that was where the sounds appeared to have come from.

Derek became fearful again that Jilly might have done a runner and he'd have a long search ahead of him, but no, the torchlight caught a flash of white, obviously Jilly ...but what was Cornelius doing to her? Surely not fighting with her was he? There was no growling, he was panting and she was making little sounds too. It only became obvious when they got closer that Cornelius had fancied Jilly. Possibly Jilly hadn't protested too much at his advances, but that was a presumption. Both must have reached *that* age, because there, in front of their astonished owners – big Cornelius was in the process of humping little Jilly.

A bucket of cold water would have done the trick, but there was little the two shocked humans could do, other than walk off towards the cottage. The dogs would no doubt join them when they were ready.

Derek wished he hadn't given in to Hammy's suggestion earlier – "let her off the lead – she'll no come tae ony hairm..." He also had difficulty visualising, if this copulation of a Labrador and a Poodle was successful, what, for goodness sake, would the pups look like?

Eventually, the two dogs appeared, slightly cowed, as if they'd been caught doing something naughty and Hammy and Cornelius continued on their way back to the hotel without going into the cottage, both appearing to be a little shamefaced...

To Derek's surprise Jilly followed him into the cottage without any fuss. Inside, he petted her and made soothing noises, and gave her some treats, and felt quite sorry for her. She very much appreciated his concern, obviously. Derek was delighted. It felt like a new relationship, a new dawn was beginning between him and Jilly. He was looking forward to taking her out a walk tomorrow.

What a disappointment when he attached the lead the following evening – she almost bit off the end of his nose...

44

To:walters424@rabrev.co.uk

From:derektee123@iamaspecialone.co.uk

How kind of you to purchase my best-selling book, and then take the trouble to read it in the depth to which you so obviously have.

Also greatly appreciated by me is someone allocating valuable time, once again as you have done, to return positive criticism to the author.

That aspect is very much appreciated.

So, it is with great anticipation that I await your next email in which I am sure you will expand your thoughts for the benefit of my future works.

Your obedient servant,

Derek Tee.

Very sensibly, Derek had waited forty-eight hours before sending that reply, allowing time to dispel some of the anger from this annoying person. However, a reply came back almost immediately.

To:derektee123@iamaspecialone.co.uk

From: walters424@rabrev.co.uk

Are you taking the piss???

If he were to be rid of this nuisance, this time it seemed wise for Derek to respond rapidly.

He had to remove some of the heat retained in this poor fellow's head.

He was probably a bitter, twisted old man who'd never had his chance in the limelight.

Derek also imagined, with all due modesty, that this poor individual was probably jealous of the success of the book and of Derek's new standing as a respected and extremely popular writer...

"And he's beginning to get on my wick," he said aloud, with feeling, to the computer.

To:walters424@rabrev.co.uk

From:derektee123@iamaspecialone.co.uk

Of course not... I was attempting the same politeness you appeared to display in your first comments, but it is obvious now that I am not dealing with a gentleman; a description which you so generously ascribed to Sailor, although from my inside knowledge, I am not sure that your assessment of him is correct.

A beer swilling, fat lout, who was willing to take a chance with any bit of skirt that might show interest, and who never learned to play the guitar properly; information, I might point out, given to me by a source very close to him for most of his performing career – so there!

Pressing the enter-button with a flourish, he sent it off, because some things have to be flushed out of your system...

Relax man, he told himself. It was the first negative response he'd received from a member of the public, and though not one of the most satisfying comments to receive, he could comfort himself that only one bad criticism should not concern him unduly.

The rest of his reading public obviously thought his writing was wonderful and worth every penny.

Even though the book was a hardback, and costing a fortune – they were buying it, weren't they?

To:derektee123@iamaspecialone.co.uk

From:walters424@rabrev.co.uk

And no doubt your perfect source of information would have been that tosser, Twister! Am I correct? Yes or no?

Go away you horrid person...

To:walters424@rabrev.co.uk

From:derektee123@iamaspecialone.co.uk

Well, you might be ...but even if you were, I am not at liberty to divulge my sources of information to you! And as a matter of fact, I am not going to, so you can just take a running jump, pal!

Take that!

To:derektee123@iamaspecialone.co.uk

From:walters424@rabrev.co.uk

Let us get something straight buddy, I am not your pal and anyway, do you know who you are talking to?

Derek heaved a sigh... This could go on forever... Get rid of the twit!

To:walters424@rabrev.co.uk

From: derektee123@iamaspecialone.co.uk

NO ...and, to be perfectly honest, I have to tell you sincerely that who you might be is of little concern to me...

To:derektee123@iamaspecialone.co.uk

From: walters424@rabrev.co.uk

Obviously...! I can tell this discussion is not going to be settled by sending emails.

Maybe the chance to meet nose to nose would influence your thinking, and as you are relatively close, it could be soon.

It appears that nothing less than a good thumping is likely to alter your approach to what I'm saying, so maybe in the future you should think of me as TROUBLE... I AM COMING TO GET YOU!

Still respectfully yours forever,

Your even more disenchanted reader.

45

The appearance on 'Early Day Chatterbox' was to be Derek's big moment. Hector would be there too, but, as Sophie put it to Derek, he would only be 'eye candy'. Naturally, it was to be important publicity for the book but the best laid schemes...

It did work out in the end, although the result was unexpected. As with many of Derek's projects, the honourable intentions went slightly askew. Being denied his moment of glory and losing the opportunity to give his planned spiel to the nation was galling for Derek but, on that special morning, a reluctant elderly gentleman became the star of a television show.

It was Tuesday, early...

Their reputations were solid: seated on the couch, always able to maintain pleasant smiles and gentle repartee no matter what might happen, Kaitlin and Edward were 'Chatterbox' presenters. Regularly, they coped with all types of adversity during a live show. However, their normally seamless performance and brilliant record came mighty close to being trashed on that morning.

Hector was reluctant to be there in the first place, and having make-up applied before appearing in front of the cameras unsettled him even more, but he endured it for Derek!

It was done with the best of intentions, but, by giving his grandson a reassuring smack on the back for luck, Hector somehow succeeded in disturbing Derek's microphone. This proved to be unlucky for Derek, and for the BBC technician who'd already been having a bad morning with equipment and didn't take kindly to the additional headache, but suddenly, they were live on air and Kaitlin and Edward were making the introductions to the viewers.

"...And here is Derek Tee, a highly successful author, with Hector, his grandad."

Derek did at least have a chance to talk for a moment, so the title of the book was heard loud and clear. He was also able to tell how the book had begun as straightforward facts about the birth of a rock band, but how along the way it became the heart-warming tale of a family re-united. Alas, he had barely scraped the surface of the many things he wanted to promote when the microphone began displaying the effects of Grandad's earlier slap.

Kaitlin apologised to Derek and to the viewers for the distorted sound. The floor manager gave some rapid hand signals summoning a sound man, and the camera swung away, leaving Derek's equipment to receive emergency first-aid, out of shot.

Then there he was, on screen, Hector sitting uncomfortably, looking into the camera's lens. *D-d-d-d-d-decoration only – t-t-to smile if I appear in v-v-v-view, and to try to l-l-l-look less g-g-g-grumpy than usual!* That's all he was supposed to do – he'd been promised, and it was his only reason for agreeing to be there! Derek said he knew what was required and that he wouldn't be involved, and he'd believed him – but suddenly, the camera lens was pointing at him. That wasn't supposed to happen!

He tried to do as they'd asked beforehand give a good impression of a smile! It was difficult as the presenters swung the attention to him because he had never felt so panicky!

"We are having more gremlins this morning, it seems. They are now attacking Derek Tee, for no reason at all," said Kaitlin with a beaming smile, into camera two, "...because I'm sure he is a very nice young man, as we'll find out in a moment when we can speak with him again." She paused for a moment and listened to instructions in her earpiece...

"Cue the music now, Kaitlin," the producer told her, "...and keep things moving."

Kaitlin introduced a sample of the music – a 'Rabid Revenge' hit that few people in Britain would have heard; the sounds of an incredibly successful rock band from the United States. "So, let's listen to an extract from an early album of 1983, 'Pressure under Decompression', which topped the US charts. This track is called 'Who's the Punk who burst my bubble?'

"Strong stuff for breakfast, eh?" chipped in a smiling Edward, and the music played. Thirty-five seconds of raucous sound hit the airwaves, then the music faded out, and there was Grandad, still alone. He was on screen, sitting stiff and straight, transfixed, with only his eyes squinting to his right, trying not to appear to be looking! *What's happening to Derek? Wh-wh-wh-where is he?*

The viewers were seeing fear...

"You liked that music, Hector?" asked Edward.

"N-n-n-n-no..." answered Hector honestly, glad that it was a question he could answer.

"While we are attempting to reconnect your grandson, maybe you'd like to read an extract from the book, Mr Smith?" suggested the ever-avuncular Edward Billston. "The one Derek would have read."

That's when a panicky comment from the producer came through his earpiece, "Nooooo... Don't bloody-well do that, Eddie baby ...this man can't talk without stammering... Edwaaaaard...", which Edward bravely ignored – and then realised he might live to regret it!

However, this was the final item of the morning, and anyway, Edward had committed himself, and in spite of the frantic message, he smiled at Kaitlin, who smiled sweetly in return. The warning had been heard by her too, and oh, how she wished that the earlier briefing, before these two gentlemen arrived on the settee, had made it clearer. She'd missed that fact too, but it was a live show – so, she continued to smile.

By their smiles they were supporting and telling each other, we could be sinking into the mire, but let's just keep it moving slickly along, as only we can!

The technician standing behind the couch, where Derek sat, was still trying to find why the unit was malfunctioning, while another had scurried off to find a replacement. It was an unusually testing time for the sound crew.

The camera covered the two presenters and a worried-looking older gentleman, who was giving an excellent impression of a startled rabbit and hoping desperately that his grandson would reappear magically beside him.

"So, Mr Smith – do you mind if I call you Hector?" continued Edward, feeling a little less self-assured.

"Y-Y-Y ...N-n-n-no," answered a worried grandad, who hadn't expected to open his mouth.

"...I believe Derek compiled this story based on the fact that the original band started life in your little town," continued Mr Billston, smiling to cover up the sinking feeling in his stomach, already regretting that he'd ignored the producer's wise words and hoping that Kaitlin was ready to step in to support.

"Y-y-y-yes," replied Hector.

"And, along the way, you found your daughter again, and a grand-daughter you didn't know existed, and Derek found his long lost mother?" added Kaitlin, behaving like the true professional everyone knew her to be, maintaining continuity and giving a natural sounding back-up to her colleague.

"Y-y-y-yes."

Edward lifted the copy of 'Rabid Revenge Revisited' from the table in front of them, knowing that extracts to be read had been carefully marked. He handed it, opened, to Hector, who coughed – professionally, he thought – but it sounded more like a squeal of terror.

Derek, now standing in front of the technician, was beginning to worry at the pressure being put on his grandad. What if he collapsed in front of the cameras? What would Gran say about that? The replacement unit was being fitted on Derek's back now, while Derek and the out-of-breath technician were clear of camera shot.

"Yes, that page there, Hector, you could read it," said Edward, pointing.

"Indeed, you can do it, Hector, we're all with you," added Kaitlin to Hector to bolster his confidence, she hoped, and then this well-known female 'smile' looked directly into the camera.

"If I might just point out to everyone watching this morning, Derek's grandad did not expect to be doing this," and she turned towards Hector, "...did you?"

"N-n-n-n-n-n-n-no..." was Hector's resigned response.

"Oh, for heaven's sake, Edward – you read it..." was the urgent instruction from control, but Edward didn't...

The old fellow had the book in his hands and was preparing himself, Edward could see, so it would be most unmannerly for him to snatch the book away. His image ...it would not look good to the viewers, so he took a chance and sat back.

Hector held the book in front of him, as far as his arms could stretch, until he could just about read the large print.

"R-r-r-r-right..." said Hector, taking a deep breath... "R-R-R-Rabid R-R-R-Revenge..."

I've blown it! Edward thought. I should have read it myself... This is bound to hit YouTube...

Edward's blown it, Kaitlin was convinced. Poor old Edward – it was something to cast at him later. They'd have a good laugh about it. Should she prise the book out of the old fellow's hands before he goes any further she wondered, to save Edward embarrassment?

Hector coughed nervously...

"Th-th-th-this b-b-b-band b-b-b-began when a g-g-g-g-group of school kids, coming together, after diligently completing their daily lessons in Newingsworth High School, found that they had a common aim in life. They wanted to make music. The music they enjoyed playing, this raucous, rough-at-the-edges, no-holds-barred type of sound, which drove their parents to distraction, was unique to them; created by them when they got together in the empty garage at Twister's house. They were quite satisfied to play in splendid isolation as long as they were all together. Initially, they did not have fancy aspirations. They were only enjoying themselves doing their own thing. Then others heard them, others who were important people in the music industry who decided the public should have the opportunity to hear this new sound too."

Hector, looked up then back at the page in front of him, paused, took a deep breath, and continued, wondering what comment Daisy would make when he got home. Derek's microphone was given the thumbs-up, but Derek remained where he was, out of camera, enthralled by his grandad's reading of the words that he had written.

Grandad was actually reading normally...

Mr Edward Billston relaxed, and turned to smile at Kaitlin, who returned the smile, as usual, the smile that now said, there ...see, there was no need to panic. We coped again...

And Hector was still reading...

"...But this would mean a difficult decision being asked of each member of this tight band of happy, innocent, music makers. Would they pursue an academic career, as had been the hope of each of their parents? Or would the music business draw them in? And if it did, would they survive in a cut-throat industry?"

The voice crackled in Edward and Kaitlin's respective ears, "That'll do now, thanks," the producer instructed ...but it wouldn't do, they thought. It was unlike the lovely pair, Kaitlin and Edward, to act bolshie, but they did on this occasion. They just sat back and enjoyed the reading.

Hector continued: "...but the move would have its downside. They would not have success in their own backyard. Instead, their backyard would be in a different country and become enormous – all the inhabitants of the cities of the United States of America grew to love them. The good citizens of America would make them stars."

Hector stopped, coughed, feeling self-conscious, and closed the book. Derek couldn't stop himself. He stepped back into camera shot, went forward and gave his grandad a great big hug.

"Grandad, you did that, without a..." and he became emotional, "...without a s-s-s-stutter!"

"Yes, I d-d-d-d-did, D-D-D-Derek, I d-d-d-did... h-h-hooorrray!"

Edward held out his hand to congratulate Hector as Kaitlin stood up to give the old man a hug and a peck on the cheek. Hector was as proud as punch, and glad, after all, to be wearing make-up. It might prevent Daisy seeing him blushing profusely.

"Good luck for the book then, Derek," said Edward, and then to the viewers, "I'll just remind you that the book is called 'Rabid Revenge Revisited', written by Derek Tee, and is available to purchase now."

"Well, it has been an exciting morning for us but that's all we have time for. I hope you have enjoyed watching today's programme," said Kaitlin, as the camera came back to her. "So, until you are with us next time on 'Chatterbox', have a good day."

"That's a wrap, folks," came this time through the loudspeakers, as the fade-out music played to the viewers. "It was touch and go, but thank goodness, WE ...pulled it off again," the producer proudly told the studio.

Kaitlin and Edward looked at each other, and smiled ...as usual!

46

Derek found it so easy to visualise the scenario: the knock on his door; opening it to discover it was the 'Disenchanted Fan'; and then being punched on the nose by that very guy. It really frightened the socks off him.

Rest easy, he reassured himself, he can't possibly know where I am ...can he?

The threatening emails were deliberately pushed to the back of his mind when he and Hector went to the television studio although, to tell the truth, the other things that went wrong that morning totally wiped any thoughts of those stupid unhelpful electronic messages from his mind. Unfortunately, at home again, the thoughts returned. They were discomfiting, preying on his mind once more.

Receiving fan messages from readers who appreciated his writing skills – grateful to him for bringing 'Rabid Revenge' to the attention of the British public – was much appreciated and gave him a warm feeling inside. That was the pleasurable part – but that one email, the only negative criticism, suddenly appearing out of nowhere, continued to upset him.

Primarily, what disturbed him most was the prospect of a good thumping. Being thumped did not appeal at all, but Derek could still laugh in a superior way. This man had exposed that he wasn't too smart. He obviously didn't even appreciate the use of an oxymoron – a good thumping indeed, the word 'good' was totally misused – though when Derek thought about it further, a thumping was a thumping, no matter the grammar!

ET's lungs were certainly healthy if the volume of his food-demanding cry was anything to go by. Derek's mind being on many other activities associated with the book's publicity caused him to lose track of the time – until ET so obligingly reminded him. This child decreed that food be due at the precise moment he wakened. Within two minutes he would be emphasising it had become overdue!

It was Friday. Derek was alone – well, not quite; obviously ET was there too and so was Jilly. Because Sally was out shopping with Mom, Derek was baby-sitting and dog-minding for a short time, on one of his rest-days due from paid work. Rob was very understanding about his having time off because of publicity commitments. He had accepted flexibility in the work Derek did for the newspaper and the Gazette, being a weekly, Derek worked at home to compensate for absences mid-week.

However, work had to be dropped immediately because, at this moment, only one thing was important, feeding little Edwin. Running late, as he was, Derek hurried to cool the feeding bottle, only too aware that each minute's delay caused the volume of the crying, coming from the tiny but powerful loudspeaker near the cot, to increase dramatically.

He hadn't anticipated having to do this. As she left, Sally said she would be back in time to feed ET, but she wasn't, hence the panic in the kitchen and the noise from the bedroom. At least Jilly was quiet. Whenever ET cried, Jilly would slip into her basket and nudge her blanket into a bundle under which she could stuff her head. She couldn't cope with ET's crying either. The phone beginning to ring only added to the developing pandemonium but, fully engaged in the final preparations of the baby's bottle, he left the answering machine to kick in. Bottle in hand, he lifted ET, still yelling, and went through to the living room.

The sound of the phone, added to the baby's yells, got to Jilly. Her little head popped out from the blanket and she was alternately barking and howling until, eventually, Derek managed to stretch out and give her basket a kick! That had the desired effect and Jilly shut-up. At the same instant the phone stopped ringing and the teat entering the mouth of little ET stopped the yelling. It was as if sudden deafness struck Derek.

Calm returned to the Manor. Relief... The silence was beautiful.

What a pleasant feeling, being alone with his little son, holding him oh so carefully, exactly as instructed every time they saw him do it – by Sally, by Daisy, by Millie: supporting the head and angling the bottle precisely as he now knew. How well Derek had learned – that everybody else knew better! He'd had to get used to it as far as handling the baby was concerned; in everyone else's eyes, he was an idiot.

So, there he was, sitting in the cottage, with a silly grin on his face, and a little bundle in his arms, his offspring, a tiny person who was totally dependent on him – and ignoring him completely. ET just lay there, making the normal strange slurping and gurgling noises, sucking away, content.

Tranquillity reigned until the sound at the door. Jilly began to bark again startling ET who stopped sucking from the bottle and, without the food to keep him quiet, resumed yelling as if it had never existed in the first place...

"Oh, Derek, why is he crying? Couldn't you even manage for the little time I left you?" said Sally immediately she walked in.

"His head, Derek, you have to support it," added Mom, who'd followed behind her, "and wouldn't it be better if you put the teat in his mouth?"

"Oh, but I am so silly!" Derek's responded, to save them having to repeat any more.

"Give him here," said Mom, taking the yelling child from his arms. Annoyingly for Derek, the moment she took him ET stopped yelling. "Was he being bad to you then, my little pet?" she cooed into his face.

ET gurgled happily.

Even the ruddy baby is making me look foolish he thought. However with Sally and Mom in action now, he could return to what he was doing earlier, although with the chattering going on and the occasional burping noise from ET, it was difficult to concentrate, and then to throw him completely out of kilter, the phone rang again.

He remembered it ringing before when he was in the midst of the baby-feeding crisis. Of course, he hadn't checked if a message was left. He rose, walked across and was just about to lift the receiver and answer when, inevitably, the piercing ring stopped. So, he went through the motions of checking who had rung earlier. There was no message but he could hear that someone had held the phone line open. It was as if they couldn't think what to say, and eventually had hung up.

Oh well, thought Derek, sitting again at the computer, it couldn't have been important. He should have known the moment he sat down the phone would ring again... This time he was a little quicker.

"You thought I wouldn't find you, didn't you? Oh, but I did," the voice said, and gave a wicked laugh, "...and I know where you live... Please make sure you are in when I call ...or else!" Then there was another laugh...

Maybe it would have been better to have missed the call, Derek thought, as he replaced the receiver.

47

"It's someone from the BBC, Derek," Sally shouted through to him.

Derek was in the process of shaving and, once again, regretted that he had not replaced his defunct electric razor. With a blade so fresh and sharp it simply took that unexpected shout to cause him to cut himself – which was not at all unusual. The shaving soap on his face quickly turned pinkish-red.

With his left hand, he took the receiver from Sally, his right hand holding the toilet paper over the cut. Another bad habit of his was wearing his shirt while he shaved and it was a fresh shirt he'd taken from the wardrobe...

"Hello" said the voice. "You are Mr Tee, the gent who was on our 'Chatterbox' programme two weeks ago? Your grandad is a wonderful person, I have to say."

"Yes, I suppose he is..." Derek realised he would never have thought of describing Hector in those words.

"My name is Sarah, and I'm a researcher for the programme. We thought you might be pleased to know that there has been a great deal of interest and reaction to your book – comments on our website, phone calls, and emails etc, the usual stuff."

"Oh, that's nice," Derek replied, foolishly removing the piece of tissue which had been stemming the flow of blood, and therefore permitting it to drip.

"We like to give feedback after an appearance, and yours created some other interest – the music. We've had a lot of queries regarding the music that was played. People want to know where it can be obtained. Obviously, the band wasn't known in this country, and apparently no-one can get the music. Everything on internet is basic history with no access to the band's tunes, other than titles. There's nothing on YouTube either, other than a video that I presume you put on – must have been before you wrote your book. That isn't your real nose, I hope ...oh sorry, I didn't put that the correct way did I?"

"It's all right Sarah. It was plastic – and I was supposed to be disguised."

"All right, whatever... But if you don't mind our suggesting it, if the public are asking for that music, you could be missing the chance of making some more cash – if you can access more of it and have the rights to reproduce it officially."

Her call caused Derek to move in a new direction – and forced him to change his shirt.

48

There could be no deviation for what had become her daily routine. It was raining which was disappointing on a Saturday but, rain or not, Sally insisted that her little boy should get out into the fresh air every day. Her rain-weather outfit and rubber boots were donned and, with ET dry in the pram, she splashed happily along the lane, making for the hotel and a chat with Thelma, if she wasn't too busy. Mom would probably be there too.

Whereas Derek forced Jilly out for walk when he chose, Sally did not, so Jilly would not want to go out and was lying asleep in her basket. Derek had been invited to go for the exercise but he had the excuse of having work to do for the Gazette. On such a rainy day he was as happy to remain indoors as Jilly. He liked walking but preferably when it was dry.

Sally had to weave the pram carefully along the path, which stretched to the main farm road, their only access to the cottage. One day it would need surfacing properly, because the pot-holes became water traps in wet weather. It would be nice to have it done but would be costly; something to be left for the future because they didn't yet have the sort of cash needed. There was a distinct chance that Alexander would be willing to assist and donate money, if asked nicely, but neither Sally nor Derek wanted to go that way. Doing it by themselves was their intention, and maybe the good sales of the book would help...

Derek's visit to Inverness, almost three months ago, was proving to have been a useful exercise, other than the inconvenience of it having coincided with Sally and Angie giving birth. Several independent radio stations had already broadcast the show and it must have helped spread the word because the book was selling well.

Without doubt, appearing on 'Early Day Chatterbox' last week had been an enormous boost to the sales, and for all the people watching who knew Hector it had certainly been a novelty. The general reaction was amazement – Hector reading from Derek's book, without a single stutter!

Up at the Old Folks Club, some even thought that, all his life, he'd been having them on; he didn't really stutter at all!

What a difference it made to Derek's concentration when Sally and ET were out of the house. He could actually think! The place was silent except for the snores coming from the dog-basket. Her snoring had only started recently, apparently something to do with the position of her head and the blanket, but now the stupid dog seemed habitually to lie this way. The noises she made were more obvious when there was no other sound. Derek could tolerate it only for a short time. There was one way he'd learned, which stopped the snorts and doggy dreams instantly – giving her basket a bit of a kick! It didn't hurt Jilly, Derek believed, but it did stop the noise so that's what he did.

He kicked – but she must have remembered from the last time and he had to jump back smartly! It was as if, this time, she had been pretending to sleep but was just waiting for him to swing his leg towards her. She almost caught his ankle and it could have been a nasty nip if Derek hadn't moved very quickly, but at least it had the desired outcome. Jilly went to sleep again in a new position and stayed silent.

At last he could concentrate properly ...for a time, but then his mind began to wander.

He remembered the question he had been asked at Bisko's book-signing: he'd panicked when the man said, 'What are you going to do next?', because he'd no idea. There had been a sudden feeling of guilt at having to admit that to himself. He still didn't have a plan, but there was a difference now: he couldn't care less.

Should he perhaps concentrate on bringing Mom and Twister back together? Was the apparent hatred displayed by Mom, when she threw the knife at Twister, simply hiding a deep longing to be with him again? Had it simply been a case of a lovelorn woman seeking the attention of her heart's desire...? Maybe he should have studied more, thought Derek, and used his natural talents to become a psychoanalyst? Then again, perhaps not...

No, being an author carried a special status, and the result of all his hard work was there in front of him. He was now part of an elite band of respected writers who had made it, he modestly realised – thanks to "Rabid Revenge Revisited".

He was becoming more relaxed by the minute and might have drifted off into a snooze if it hadn't been for a noise at the door. Someone knocked! Sally and Mom, back already? Good timing sweetheart, he thought in a woozy way, she can make me a mug of coffee.

"Can you manage?" he called out, then, remembering Mom always expected the door to have to be opened by a key, he added, "It's unlocked. Just turn the handle and come in!"

"Ahhh... So, this is the famous *Sweaty*..." said the voice.

"Mom?"

It obviously wasn't... Mom didn't have a deep, male voice. Derek was suddenly wide awake. He jumped up from his computer-seat and turned around.

"What? Who? Where have you...?" Derek spluttered. "What are you doing walking into my house? Who are you?"

"If you think back a few moments, Sweaty, you might recall inviting me in," the man replied.

"How do you know I am Sweaty? Anyway who are you?"

As he said that, Derek looked over to the dog basket to be sure that his little guard dog was ready to spring into action the moment she was given the command. Derek knew that she would strike terror into the heart of this bloke if he started any nonsense.

Jilly lay, peacefully asleep – not even a twitch!

"I, young man, am the 'Disenchanted Fan' who sent you an email. You might recognise the name..." but, as he said it, all Derek could think, seeing the rain dripping from his coat to form a pattern on the floor around him, was that Sally would be annoyed. Worse still though, this fellow was inside the house wearing shoes that were covered in mud and he had left footprints as he'd entered – she'd kill him for that!

Derek brought his thoughts back to himself and why this figure stood before him. Of course he recognised the name, and he remembered something that this man with the easy-to-remember name had promised to give him – a good thumping!

His voice on the phone sounded menacing, but having him standing so close was terrifying! His face seemed vaguely familiar though. *Should I know him,* wondered Derek? It was an upside-down face, with a greying beard and a bald head. If reversed, as it might have been when he was younger, he could almost be considered handsome. He looked about his Mom's age to Derek (and slimly built too). If this gets serious, Derek wondered how he should he react. Should he go for him and wrestle him to the ground? Just a minute... he wouldn't even consider trying to wrestle Mom to the ground, so what chance would he have against this guy? Maybe not, he decided.

"How did you find out where I lived?" Derek demanded, deciding to keep him talking until help arrived in the form of Sally and Mom, and ET of course.

Jilly had started snoring again...

"Blame yourself. In your book you continually referred to your local knowledge; 'they all went to *my* school'; 'the cafe *I* use in town is the same one that they used as their base all these years ago'; '*my* friend Anton who still owns the cafe' etc... It wasn't a difficult problem. You couldn't have been living anywhere else other than Newingsworth."

"But you called me Sweaty, and you found this address – how?"

"Thank your dear friend, Anton, for that. Boy, can that bloke talk? It was lucky for me though that he was in today, he doesn't come in every day now that he has retired, he insisted on telling me. However he was delighted to explain in great detail how he'd started the idea in your head, and, yes, of course I was welcome to know where you lived, and that your real name is not Derek Tee. Then your very informative boss Rob helped too. Both were delighted to help *Derek's uncle*..."

"Very smart of you," Derek offered, hoping he'd made it sound like a compliment, rather than sarcasm because he wanted to keep this man calm – obviously a psycho! "Maybe it would make you feel better if you explained in detail what you found wrong with what I wrote, and perhaps I could understand your frustrations..." Derek liked the way he'd phrased that. Maybe the psychoanalyst idea had been a missed opportunity right enough... Should he invite the man to lie down on the couch?

"Well, for starters, how about you having called Sailor: 'A beer swilling, fat lout, who was willing to take a chance with any bit of skirt that might show interest, and who never learned to play the guitar properly?'"

"Ah, now, wait a minute," said Derek, "That's what I said about Sailor in the email, not in the book, if you are going to become finicky..."

"Look mate, what is worse, you said it without knowing the person, or asking questions of him, or even having seen him at any time..."

Why was so much concern being displayed on behalf of 'Sailor' by this disenchanted fan, Derek wondered in the passing? Was he a relative maybe? Or, could he be his agent?

"So why should you not deserve a good thumping?"

As the feeling returned that the face seemed familiar, Derek resisted the urge to ask if he realised that he was using that oxymoron again, but these thoughts were abandoned as the older man started to remove his dripping coat, and then his jacket, menacingly... Drastic action could be necessary or else someone could be receiving a good thumping. Think quickly!

Jilly, yes, use Jilly! Derek side-stepped towards the basket, turned and gave it a sharp kick. He yelled at the same moment, "Kill, Jilly, kill!" with the fleeting thought in his head, that in this defensive situation, no jury would convict him for taking desperate measures... *So, hell mend 'im!*

49

The moment Derek's book became available to the public it was purchased and read avidly by Mabel. She felt involved. It couldn't have happened without her. It was she who had helped mix the cement for the ground floor of its construction, she told herself, feeling a vicarious tingle. She, who controlled all communication into and out of the office, had been the vital link, the go-between.

It could certainly be claimed that an essential part of the book's development was thanks to her. She could have been awkward and prevented the contact, and, without either of them being aware – it had been in her power to do just that – but she used her strengths in a positive way.

There was a downside though. Since the issue of the book, she had noticed even more changes in Mr James Hoist. To her eyes, her boss, the boss of The Fort Knights Music Agency, now appeared to be burdened by a lifetime of regrets caused by what he'd allowed to be exposed on the pages.

His behaviour changed when he returned from that pre-launch party up in Newingsworth earlier this year, when he discovered his son – and his daughter but the part Mabel had difficulty in accepting, imagine being there at the party and not actually meeting them!

Of course, he was bound to have been affected by having a carving knife thrown at him by the woman to whom he had once made love – sorry – twice made love! Not pleasant... That had encouraged an early departure; hence the failure to meet his off-spring. Not what one would call pleasant memories for him, were they...but the fact that he agreed to perform at the party – that had really surprised Mabel!

Before the event, she reckoned it would be cathartic for him; a breakthrough that she could take delight in observing and, as the big day approached, it had been a pleasure to see him showing fresh determination by turning back the clock almost. She suspected him to be a natural entertainer, though in the many years she'd worked with him, he'd hidden it. It was not something he'd ever wanted to open up to her about – she assumed that for some deep, dark reason the night had turned out to be a big disappointment, affecting him deeply.

It was many weeks after his initial contact with his newly-discovered off-spring before he could even tolerate hearing words like 'dad', 'father', 'family', 'parenthood', 'marriage', or even 'responsibility', without shuddering uncontrollably, the poor man. There was much sympathy from Mabel, but a good chance he'd never even noticed it! It was so clear to her, he needed loving. He didn't realise that of course, but it was obvious to his dedicated and caring secretary, and she determined to do something about it. Recently, she'd learned a great deal about the man she worked with and, as a consequence, felt well involved...

Recently, he'd become more open to suggestions and ideas, and was willing to be guided by her. She was a married woman herself, so there was never anything other than a good platonic friendly relationship in these talks. The unspoken threat of the ex-boxer husband hovering in the background no doubt made sure there would be no thoughts of hanky-panky!

Since there had been a suitable cooling-off period after the confrontation with his old lover, Mabel reckoned the affair should be considered calmly by all. She was also aware, from her conversations with Derek, that Millie was going back often to America, but spending a great deal of time in this country too, which meant she could be contactable, and now seemed about the right time for some action, although no doubt it would require a kick-start. Mr James would do nothing himself. Gentle encouragement was required. All men were like that, always hoping the problem would right itself without them having to take action...

"Send her flowers," Mabel suggested to him one day. "All women are suckers for flowers, I can guarantee."

"Send flowers to a woman who tried to kill me? Are you nuts?" was his retort.

Not the answer Mabel expected, and she was taken aback, but she was not one to give up at the first hurdle. Unfortunately, he was less than convinced by her reasoning.

Why can't he see it, she asked herself... "At the party," she explained, "the little altercation had only been Millie's way of asking if you still remembered her. Let me put it this way," and now Mabel spoke as if to an idiot. "Look on her as a little Cupid, firing her golden bow. For the carving knife, think – golden arrow."

It was so glaringly obvious...

50

Hearing Jilly's persistent barking caused Sally to think something serious had happened. Mom had not been quite ready and stayed behind at the hotel to follow on shortly. Although dressed for rain Sally had come ahead hoping to get home during a dry spell. The barking made her anxious and she speeded up but, in rushing, she was failing to avoid many of the water-filled potholes. Surprisingly, ET managed to continue sleeping through all the bouncing as each plunge caused another splash.

The noise coming from the cottage was disconcerting. It wasn't like Jilly to bark so much. Sally worried about what could be happening to her – her little darling – she sounded upset.

Throwing the front door open, the pram was pushed inside the small hall. She slipped off her wellingtons so that there would be no mess in the living room and, lifting little Edwin up in her arms she hurried in to where the barking was continuing.

She could see immediately that Jilly had had a fright of some sort. Her darling little white poodle was simultaneously barking, and shivering, but the barks then changed to a pathetic howl as Sally went over towards the basket with a sympathetic look on her face. Holding ET on one arm, she lifted the lightweight dog up in the other.

"What is wrong with my little Jilly, then?" she asked the poodle, face to face. "Tell Mumsy all about...!"

She stopped suddenly because there, lying on the settee with one shoe off and with his sock off too, was Derek, holding both hands over his face. Her husband had blood seeping from an ankle wound. A noise behind her caused her to turn around to face the man who was coming from the kitchen with a damp cloth in his hand.

"Hello," she said automatically.

"Hello," he responded, continuing passed her and bending over her husband, applying the damp cloth to the ankle wound.

"What is...?" she started to say.

"He should have explained to the dog beforehand who he wanted her to attack..." the man told her. "If you don't do that, and he didn't," he continued, "...it can turn into a kamikaze mission, as this idiot found to his cost."

Sally was standing open-mouthed with a baby on one arm and a poodle on the other, with no idea what he was talking about.

"Derek, are you all right? Talk to me, please. What is going on?"

Derek removed his hands from a pain-filled face, and glowered up at her. "It was your stupid dog again! It's never liked me. It bit my ruddy ankle..."

"What did you do to her? You've never liked her either, have you Derek?"

Here we go, he thought, I get bitten by the ruddy dog, so it has to be me who is at fault... Derek was feeling sorry for himself, currently with a pain in the ankle, and no doubt a 'good thumping' still to come from this big bloke standing over him – and with him incapacitated too. Life was most unfair!

"Anyway, who is the friend who's helping you? You haven't introduced us. Would you like a cup of tea," she asked Derek's friend.

"It is better if you don't know who I am. It was a private matter between me and Sweaty and you shouldn't have to be involved."

"You are obviously a very old friend, to be calling him Sweaty," Sally laughed. "He never gets called that nowadays."

Derek's friend ignored Sally and turned to the prone figure on the settee.

"We'll continue our discussion some other day," he said bending over so that his nose was extremely close to Derek's. "I'll be back – Sweaty..."

As Derek pulled his head back, the man straightened up and turned, picked up his jacket and coat, and went to leave. That is when Mom appeared, a little out of breath because the rain was restarting and, having forgotten to bring the hotel umbrella, she'd attempted foolishly to dash.

"Oh hello," Mom said, eying the visitor up and town appreciatively. "You are a nice big boy..."

He hesitated, not sure what to say, but was unable to get passed this woman blocking his exit, and who was making no attempt to move out of his way.

"Just a doggone minute..." said Millie, "...don't I know you?" and bent towards him, making him a little uncomfortable. "You've got no hair on top now and a beard, but that face – look at me again – yea, even though it's been nearly twenty years..."

Just let me pass, he wanted to say. All he saw in front of him was a female, a good looking female admittedly, one he didn't know though she thought she knew him. Who was she? There had been a lot of women in his life.

"...Yes, and jumpin' Jehoshaphat!" said Millie, as a grin spread across her face. "Look who it is... If it aint my old buddy, Theo! Theobald Walters! Well, I'll be doggoned!"

At that name Derek's pain immediately left him! He was up on his feet, with one shoe off and one shoe on, and hobbling rapidly over to grab the visitor's hand. That name! It suddenly clicked!

"Theobald Walters! It's *Sailor* isn't it, I should have known...!" Derek said in an awestruck voice, realising now why the face had appeared familiar, though a little different from the newspaper photos of the band's early days.

He'd searched for information about this man for months when he was preparing the book, and at last he'd found him. A mass of thoughts were running through his head, including: Could this be the direction I should be going in the future – towards 'Rabid Revenge Revisited – Part Two'? However the reaction from this man, who had become an absent hero of his, was disappointing...

"This is none of your business, boy," the man retorted testily, shaking loose Derek's hand. "It's me this lady is talking to."

"But this is Mom, my mother... Sailor, this is Millie!"

The visitor stood and looked at the woman.

"It *is* me, Theo. Do I look so different?" she asked, hoping that he would answer like the gentleman she remembered.

"To be honest, you look much nicer than I remember," he said, going suddenly soft, and sounding as if he really meant it.

Would you listen to the patter! Polished to perfection! More like the answer a cocky conman would conjure up – and a little different to the way he was talking to me, thought Derek.

"I thought you'd be in the States," said Millie. "Are you still working?"

"Yea, I was doing a solo gig in Dundee last weekend, and that's why I came south; a chance to meet *Sweaty* – the author of a great book."

Derek considered that that part was said with a bit less sincerity than his previous comment about Mom.

"It must feel nice to come face to face with the author then..." she added.

"Sure is," he said with a glance at Derek. "Me and the author are already very close."

"So, where are you staying then?"

"Nowhere yet, I've only just arrived. Is there somewhere you could recommend in this town?"

"Why not come back with me to the New Farmhouse Hotel along the road. I'm sure they'll find a space for you."

With eyes only for each other, the two of them went out the front door making no further comment to the occupants of the cottage, leaving Derek with one shoe off, and Sally with a baby on one arm and a white poodle on the other...

51

Derek felt let down by that damn dog. The hatred it felt for him was obviously deep-seated, as demonstrated by the bite on his ankle. Incredibly, the person who'd appeared with the intention of giving him a 'good thumping' had shown more compassion and tenderness than this bloody dog ever had, and Derek didn't put his lead on every night, and take him for walks, or have to pay for his tins of dog-meat.

She'd tasted blood. Every time Derek glanced her way, the sharp little teeth came into view, and it wasn't a smile... Jilly was supposed to leap to my aid, and chase the guy off, instead of choosing to fight for the opposition. Look at her even now! She is sitting in her basket watching me, daring me to go near her again.

"...As for my 'friends', eagerly disclosing where I live. Grrr..."

The threat of the thumping hadn't gone either, had it? At least he was nice to Mom, wasn't he, when he left... Maybe Sailor would come back and say 'Sorry...'

Yes, that would be nice – but Derek wasn't holding his breath!

He'd been out of Britain for much too long. He'd come back to perform and after doing the gig, the intention had been to follow up with a visit to Edinburgh, and maybe even Glasgow; do the tourist circuit. There was no rush to return to the States – no gigs planned in the near future and no little lady sitting waiting for him either.

Sailor, since leaving the band, had promoted himself. No longer was he a common seaman, he was now the Captain, 'Cap'n T', the name he used as a solo artiste. When in Dundee, he had taken time to wander around the town's centre. Staying cooped up in the hotel bedroom of any town or city where he had a gig was not his style. He hadn't been there before – it was his first time in Scotland – so, it was a good opportunity to have a look around. From what he knew about the place it was supposed always to be wet, but that was obviously untrue, and as for the kilts...

So, he'd intended to do the gig, go to Edinburgh, then across to Glasgow; no rush. That was the plan – until the chance discovery of 'Rabid Revenge Revisited'. He noticed the book about his band. displayed prominently on the shelf of a Dundee bookshop.

Who is this guy Derek Tee? Never heard of him... and what qualified him to write a book about Rabid Revenge and without even contacting the most important member of the band? That is definitely cheeky!

So, the book was purchased, the walkabout terminated, and back to the hotel room he went with a lot of reading to do. How could this have been written without his being involved? As he read, he noted some things that didn't sit comfortably with him. They weren't seriously wrong, but they were highlighting some aspects of his life that he would have preferred not to have aired, and of course no-one had even talked to him before printing this.

By the time he'd read the whole book, he had worked up a real bad humour and it had to be gotten out of his system, and only one person could be to blame – the author! From what he'd read, it looked like this guy lived in Newingsworth. He talked about familiar things the way a local does, so a visit there instead of the Scottish trips would be a good idea; Scottish cities could come later, and it would be interesting to visit Newingsworth again after such a long time, to go 'back home' – but first he'd made use of the email address.

So, to Newingsworth he went...

Returning to one's old hometown, after a long time away, living in a far distant country, can be an emotional experience. For most people, while distant, there is usually nostalgia felt for friends left behind, and the visualisation of old haunts, and how the feel of the place is remembered – to be replaced by the delight of the real thing on arriving. However, reality after nearly thirty years is that friends have moved on or died off, and modernisation has cleared away a great deal of the old haunts.

Theobald Walters, remembered where they'd performed in the early days, and being long before anyone thought it possible to ban cigarettes indoors, the venues had been generally dark and smoky basements. Even at the time they felt claustrophobic. He had no desire to return to look there.

As for friends, there had been few. When they formed the band the members became a very secretive tight-knit group, involved almost only with one another as they developed their musical talents. Schoolmates for them were tolerated rather than befriended, even though these very schoolmates looked to them in wonder, recognising and supporting their talented performances. When they were in America, they changed the name. They became 'Rabid Revenge'. Back in Britain, the reputation of the old band and the band members faded.

Surprisingly, there was little publicity back in the UK for the newly renamed band and they were totally forgotten by most of their earlier followers. New heroes were appearing on the UK music scene, good musicians to take their place in the affections of fans, although, even these replacements were absorbed and loved only for a limited life – stars for only as long as a fickle British public allowed them to be.

Having formed the original band in Newingsworth while they were still at High School, and being founder members, Millie, Theo, James and Jonathan, knew each other very well, but, after five years with them in the 'big time', Millie left. With a roving life being requisite for a rock band, close and regular contact between Millie and her ex-school friends gradually diminished.

Theobald Walters even lost touch with his son – a long time ago. He didn't know that Sam had moved to the UK or that he was married, or that he and his wife, Angie, had a new baby. In fact, he knew nothing – no, that's not true. He knew his own father was in a bad way, because he was paying for his care at the Slatterfoot Nursing Home. Contact with his father's neighbour had highlighted a need, confirmed by his father's doctor. The transfer to care had been a very private affair, arranged remotely and sadly without personal contact, relying on the services of a local solicitor to arrange the detail. Staying away from his father was his cowardly way of coping.

Even though he told himself it was not infectious, he was afraid of the inevitability of going that way too.

It was naughty of Millie to invite Sam and Angie to bring little Annabel for a meal with her, but without telling Theo what was about to happen. Theo wasn't mentioned to them either. Maybe she should have considered, medically, that when they all came face to face, there could be serious consequences for the older man but, thankfully, Theobald's being struck dumb didn't qualify as a major medical disaster.

Sam, seeing his old man for the first time in more than six years, was delighted, and proud to be able to introduce his family, and there was plenty to talk about. Back in the days when he was 'Sailor' Theo had known Angie, but only as a tiny baby in Millie's arms. Now Angie had her own child – his grand-daughter – and Sam, now a successful teacher here – a smart cookie and his boy...

"Grew the beard to compensate for the loss of head hair," Theo explained, in response to his son's comment that there was something different about his appearance.

Sam told his pop about the visit to his granddad.

Next day, feeling ashamed, Theobald Walters plucked up courage and visited his old man. Was it worth it, he asked himself later? As expected, his father had been happily ignorant of who this visitor was. As he left the old fellow behind, Theo waved, and smiled, and tried to hide the tears.

Discovering Millie again was a combination of shock and delight for Theobald Walters. Similarly for Millie, meeting this old pal after such a long time was wonderful, and there was lot to catch up on.

Thanks to Millie, a truce was declared between Cap'n T and Millie's boy. Any distorted information used by Derek, she explained to Theo, was fed to him by Twister, and, as far as she was concerned, the passing of the years had made James Hoist worse than he had been before. Theo's justification for 'getting back at the author' was therefore successfully removed. Winning Theo round to her way of thinking had been easy so, obviously, the knack of twisting men around her little finger hadn't left Millie, but this time she'd used it to good cause. Mom was the one Derek would have to thank for the removal of the 'good thumping' threat.

When she thought back to her days as a vocalist Millie remembered Sailor well, a great guy in her eyes back then – but only most of the time, because he'd been unable to resist temptation. All the blokes had reputations for being highly sexed and took advantage of 'free offers' from the female fans. Anyway, who was she to criticise them. Unlike her, at least the others had stuck together through thick and thin and functioned professionally together until the end. When they gave up, they must have known each other very well – maybe too well...

His performance in Dundee had been one of only a few he was doing nowadays.

It wasn't the money; he wasn't short of cash; he sang because it still gave him a buzz to perform and he was delighted that people still came to his occasional concerts, this one having been arranged by an expat American living near the city. The night was shared with a local star, and that had guaranteed a good turn-out. Being paid good money to go on stage for his own enjoyment? He couldn't grumble about that!

Now in Newingsworth, there was no need to rush off anywhere. Staying at the New Farmhouse Hotel was agreeable so he might as well put his feet up here for a while. Everything in the hotel was new, the surrounding countryside pleasing, Thelma and Hammy had made him feel very welcome and, of course, Millie was here too...

52

Mom was visiting, yet again, but this evening she was much appreciated. For Derek and Sally, having a baby who had a vocal strength that many an opera star would envy, was driving them crazy. Then Millie arrived and took over.

Her baby-calming technique worked beautifully, ET became mesmerised – and silent. She was simply walking up and down the room with the little fellow over her shoulder, patting his back gently as she sang quietly in his ear. Neither Sally nor Derek had been able to stop the crying, but they hadn't tried singing to him. It was a solution that would have occurred to them as neither possessed a decent singing voice. The soothing music did it, and answered the question Mabel asked a short time ago. Yes, Millie could still sing ...beautifully.

After placing him in his cot ET gurgled in a contented way and they were all able to relax. There is nothing quite like the continuous crying of a young baby for setting nerves on edge, when everyone is clueless about how to stop it.

"Can I top up your glass, Mom?" Derek asked gratefully, knowing there was little chance of her refusing.

"Oh, I shouldn't Sweaty ...but go on then, just the one."

"I haven't heard you sing before," said Sally, beating Derek to the comment. "Have you done much since you left the band?"

"No, Honey, only now and again, and I kinda miss it. There's never any reason these days. A bit different for Sailor – tells me he is still performing, though not so often now. I didn't know he had changed his stage name to 'Cap'n T'. Didn't like to say to him but it sounds to me like he's selling fish fingers, or something! Says he still enjoys it. He goes solo sometimes, voice and guitar only, other times, a small backing group, but it was unusual for him being over here for a gig. It turned out a big success too, and maybe he should have done a few. He was sorry to have to go back to the States."

"If you had a chance to sing professionally again, would you take it Mom, and maybe do it over here?" said Derek.

"Sure thing, Sweaty, and I could sing some of the countless songs I've written over the years, ones I've never performed for an audience. I would love that dearly..."

"Solo, or with others?" he continued.

"It's good to be with others you know; but I don't think that's very likely."

"How about singing with an ex-partner?"

"I doubt it, unless you could persuade Theo to remain here permanently..."

"Oh no, I was thinking more of James... Yes, you and Twister singing together..."

There was a deathly silence in the room, except for the burbling coming from the cot. Derek couldn't really be sure what his baby son was thinking of this brilliant idea, but it was obvious by the look on her face that he had not won Mom over...

53

Mabel was not ready to give up the romantic notion of bringing together two people – two who had loved each other many years ago sufficiently to have produced two children, and she was convinced they just needed a little shove to make them happy together again.

The cost of the bouquet could come out of petty cash, which she controlled. The flowers were not yet organised but she had already downloaded a suitable card from the florist, it just required a personal message.

"Just write 'Please forgive me'," she instructed her boss.

"Get stuffed!" he told her.

"What? What's wrong?" she queried, a little upset at his rudeness. She was only trying to help him.

"What have I done to require forgiveness – she threw the ruddy knife didn't she?" he retorted.

"You obviously do not understand how it has to work, do you?" she replied with a disdainful expression on her face. "You have to realise that for a woman in this situation, the man is always in the wrong, even though she may not have been totally in the right ...ok?"

He wasn't in the mood to argue. It was simpler to give in and do what she asked, even though he hadn't a clue what she meant. So, he wrote 'Please, oh please, forgive me' simply to get rid of it and she went away with the card in her hand, triumphant!

She had already decided that the personal touch was required so, on with her coat and out of the office she went – after unplugging the telephone system and the computer so that he wouldn't be tempted to get involved in her side of the business. He was no good with technology.

Her chosen florist was only a few minutes a walk along the road. Deliveries could be arranged by them efficiently and discreetly and they could be trusted to supply a quality bouquet to suit any occasion, provided the request was explained correctly.

"I would like you to make up a nice large bouquet for me, one that says 'Sorry' in a big way, to a lady. It's not from me, of course, it's from a man," she explained.

With the destination name and address added to the form, the card to accompany the flowers was handed over with the cash. Mabel's pleasant smile was returned by the lady serving, and the deed was done. She left the shop with the receipt for her records.

So job over, feeling good inside, she retraced her steps to the office and plugged the connections back into the sockets, pleased to note that he hadn't attempted to interfere with anything during her short absence. She sat down satisfied with a job well done. It would just be a matter of time before the phone would ring and she would permit Millie to speak to – and say thank you – to sweet Mr James.

Hammy was doing Temporary Desk Duty when they were delivered. He always felt uncomfortable in the presence of 'flowers', especially expensive looking bouquets. They were signed for at the desk and they were then his – to pass on, thank goodness!

Delivering them right away seemed best. Feeling a little foolish at having to carry 'flowers' along to Millie's room, he hoped sincerely that he would not bump into anyone. He was never comfortable holding 'flowers' and would rather be dragged across hot coals than enter a shop to buy any, never mind being seen bringing them home...

Her afternoon nap being disturbed resulted in a tousle-haired, sleepy-looking woman opening the door to Hammy. Normally she preferred 'her fans', as she still liked to think of the general public, to see her only when well made-up and with not a hair out of place. Thank goodness it was only Hammy ...but a bouquet, how wonderful, who is it from?

"A card, Hammy, is there no card?"

"Och aye, is it no' there. Ah'm sure it wiss a minute ago. Ah mussed huvv dropped it..."

Back along the corridor he went and sure enough there it was on the floor beside the desk. He looked at the envelope. It wasn't sealed, so he had a wee peep inside.

'Please, oh please, forgive me!' it said. He carefully replaced it, closed the envelope again, and took it back along the corridor. He knocked and the same dishevelled person appeared, but this time the look was one of curiosity and anticipation. Who sent the bouquet?

She took the envelope from Hammy, opened it, and read the words. Hammy could see a little tear appear in her eyes, and if there was anything worse than having to carry 'flowers', it was standing in front of a woman with a tear in her eye.

"Oh Hammy, thank you so very much," she said, stepping forward, hugging him and planting a kiss on both his cheeks. How embarrassing! Now as far as Hammy was concerned there was nothing worse, than...

She closed the door.

Hammy shuffled away, hoping he would not bump into his wife or anyone else for that matter, at least not until he'd calmed down.

As Millie laid the flowers on the table, she realised there was no container large enough for them in the room. If she rang Hammy he'd bring one along she decided. She looked again at the card: 'Please, oh please, forgive me' it said.

"...But Theo, you lovely, silly man – you did nothing wrong..."

Mabel was most disappointed when no call came from Millie for sweet Mr James...

54

"A race – that's what we should be doing – having a race!" exclaimed Alexander, as they crushed through the door together into the Torrid Hedgehog. Alexander was the only one showing any enthusiasm, partly because it was his idea and partly because he was the only cyclist not gasping for breath and able to speak. "...And if we decide on a course, we could do it every week and keep a tally of our individual times for a league table."

"Yea...yea..." was the general response, everyone else being more concerned with getting to the bar, and having the pleasure of tasting one of the delicious real-ales sold here, than in the organising of any stupid exhausting races.

Hector and Hammy had it easy being on the scooter so no need even to think about getting involved! Anyway, being the elders of the group, they were considerably slower at dismounting from the scooter, parking it up, stretching stiff legs, and removing helmets to hang on the scooter handlebars. At least, being last, the pints would be there waiting for them at the counter. For them there was no rush. As usual, their drinks were there along with refreshments the others had also ordered for them.

It was a pleasantly warm day but, for Hector and Hammy, travelling on the scooter always felt chilly. They were just sitting. The other four, having been highly active, were perspiring visibly even though they wore only lightweight clothing. Of course, the common feature of all their wear was the safety helmets; slightly flashier in style for the cyclists.

"Have you ever fancied getting a licence to drive a scooter?" Hector enquired of Hammy, because he fancied some of what the others were downing, rather than the non-alcoholic drivel he was stuck with. "What'll it be?" he was always asked, "A pint of orange, or is it maybe a lemonade today, or are you going wild with a Coke?" What a tantalising selection!

"Are you tellin' me that ye'd let me drive your wee bike?" replied Hammy. "Ah dinna believe ye would do that. It wid mean ye couldnae drink yer lovely lemonade... An' ah wouldnae be able tae drink ma beer. The answer's – *naw*."

Hector chose orange and, because he was becoming well known by the landlord, it was topped by a little cherry. "Well, how do you like this place, Pop?" Sam asked Theobald Walters. "...A bit different from back home."

Sam's dad just gave a smile. For him this was all a novelty.

Millie had worked on him. Having a very good friend at odds with her son discomfited her, so she took it on her shoulders to change the situation. It took a lot of persuading to convince the 'disenchanted reader' that he was going at it the wrong way. Derek was really a good guy, so his annoyance had been transferred elsewhere. His target now was Twister!

With her friend Theo no longer a threat to him, Derek was told by his mother to stop being silly and to come to the hotel and shake hands; make her friend feel welcome in the country. Reluctantly Derek did so.

"Introduce him to the others, please Sweaty," Mom requested. "He could do with some friendly male company in this place."

Mr Theobald Walters was therefore with 'friends'. He had been accepted, 'sort of'. Permitting him to be sworn in, as a member of the Newingsworth Mafia, Male Section, had not been a decision taken lightly by the existing members of this elite group. There was still suspicion...

Derek had met the others and told them what Mom requested. He was no longer under the threat of a good thumping, they were told, but they weren't so easily convinced. Maybe he was a nicer bloke than originally thought, Derek added. That was conjecture, the others said.

Very little was known of him other than his ex-membership of Rabid Revenge. Yes indeed, a friend of Millie's a long time ago, but they had lost touch, so was her judgement to be trusted? He still had a home in America, they knew that, but what did they *not* know?

There was no getting away from it; 'a good thumping' had been threatened. This sort of behaviour made them all mighty wary of him, even though the threat had apparently been lifted. They all agreed. This man couldn't be invited to join their little Mafia clique without more checks and Hammy would be the one to make them.

As the New Farmhouse Hotel was proving popular and paying customers generally filled the rooms, Theobald Walters had decided on a similar arrangement to Millie's. Hammy wished he still had enough money in his bank account to do that sort of thing: have a room kept especially, paid in advance: his, whether or not he was in the country. Convenient for Theobald Walters and good for the hotel, but for other reasons Hammy was happy too. While he was staying in the hotel, Hammy could keep an eye on him and get to know more ... the power of whisky can be wondrous.

It became obvious, very quickly, that Theobald Walters liked whisky. Standing chatting, then sitting chatting, while being plied with drinks on the house caused to him to relax. They had a pleasant mellowing effect on him. In fact, both he and Hammy became quite loquacious, and confidences began to be shared. After a few glasses, he admitted to his Scottish drinking buddy and host that it had been a bluff when he challenged Derek and that changed Hammy's attitude towards him.

"He is really jist a big saftie, ye ken..." he reported back to the other males. "He's aw wind, but he couldnae burst a paper bag!"

The males in the secret clique then voted on whether he should be permitted to join. They had to consider also, if they let him in, would he be capable of keeping secrets; it wouldn't do if he turned out to be a ladies' man who would blab to the females about what they were up to every time he drank whisky! In the end they all agreed that maybe he wasn't such a bad fellow after all, or at least he was not any worse than they were. Of course it was difficult for Sam's vote not to be biased; after all they were talking critically about his dad.

So, they were all agreed... Theobald Walters, aka Sailor, aka Cap'n T, would be taken on as a fully paid-up member of the Newingsworth Mafia, Male Section, and, from now on be known, exclusively to the members, as 'Baldy'.

So, Baldy was out for the first time with his newly discovered friends at their favourite pub in the country.

For the outing to The *Torrid Hedgehog*, Theobald Walters had the use of one of the hotel's spare bikes. He found that pedalling it was extremely hard work but it seemed to him that he was the only one with a problem. For the others it appeared to be a relatively easy journey. What he didn't know was that his bike was ancient. Derek had spruced it up a bit but, basically, the machine Baldy was using had been Hector's: the bike from his pre-scooter days, the one that was used on his paper-round for many years, the one that had received very little maintenance, the one that squeaked...

So when Alexander brought up the idea again of a race, Baldy was even less enthusiastic than the other two, but he was enjoying the company and the location, and the ales, although not overly happy about the nickname they'd allocated him. He sampled a few beers, and when it came time to leave, he was in as happy a frame of mind as the rest. Needless to say, 'happiness' excluded Hector, the grumpy tee-total scooter driver!

It is amazing what a few drinks can do. Baldy felt better, returning home on the bike; the sound of the squeak became reassuring, even though it was still hard work pedalling the darn thing, and it was a struggle to keep pace with the other three cyclists. He was afraid he might get lost if they got out of his sight. When Hector realised how difficult it was for their newest member, he and Hammy tootled along behind him on the scooter, shouting encouragement. Hector was thinking back a few years, affectionately, to when he used to pedal that same, wonderful bike.

Second wind kicked in for Derek and Sam, and though they were not as fit or as strong as Alexander, and Spider as cyclists, they could put up a good burst of speed, so with a nod and wink to each other they suddenly pushed ahead of the other two, much to their consternation, and it suddenly became a race!

With little traffic on the road, they took risks on corners, maximising the advantage of downhill stretches, and were soon way ahead of Baldy and the scooter pair, having totally forgotten about them. All four were seriously pushing each other.

The silence of the countryside was disturbed only by the whoosh of tyres on the road and the gasping breaths of four only moderately-fit people. Of the group, Alexander was out in front again, and almost neck and neck was Spider, followed closely in their slipstream by Sam, with Derek holding a very tight fourth position.

That's when they came round the corner ...*and into the rabbits!*

Alexander and Spider hit several, holding a straight course with difficulty, as the furry shapes panicked and went everywhere, bobbing around and scattering; Sam slipped through unscathed in the middle of the road, but Derek couldn't help himself and, trying to avoid them, he swerved at high speed and hit the road edge. With all control lost, and eyes tightly shut, he flew over the handlebars!

A tree stopped his forward momentum.

Eventually, when they reached the corner, the horrifying sight which met the eyes of Baldy, Hector and Hammy, was of three people jumping off bikes and rushing over towards the mangled steel and rubber, and the crumpled figure, beside a large tree...

55

My head is still painful. Small wonder – that damn tree! How is the bike? Can't remember what happened after, but, no matter, here I am, at the airfield. Ah, is this my instructor? The gent who is coming in my direction will be the one I'll be flying with, I presume, but how did I get here? Did Sally bring me? I can't see her. Where is she? Gawd ...my head is really fuzzy.

Wonder which plane I'm going up in.

Oh dear, I don't feel too good. My stomach... must be butterflies. After yesterday, I suppose I shouldn't be surprised my stomach feels strange, as well as my head. In fact, all my muscles ache! But, I mustn't complain, I am the birthday boy, and mustn't seem ungrateful. Any moment now, I'll be enjoying my treat.

Quite a surprise – didn't think I'd be given anything so lavish. 'Fly a plane on your own'. Hope I can cope, never having driven anything before, and especially after me proving that I can't even ride a bike properly! Told me yesterday morning, a day in advance – then apologised for it being a day early – sorry to spoil the surprise, Sally said, but that was so that I wouldn't be tempted to go out drinking with the others. That sort of celebrating wouldn't be wise for a budding pilot, now would it?

Fly an aeroplane with a hangover, no thank you, although this head feels as if I've had a few? It's a family present, not just from her, she said, so the guys shouldn't have invited me out anyway. They'd know the plan – although that could have been a good reason for that lot to deliberately get me sozzled... but did we go to the Torrid...? No, that was ages ago – wasn't it?

I am not sure that I'm looking forward to this... Can't chicken out though – unless I can think of a good excuse!

Flying off on holiday is bad enough ...didn't like that either, even though it was a large plane. The pilot was supposed to know what he was doing; experts are supposed to fly the big ones, but he could have fooled me! He should have known which knobs to twiddle and the right levers to pull for that job, so that passengers could relax. Not on that flight... Bloody amateur, the way it felt. Could have been on auto-pilot – or maybe the stewardess was in control!

No, that flight to Tenerife was not much fun. The landing – it was like it was the first time he'd ever done it. Could have been, I suppose. Everyone has to do something for the first time. Boy, did that plane bounce...? Jarred my spine, it did, and that could have ruined the holiday. I wasn't the only one. It gave Sally a bit of a fright too. You can understand why they clear all the drinks and containers and loose bits away before they land, can't you.

I'm feeling a bit lonely standing here – like the proverbial prune looking for custard... I thought my man was on his way over. Where's he gone? Couldn't have been him....

Oh, it's starting to rain. Where is my instructor? Ah, at last... Looks a bit old fashioned in that get-up, must be to create the right atmosphere...

"Good. You are here on time anyway. Have you had your posting yet?"

"Posting? What do you...?"

"No, don't suppose the lads at the Ministry would want to tell you where you are off to, until after I've rubber-stamped your form. Right, get that on."

A leather helmet - this looks the sort of headgear the pilots used when flying began – in the old biplanes...Where's the communication system? Must be separate headphones inside in the cockpit.

I'm getting a bit chilly – should have gone to the toilet – not helping the nerves, or the headache. Better not say. Wouldn't want him to tell me I can't fly because of a stupid headache, especially not after them all going to the bother of arranging this for me. It'll be good to get inside, out of this cold wind. I suppose training planes have heaters.

"Put these on please." Goggles...? What do we need goggles for? Isn't the windscreen enough?

"Follow me, my good fellow."

Easy up, man, marching off as if we were in the forces... Where's our aircraft? These are museum pieces – biplanes, open cockpits. God, imagine flying in one of these. It'd freeze the goolies off you, I'm sure. Why are we stopping here?

"Climb aboard then. Let's get it over and done with. A bit of a storm brewing, I think."

He must be giving me a look at some of the older models before we have the lesson. Good value for money certainly, but I'd rather get on with it, in the real thing. Why is he clambering in the cockpit behind me? He could have just leaned over to explain about this one. And my head's feeling worse... The other guy, standing beside the propeller; they used to have to crank the propeller for these machines – saw that in the films.

Hmmm, I never expected to have the chance to sit in the cockpit of a biplane. Interesting, yes... but can we just get on with it? Can we get to our plane? I'm freezing...

"Right, get her going then!"

He's shouting to the bloke on the ground. What's he doing? He's turning the prop ...starting up the engine – oh my God – we're not going up in this, are we?

"Got your straps fastened? Keep clear of the controls. I'll take her up."

Where did the voice come from? It's a speaking tube. Where's the end I speak into? We've to communicate with each other by using that – good grief...

"How do I speak to you when we're in the air?" I'm shouting to him as loudly as I can, but he can't hear me above the noise of the engine. How do I speak to him...?

"Chocks away..."

Oh no – we're moving. I don't want to go up in this... I don't need a birthday present... He's got me mixed up with somebody else. This isn't my birthday present... I'll shut my eyes. It's not happening to me.

Oh my God, this could be Sally's retribution – for me and Sophie.

I'm sorry Sally I shouldn't have hidden my meetings with Sophie. I should have been honest with you. There's no such person as Josephine, and anyway Sophie is a really nice person. There's nothing going on between us. Yes, it looked to you as if we were going to be naughty, but I wouldn't have ...although she has a lovely body... But my goodness – she's only my publisher. Hon-est!

Oh, what's happening now? The engine sounds different. Should I look...?

Heavens... We are in the heavens... We are flying...

"Ok Private Sweaty – you can take over now. Let's see you put her through her paces – and remember you could be firing a machine gun, as well. It's all yours."

What does he mean, take over? I don't know what to do. He's told me nothing about this.

"I can't do it... I can't fly an aeroplane. I'm not who you think I am. I AM NOT SWEATY – I'M DEREK!"

He can't hear me. Help, what's happening? We're starting to dive... Is he going to do something? He isn't – he's leaving it to me... The man's a fool. This stick – I'll pull it. What's it doing? We seem to have levelled. Did I do that? And these pedals – what do they do? Whoa...

"That was a bit rough on the old tail fin, Private Sweaty. I have a bad headache too, you know."

Why is he calling me that...? Does this man know what he's doing? I'm supposed to be receiving instructions... And he should be calling me Derek ...or Mr Toozlethwaite!

"Take us down lower, man. Remember if you are on a reconnaissance mission, you have to fly low enough to estimate the troops in the trenches – but not get shot in the process."

What is he talking about? I'm not going to war. He's living in the past... Right – I'll take it lower if that what he wants. Be it on his head – so, if I move the stick like that... I'm controlling this thing... yes, we are dropping... Ooooh... Is that too steep?

"Good God, man – where did you learn to fly?"

He thinks I can fly...? What's happening to me...?

"I've had enough of this, old chap. I'm going to leave you to take it down yourself. I'll jump now – before we get too low. See you back at base, old boy. I'll be most disappointed if this parachute doesn't open. What ho!"

What's he doing? He's climbing out of the cockpit... He's jumping out...

"Don't leave me..."

He's gone...he's gone, and I'm alone in a biplane and I'm...

But I recognise where I am. There's the hill we cycled down yesterday. I'm near to Little Typington... And there's the *Torrid Hedgehog* again... Is that Sally I can see? She's with Gran and Grandad, and Hammy. Thelma and Angelina are waving too. Where are the babies – ah, yes in their prams with Sam, and Alexander and Muriel. They are all here – isn't that nice, and Mom's waving too.

I'll go round again... This is much better now! I can see Josephine too, or is it Sophie... It is Sophie. No, don't take you clothes off, Sophie, not again, not in front of Sally and all her friends. I can't look...

I'll look elsewhere – there's the tree I crashed into, but I don't see my bike.

I'm getting the hang of this... Let's go round in another circle...

What? Who tapped my shoulder?

"Surprise – Derek, it's us!"

"Mom – Dad – what are you doing here? I'm in the middle of a crisis."

"Yes, we know, but we smuggled aboard – so that we could share this experience as a family – together."

"You can't be together. Mom, you said you can't stand the sight of him!"

"Don't be silly Derek. At a time like this – all you need is love."

"No, I don't need you to start singing – I need someone to fly this airplane!"

How do I stop the engine? How do I slow it down? What am I doing here?

Oh ...oh no ...that tree again... it's getting awfully close... I'm going to crash into it... Could I land on the branches? What if I don't...? We are...

"Hold tight everyone – we are going down.........!"

My eyes are closed... Sally I love you... My eyes are still closed... Oooooooooooh...

"...I am still here... Are you still there? Mom, Pop!"

I've landed on the... on the... on...

Should I look...?

"What happened?"

Derek opened his eyes: bright lights... The goggles, he wasn't wearing goggles, it was an oxygen mask.

"Where...?"

He felt a warm hand gently take hold of his. It was Sally. She burst into tears...

56

Twister was not at the hospital, in fact no one thought of telling him about the crisis. This was mainly because contact had only ever been between Derek and Twister; no other members of the family were involved. It just didn't occur to anyone to say, so he didn't know, and therefore, Mabel didn't know either.

Several weeks after Derek's accident, Mabel decided the romance should be progressed forward to a new level, but not surprisingly, her boss actually wanted little to do with it, and was being a very reluctant participant. She needed Derek's help, totally unaware that he had been hospitalised, concussed, and oblivious to the normal world for twenty-four hours. If she'd met him face to face, she might have wondered if his nose had always looked like that, the result of a brief involuntary sliding contact with the ground prior to smacking into the tree.

As it was, when she contacted him at work, she was surprised to learn that he had only just returned, and she couldn't have been more sympathetic. All conversation between the two had been on the telephone. She thought of Derek as a good friend – he thought of her as the essential link to his blood relation. Disappointingly for her, Derek was unable to answer her query immediately. Did he know if his mother had received the flowers from her boss, dear Mr James?

Derek was amazed that his natural father could have gone to that sort of bother, but surprised and delighted to be asked the question because it meant he was still interested in her. Even after the knife-throwing act, the idea of getting them to work together as a group had not died the death yet, so he promised to find out for her. He promptly rang Hammy to see if he had any record of the delivery at the hotel.

"Och aye, ah mind weel o' that," Derek was informed. "An' sure, she goat them flooers a' richt. Ah delivered thum tae her masell, an' ah remember there wuss a wee drippy tear in her eye..."

This was good news to Derek because a tear indicated emotion and so there obviously must be tender feelings still there for Twister. She'd said, "No way," when he had asked her about them singing together, but was probably just putting on an act, not wanting to display her true feelings. So, the plan still had a chance. Between them, he and Mabel would get his parents together again, he thought confidently, and called Mabel back. She was pleased to hear the bouquet was received and that it had been much appreciated.

"What should we do next, Derek?" she asked.

"No idea, but tell you what, is he available to talk just now, because there is something that could be done?"

"Oh sorry, Derek, he gave instructions not to be disturbed for about an hour and a half. He has an important client with him. I can't tell you who it is, but if you watch the music programme on Tuesday evening... No, I mustn't tell you any more... That was naughty of you trying to wheedle it out of me, Derek."

"Sorry," he said automatically, "then you could give him a message. Would you tell him to keep a week on Saturday free? My father-in-law is arranging a special late-birthday treat for me. Because of the accident, I missed what they had planned. It would be good if Twister can be there. I could talk through an idea with him then. It is to be fancy dress, I'm told, so he can maybe think about a costume, oh ...and Mom won't be there. This is to be just for the guys..."

Hmmm, a fancy dress party for males only? If Mr James attends that he'll have to have a good costume... What should I organise for him? It will have to be something very good...

Mabel was good at organising...

Derek was not sure what the party plan was. Alexander was playing the cards close to his chest. It was to be a surprise, but males only? What did he have in mind? Surely not a stripper! Hector and Hammy couldn't cope with that sort of thing at their age, but then again Hammy was recently married... Anyway, that was old-hat, and holding it on a Saturday afternoon? "We're having it when the females are at the hotel doing their thing, and we won't be bothered by them; just leave it to me," Alexander had said. So ...what did he have in mind that we shouldn't be caught at, Derek wondered apprehensively?

He might have a chance to win-over Twister at the party, if he appears – and to convince him that he should perform again as a duo with Mom. Twister should be able to open all the doors for them with the contacts he has as an agent. Derek himself would do the publicity and have a go at writing songs. He'd always fancied having a go at that – it shouldn't be all that difficult. He'd written a book, so song-writing could be his next success...

Derek wondered if Andy Woodstock would like to come. He hadn't seen Andy for a while. Sophie could give him a lift, because she'll probably be in Newingsworth as usual to do her 'Josephine' act. Yes, it would be nice to see the guy again.

57

It was Saturday afternoon again. Derek and Sam, with their normal outings to the *Torrid Hedgehog* sadly curtailed, were at the cottage making-do with proprietary cans of beer instead of the speciality ales for which they had rapidly acquired a taste. They had been warned not to drink too much. Even by choice there was little chance of that because this stuff tasted poor by comparison, but because they were baby-sitting, commandeered by their wives who had other things to do, the 'stay sober' was an order. Unfortunately, the *Torrid Hedgehog* had been a 'cycle too far' since Derek's painful crash.

Any suggestion of another visit to the country pub had been avoided by the others, in deference to Derek's fortunate avoidance of serious repercussions. They were being martyrs too.

For Derek, not cycling to the Inn was due to an inability ever to get on his good old bike again, not that he'd lost his nerve, oh no ...it was the bike's fault, being a mangled mess. It wasn't worth repairing, and he wasn't buying another yet. He would, but for a while he was basking in the glory of being, in the eyes of the others, 'precious'.

Other than during the weekend of Derek's accident, in no way were the goings-on of the Newingsworth Mafia: Female Branch, inhibited. They were continuing to have their usual get-together on Saturday afternoons, doing whatever it was they did, about which the males still hadn't a clue. The males thought they were being smart keeping their activities secret too but they weren't: mints fail to hide alcohol fumes!

Alexander was more eager than the others to know what his wife did, but no-one would tell him; he'd given up asking his wife. With male meetings temporarily curtailed and Hammy being around when the female group met at the Hotel on Saturday afternoons, Alexander asked him to find out, but Hammy failed.

"Ah dinna ken whit they dae. They urr in the room and close the doors ahint them, so ah canny hear onythin' – an' there wid be hell tae pay if ah goat caught peepin' in the windaes!"

It was all very silly because there was nothing to be secretive about. It was very low key, and to say they were a 'close knit' group would come surprisingly close to the truth.

Their Saturday afternoons included almost constant chatter obviously, because they were female, but it was also a hive of industry, currently churning out hand-knitted woollies for charity babies, having many weeks ago completed the wardrobe needs of their own little ones, Edwin and Annabel. As a team they were not short of ambition because they were now targeting a move to a higher level of garment – woolly jumpers for their males.

Here the little group sat in a circle and since Derek's accident, with no babies to bother them, the diverse conversations flowed continuously. There were moments of high drama occasionally when a dropped ball of wool rolling on the floor led to entanglement with another and one person had to stop knitting for a moment to untangle them. It didn't get much more exciting than that.

Thelma, Millie, Muriel, Daisy, Angela, and Sally, and the special member who came up from London each week because she truly enjoyed their company – Josephine – all clicked away merrily like a collection of wind-up clockwork toys.

It should be pointed out, though, that one didn't click quite as efficiently as the others. When they started the knitting-bee many weeks ago, although she was a lady of mature years, Josephine was the only one of the group who had never in her life knitted. Did she allow that to stop her coming to the meetings each Saturday? Certainly not! She wanted to learn.

The others were impressed and patiently, each week, she was given tuition, but Josephine was an incredibly slow learner. Sensibly, one person was not permanently landed with the problem. Because of the frustration level of whoever would be tutoring, they agreed who it would be before each meeting by drawing the short straw.

Encouragement was offered... "You are doing fine. Have a go yourself now," but nothing worked.

The minute she was left to try on her own, she was lost: "Have I done that wrong again?" Or, "Was it two plain, one purl, or one purl and two plain?" It seemed to the others that no one could possibly be as inept as Josephine. "Can someone pick up this stitch for me, please? This large hole is getting bigger!"

Then suddenly it all clicked! Two weeks ago she'd succeeded in producing her first set of bootees. Unfortunately the wool she'd been using had been knitted and ripped out so many times that it looked dirty, and the bootees had to be thrown away. No self-respecting baby would have worn them, even little charity babies.

Josephine loved the company of the others.

Sometimes, when the fathers refused to baby-sit, the babies appeared at meetings, and she treasured the chance to hold them, marvelling at their progress. She was grateful for the patience the others had shown in teaching her to knit, a skill that her dear-departed mother had failed to instil in her as a child. However, wonderful though the achievement was for Josephine, her alter ego, Sophie, was considering ending the charade. It could not go on forever.

Being part of this tight little group of friends was a new experience. She liked them, and the feeling was mutual, but, it was Josephine, a character she'd created, that they knew and liked, not really her, Sophie. What should she do? It had to end sometime.

The Saturday meetings had been running for months. A lot of miles were being clocked up, driving from London and back once a week, but that wasn't a good reason to stop. Andy had commented about her being away so much; she could live with that as well; he usually worked weekend shifts anyway. There was the hassle of the make-up, the grey wig, the old-style clothes, the acting, but she was enjoying all that... So, why stop?

It was the deceit!

Sophie wanted simply to be liked for being herself!

Being naturally blonde and attractive, with a figure that wasn't too difficult to keep in shape, and having a way with words that guys always found inviting were talents that caused her to be envied, and often disliked, by most females she'd tried to befriend.

When she and Andy became partners, she stopped flirting automatically, as she used to, whenever she met a male. Some people didn't seem to appreciate that yet. Sally for example. Sally retained a particular grudge against her for a sad misunderstanding.

Yes, there was a reason, but surely not one good enough for carrying on the bitterness forever? It was amazing that Sally had not recognised who Josephine actually was.

"Oh dear, what have I done," howled Josephine, suddenly realising that she hadn't been concentrating on the needles, the wool, or the pattern. "Could someone help me...?"

The others, knitting and chatting being second nature to them, looked at each other despairingly. Not again! Wouldn't she ever get it right?

58

Eventually, she did – get it right, that is – last Saturday in fact. For her achievement she had received a well-deserved round of applause, and then went out of their lives.

It was so ironic they told each other later: Josephine's success, in knitting a respectable pair of baby bootees for the first time ever, on the day of her departure. If only they'd known it was to be the last time they would be seeing her, they could have said farewell properly, but regrettable though it was, missing a proper farewell, they all agreed that she did leave in a blaze of glory. However this fact was not realised until they were well into their current meeting.

The journeys Josephine made every week were long, particularly for a woman of her advanced years: Saturday after Saturday. It was a display of the dedication she had towards each and every one of them – and to her knitting, but today, they were worried when she did not arrive at her usual time. A perfectionist when it came to timekeeping, she knew that tea was brought to them promptly at two o'clock, so for her to be fifteen minutes late was unusual.

"I hope she is all right," said Sally, "...and that she hasn't had a breakdown, or an accident."

Serious knitting was already underway with all seated in their customary positions in the circle, but today one chair stood vacant: Josephine's. It was left in place in the hope that she would eventually appear, and the attending members of 'The Mafia: Ladies Section' got on with the serious business – knitting.

Sally and Angie were taking advantage of husbands who were available, both having skipped out again without babies. Thelma was now more confident in Hammy's capabilities, and pleased to be able to leave him looking after the Hotel. Muriel started another ball of wool knowing Alexander was at the drama group's clubhouse instead of out drinking, and Daisy was wondering if Hector had stayed awake long enough to see the start of the football match on television. Millie was absent. She was over in Detroit again and missing the get-together, but due to return to Britain later that night

At half-past-two the door opened, but it wasn't who they were expecting; it wasn't Josephine entering. She about the same height but very different from the little old lady they had grown to love. The figure before them was at least half Josephine's age and wearing modern clothes, which showed her slim but curvy shape to advantage.

"So sorry to be late," she said. "Josephine told me you'd be here and warned me to leave home early to make sure I arrived on time, but I'm afraid I didn't! I'm Sophie Clerkenwell-Brown."

"What the...!" Sally gasped ...and they were all staring at the person talking; Sophie Clerkenwell-Brown, she'd said!

Knitting froze in the middle of rows!

Angelina, had no idea who this was, having never clapped eyes on her before; Muriel and Thelma thought that she seemed familiar and wondered why the thought should be associated with Derek, and Daisy had a vague memory of the voice, somewhere recently – someone standing beside Derek – but where?

Sally knew exactly who it was and where she'd seen her and who she had been with! Only seen for seconds but not forgotten. The cheek of her, fumed Sally silently, daring to walk in here so brazenly, and knowing I'd be here too!

"Forgive me for bursting in but I came with a message from Josephine. She won't be coming back," Sophie continued.

"WHAT...?" was the collective response from the knitters. This was totally out of the blue. She had given them no warning that she would be leaving them – why? Was it something they'd said? Was the journey too much for her?

"Yes, she told me to inform you that it's for the good of her health, you know. She is going to live in Spain for the rest of her life. It's just something she has to do, but she didn't want to tell you all too soon. She couldn't handle the tears."

There was a stunned silence from her shocked friends. Sophie had the floor – and their attention. Keep talking, she told herself, *and don't let Derek's wife get a word in because she'll want to attack me before I've won her over.*

"You all knew that Josephine was unwell, I presume..." she hesitated. All she received back were blank looks. "You didn't know? Did she not tell you...? What a brave woman. She kept it to herself for such a long time. Am I the only one she took into her confidence?"

Still the same blank looks, so she ploughed on...

"Did you not notice...? No hair, the wig?"

"Oh, yes," said Sally, suddenly feeling uncomfortable and guilty because she'd said nothing at the time or afterwards, no sympathy offered when it should have been, even though she had guessed it was probably serious and now it was too late.

The others felt uncomfortable too. They'd talked about it together after the night out at the *Torrid Hedgehog*, when they'd all been drinking too much, and Josephine had helped them all home. Yes, they'd seen her head; they'd talked, but only to each other and not to her. "The end had to come, but she was determined it had to be on her terms," Sophie said with tears in her eyes, "and now..." she sat down on Josephine's chair and began to sob. Deep inside, she was giving herself full marks for the acting bit.

The others fidgeted uncomfortably. What could one say at a time like this? And this poor girl had to bring us such a sad message.

"She was only an aged colleague, but she seemed like a mother to me," said Sophie. "She wanted you to remember her and asked me to give each of you a little trinket, as a keepsake."

Sally had tears in her eyes now too, as she thought how Josephine had bravely said nothing about being ill, nor had she ever complained about feeling unwell, and although no-one considered it correct to ask her to her face, they had known ...they'd known but had not offered her comfort... In her time of need they'd failed her.

Sophie opened the bag she was holding.

"It was only yesterday. You can't know what it was like for me having to say goodbye to someone who'd taken the place of my own dear mother, and knowing that it was to be the final hug..." She took out her handkerchief to dab her eyes, and reached back into the bag again. "The trinkets from her gold bracelet; she wanted each of you to have one."

Sophie handed one to Angie, then to Daisy. Thelma was delighted to receive hers, as was Muriel. When she came to Sally she stopped and looked her straight in the face.

"Sally, Josephine asked me to give you a very special hug, and to ask you to tell Derek that she's sorry she won't be seeing him again – she loved him, like a son, you know – and you have a trinket."

Sally stood up as Sophie leaned forward and they held each other close for several sobbing moments. They parted and Sophie held Sally at arm's length, giving her a sad sharing smile, before placing the last little gold trinket in her hand.

I've totally misjudged Sophie Clerkenwell-Brown, Sally thought; she is really such a lovely caring person.

"Oh ...and there was something else she insisted I was to give to you, Sally," said Sophie, "...her silver-grey wig."

At that, Sally felt really emotional – and just had to give Sophie another big hug.

59

It probably would have been just as bad at any other time to hear Sally say that Josephine had sent good wishes to him because he would never see her again. She was not returning to Newingsworth ever, because she was about to, you know – die – but in the middle of changing ET's pooh-filled nappy the shock seemed more severe!

The book, he immediately thought; this was only his first one, successful yes, but there were more to come, if only Sophie helped and encouraged him. He needed Sophie's help in the future. Die? Surely she couldn't possibly be dying; she was as fit as a fiddle! She must be going away, but where? Why was she abandoning him? Was this the fault of Andy Woodstock and some stupid idea of his again? She couldn't do this to him!

When Sally then began to tell him how Sophie had been so thoughtful and gentle when she brought them the sad news, Derek thought he'd misheard. Concentrating on nappy-changing was difficult enough normally, but being distracted by conflicting information at the same time was testing his multi-tasking capabilities to the limit.

Didn't Sally say only one moment ago that Sophie was going away for good? No ...and it took a moment to permeate his brain; she said Josephine was going away... Ah, that's what it will be, but ...wait a minute, had he misheard something else? Didn't he hear Sally actually say something pleasant about Sophie Clerkenwell-Brown? They had been face to face and they hadn't scratched each other's eyes out?

"We are having a golf day tomorrow," Sally informed him, "...ladies only. You are baby-sitting again, Sweaty dear. We are going to test out the new course. Thelma says it's not yet completed, but it's good enough to have fun. Nothing we could do will ruin it."

"What, all of you? Even though none of you can play golf?" scoffed Derek.

"Thelma can, and Sophie can too, and they will teach us. It can't be all that difficult."

"Sophie can?" he said, and then realised that he'd said out loud a name that had been taboo in the cottage ever since the day Sophie fell in the muddy stream, and... No reaction? Wow!

"Yes, well, she says she can," his wife informed him, "...but I would think she's the kind of woman who could turn her hand to anything she wanted to – and do it well."

Derek found this hard to believe. This was his wife talking nicely about the woman she'd hated for months, but hold on a moment, all this talk was putting him under too much pressure – this clean nappy, it is backside foremost! Sorry ET, I'll try again... ET just gave a sigh. He knew his dad's skill-level better than anyone. A nappy being put on the wrong way by daddy was not at all unusual...

"She's staying overnight at the Hotel specially to join us for the game tomorrow; she is a lovely girl; I hope I am in her team."

Sunday turned out to be a beautiful, fluffy-clouded, no-chance-of-rain sort of day – perfect for the golf match. The phone call from Thelma, that Sally answered, was to say that the other males would be coming over to support and cheer for the teams and would Derek be coming too?

Would he actually be allowed anywhere near Sophie when she was not Josephine? Derek felt apprehensive...

The loyal supporters stood attempting to look eager, and show that they were glad to be there: Hammy with Cornelius, Hector, who'd popped into town on the scooter and brought back Anton to give him some fresh air, Alexander, who'd come on his bike, as did Spider, and Sam with Annabel in his arms. Baldy was there too, being called Theo, or Theobald, by the males because there were females present. He was back in the country again after a quick trip to the States. Of course, Derek was there with ET in his arms.

The dogs also came with Derek and Hammy, who hoped to avoid another walk later in the day. Jilly, determined to dodge the attentions of Cornelius, was constantly wrapping the extending lead around her master's legs.

Cheers and whistles from the waiting mob greeted the lady golfers as they came out of the hotel together, chattering as usual. There were seven eager females, with two sets of golf clubs between them. The teams would be uneven and the golf clubs would have to be shared. However, considering the standard of the course and the capabilities of the players, these were small matters.

Over their shoulders, Thelma and Sophie each had one of the golf bags, whereas Thelma, being a sturdy mature lady, was carrying her bag with little effort, Sophie appeared to be wilting already under the weight of hers.

Sally had already noticed one thing in particular about Sophie; here were the rest of the females with faces scrubbed for the fresh air, with no make-up. Sophie wore make-up and it was perfect. She did look good though. It was a very unusual shade of lipstick she used, Sally noted admiringly. Yes, a very attractive girl...

Derek would willingly have offered to carry the clubs for Sophie, but there were three things preventing that: firstly – he was responsible for the safety of ET; secondly – at the end of a lead was a dog that was beginning to yap at everything. Thirdly, he was afraid of a negative reaction from Sally if he showed any interest whatsoever in Sophie.

So, to team selection...

With Thelma and Sophie as captains, the coin was tossed, and Thelma had first choice. She went for Angie; Sophie went for Sally, followed by Muriel to Thelma and Millie to Sophie. That left Daisy looking sad because nobody appeared to want her, which was always the problem at school she remembered, and, considering that to have been over sixty years ago, her memory was ok.

Thelma diplomatically suggested that someone would be required to be referee. "Would you be willing to do it?" she asked Daisy.

"Shouldn't I know the rules?" was Daisy's response.

"Nooooo..." came back as a chorus from everyone there, and that made her feel better.

The course was not yet complete and the putting surfaces would not be acceptable to a professional. Maybe even a discerning amateur would choose to play somewhere else, but these had been cow pastures a number of years ago, so it was small wonder it was taking time to perfect.

Thelma was pleased with the design; all her own work. The physical part had been largely thanks to Hamish Macintosh Esquire, and a small team of ex-builders who also played golf and from experience knew a great deal about hazards. They had enjoyed themselves, doing something other than move bricks and concreting. Already they had played nine holes, and were proud of what had been achieved so far. Of course, Hammy only did caddying – no chance of him playing. He'd decided previously that golf was not his strong point. With a wife who'd been a champion at school it seemed wiser not to risk being constantly criticised and humiliated, by his failure. He had tried, one day when he was alone, and proved to himself that a golf ball was too tiny to be hit regularly, and Thelma had also made it clear that he was supposed to hit it in a chosen direction... "Nae chance!" he'd told himself.

Thelma and Sophie were proving to be competition for each other as they played out the first hole, finishing level. Not bad considering that Sophie arrived via a bunker. Thelma had not played for many years but was satisfied that she was still capable, a little rusty and less supple perhaps, but not bad. Sophie showed herself as a skilled performer too, obviously wanting to shine and be liked by her peers today.

Then it was the turn of each of the team members to have a try.

There was no preamble for Millie, though she'd never tried this with a golf club before. First on the tee, she placed the ball, swung, and surprised everyone, especially herself, by hitting it! It didn't go far, but she'd hit it straight and for a reasonable distance. "Amazing," she exclaimed, and they all agreed!

Muriel had been out practicing in her back garden at Cloverton with a broom handle for a large part of the evening before and it paid dividends. After she'd taken about a dozen practice swings, she stepped up to the ball, and hit a beauty! Beginner's luck she said modestly. Thelma smiled and was in total agreement, until Muriel surprised her by hitting another beauty at her second shot. A third time out of the rough – and hit well too. Thelma was glad she'd picked her – until it came to the putting. Oh my goodness! Muriel was clueless at that!

When it came to Angie's turn to drive from the tee, she and Sally both started giggling and couldn't stop. Angie kept missing the ball, but then had a lucky hit and she was on her way.

"You've taken eight strokes so far, but because I like you we'll just put down four as the score," Daisy, the referee, informed her. Scoring became more complicated for Daisy though when Cornelius stopped being the well-behaved dog staying with his master, and decided he would 'fetch'. He went lolloping after Angie's ball, found it immediately, very carefully lifted it in his mouth, and returned it to Angie who was still standing on the tee. Cornelius then stood wagging his tail until Angie eventually patted him, and Hammy put on the lead.

Then it was Sally's turn.

In sight of this tee was the water feature, the large expanse of water lovingly created by Hammy and his team, and just beyond was the cottage, Toozlethwaite Manor. There was no denying that the large pond enhanced the view from the French windows at the rear of the cottage. Hammy intended to add a wire fence somewhere along this route because he didn't want any stray shots to land in the garden, particularly with the chance of little ET being in the pram, or when older, out playing. Where exactly the fence should be had not yet been finalised.

Sally was delighted to be in Sophie's team, and wanted to do well for this lovely talented person, but her first swing caused a jarring of her arms and wrists as she hit the ground. She felt foolish as she looked at Angie, and they started to giggle again. Another try, with a bit more concentration, and 'crack' – she hit a really sweet shot and the ball landed near to the front edge of the pond.

"Now you can use a lofted iron and get it safely over the water. It's easy," said Sophie.

Sally took this new club, the iron, from Sophie.

"Just swing it nice and easily again and it'll fly to the other side," Sophie promised.

So that's what Sally tried, but again the ground was whacked. Her wrists hurt and the ball scarcely moved.

"Let me show you how easy it is," Sophie offered, and took the club from Sally.

Sally observed the body movement as Sophie ensured her feet were firm; it was a sexy bottom wiggle. Derek following behind them noticed it as well, but made sure Sally didn't see him looking.

It was important to impress Sally, thought Sophie. I must do this very well if I am to become a good friend. Just relax, she instructed herself, but she felt tense. She swung back. It didn't feel comfortable, so wisely she stopped and re-addressed the ball. The bottom wiggle, the swing back, the forward stroke – it still didn't feel right but, too late – she'd hit it!

"Oh no..." was all she could say, as she saw the effect of the tense swing.

The ball was curving towards the cottage.

"Fore...!" she called out instinctively, then realised that fortunately, there was no-one in Toozlethwaite Manor to be injured because they were all behind her watching. Unfortunately, the ball was still going in the wrong direction – there was about to be damage – it was going towards the French windows...

*Crashhhhhh...*went the glass.

"*Ohhhhhhhhhh...*" came in unison from the surrounding watchers...

Sophie looked at Sally.

"Sorry..." she said timidly. It may have started well yesterday, but after this, Sophie guessed, the long-lasting friendship she'd hoped for, with Sally, could have come to a premature end.

60

Neither Derek nor Sally could get Josephine out of their minds.

For Sally, Josephine had become a good friend, but now she was gone and sorely missed and without a final farewell having been possible. Sally tried consoling herself with the thought that it was the way Josephine herself had chosen. Would they ever hear of her again? When the end came, would they be made aware?

For Derek, Josephine had become a safe contact for him; a harmless old woman who no-one had really noticed and that Sally had accepted as a friend; the only female publisher with whom he had been allowed close contact, and now she was gone.

However, Sophie, having got away with the deception, had thrown off the disguise and become accepted as herself. Even after damaging the French windows, Sally still thought she was wonderful. How Sophie had managed it Derek was unsure, but he admired her talent as both an actor and a publisher. He owed a lot to her and all because of a chance meeting when he'd been wasting his time training for a marathon. If she hadn't stopped to help him she wouldn't have ended up stripping for a shower and he wouldn't have been doing penance for ages because of her!

As Josephine, she'd been a Saint who'd helped him enormously with the book and to whom he would be eternally grateful. Flipping heck! When he thought about it, as Sophie, she'd caused his life to be a misery! And here she was back again, as Sophie! He would have to tread carefully in their relationship, but she was getting away with it. She would be continuing the weekly visits to Newingsworth so he could invite Andy to come up with her next Saturday, for his delayed birthday celebration, if Andy could sort out his shifts.

The celebration was still to be males only: Alexander's treat. It was to be a surprise and he was organising it all, but wouldn't tell Derek anything about it. Various people were being contacted. It would be the Saturday Male Mafia Group only, i.e. the pedal-pushing blokes and some hangers-on.

Derek wasn't overly happy about the secrecy, particularly as it was his father-in-law who held the secret. Having landed him in deep trouble once before, not surprisingly, Derek would be very cautious about what the end result turned out to be – anything questionable and he'd be out, like a shot! He was not going to let himself be dragged into trouble with Sally again, thank you very much!

61

It was Saturday afternoon, and Sophie had driven up from London bringing her lovely Andy with her this time. Whereas she would be making her way to the New Farmhouse Hotel, still feeling guilty for smashing the French windows with the golf ball, he was going to join friends somewhere secret to have a late birthday celebration dinner for Derek.

The broken window was on Sophie's conscience. Sally had said not to worry about it at the time, these things happen unfortunately, and the emphasis placed on the last word made the forgiveness seem a little less than sincere; as some people can become touchy about the smallest things, Sophie was unsure if they'd let her join the knitting bee...

As instructed by Alexander, Andy requested Sophie to drop him off a few streets away. He knew his way around, having pounded the streets of Newingsworth, Slatterfoot and surrounding districts, for many years in uniform. Most organisations in the area had been visited by him at some time or other over the years, in uniform and in plain clothes. He was not acquainted with the Slatterfoot Amateur Dramatic Players clubroom but he knew where it was and that was his destination today.

Coming from the opposite direction Derek recognised Andy and waved. As they stood outside shaking hands and having the usual 'not seen you for a long time' pleasantries, they could hear raised voices, though it wasn't possible to make out what was being said. It sounded a jolly noise, although a few negatives could be heard as they entered the building and walked along the corridor...

"It disnae even fit me!" Hammy was proclaiming.

"Of course it does," yelled back Alexander's voice. "Just pull in your belly!"

"Ah've *goat* it in..."

As Derek and Andy followed the sound of the voices and opened the door, they were greeted by male bodies in a state of partial dress or undress, all shouting ribald comments at one another, and more disturbing to Derek, were the clothes they were all attempting to squeeze into. They were of the feminine variety. Each had a large name tag pinned on the outfit and it wasn't the name he knew them by... all were changing into the sort of apparel that led to Derek's downfall not all that long ago.

Some were in the advance stages of make-up application. Who was who? The voices were recognisable but the visions before him were uncertain. James Hoist was not present, as far as he could tell. Had Alexander failed to contact his dad? That could lead to ill feeling because Mabel would have primed him that he was to receive an invite.

And over there, in the corner, must be one of Alexander's friends; Derek didn't recognise him. Wasn't Alexander inviting only friends of Derek? The figure minced over towards him. In the full outfit, including make-up, was Alexander himself, or rather 'Zandra', as the label on his dress said. He was a redhead today, with a short bob and not the long flowing locks that seemed to be fashionable with real women.

Why did I agree to go along with Alexander's suggestion, thought Derek, it got me into a lot of trouble last time? I didn't think he would dare... I'm a fool. I should have known...

"Oh no, not again; this is not for me..." Derek muttered, and moved towards the door. Under the circumstances, Derek was quite happy to abandon Andy and leave him to fend for himself, but Alexander was too quick and blocked his exit route.

Derek needn't have worried about leaving Andy behind. He was standing with a big grin on his face, and didn't appear to mind the prospect of dressing-up in female clothing like the rest of them.

"Come along now, Derek," said Zandra. "This is your big chance to have some fun – without getting caught this time. We are all here to look after you."

"Oh no..." said Derek emphatically, "I am in no way going through all that again. Sally would flay me alive and leave me out for the crows to peck if she knew I was getting dressed again as a female!"

"Relax man," insisted the cause of the problem the last time. "Sally will never know, and it's not her clothes you'll be wearing. We are not staying here. I've arranged a secret location for a meal and some drinks and it's all being paid for by me."

Having the use of the Slatterfoot Amateur Players Clubroom, Derek supposed, was not too surprising seeing that Alexander had become a leading light in all their productions. As a consequence, he was now the Club President. He would obviously have easy access to the keys, but would he be able to ensure that none of the other club members would appear and find this lot all in a state of undress, or otherwise?

The others had been there for a while and had been using the little theatre's dressing rooms along the corridor, sitting in front of the large mirrors receiving lessons from Alexander in applying make-up. The application for most was apparently successful but not for Hector – he looked more like a clown!

"Who's that over there, with the pink sweater and the big boobs?" Derek asked Zandra, indicating the stranger who was very carefully applying eye-liner and making a good job of it.

"Don't you recognise him? That's Baldy! He's shaved off his beard; did it today for a very special female friend apparently, a friend who preferred him without bristles."

"I thought he was still in America," said Derek.

"Came back this morning, he told me," said Zandra, "...some unfinished business with a lady to deal with."

"I'm not sure if he likes me much," said Derek, "He pretends he does but I think he still holds a grudge about what was in the book. Maybe it's a good job you didn't invite Twister. The two of them would probably have argued all night, and I wouldn't like having to separate them if they started to fight..."

"What made you think I've not invited Twister; he's meeting us at the destination."

"Oh!"

"Anyway, this is not getting you ready. I've chosen a nice little outfit for you from the club wardrobe."

"I'd rather not..."

"Now don't be silly. Remember it's all being done for you. Sally will never know, so, let's get that jacket of yours off and check that this lot fits. The transport will be here shortly..."

62

Derek recognised the road they were travelling on, and made a confident guess as to where the white stretch-limo was heading. He'd cycled this way many times. They were on their way to the *Torrid Hedgehog*, he was almost certain, and when they did arrive he was proved correct.

Now, this may seem to be an anti-climax for a birthday treat, to arrive at a surprise destination you have guessed beforehand but, in Derek's case, it was more than that, it was horrifying!

He had already made a fool of himself here by climbing out of the toilet window, and although the landlord had apparently accepted that it wasn't him but his double who did it, he was chancing his luck returning dressed like this, and particularly with Andy as part of the group; both looking ravishing in mini-skirts, wigs, and full war-paint.

The regulars were surprised to see the long vehicle draw up outside their country pub and, as eight females tripped out of the limo, each wearing a lapel badge, they peered from the little windows to observe the arriving talent.

To the eyes of the regulars, the make-up applied by Alexander to each face had created six luscious dolly-birds; but much nearer the mark, describing two of them, was 'passed-it'. Alexander had not been able to help the old 'beauties', Hector and Hammy, because of their body shapes more than anything else and they were lumbered with lapel badges showing respectively, 'Winnie', as in witch, and 'Haggard', as in ...well, haggard.

The rules to be applied this evening for the merry band of 'ladies' was that only lapel names were to be used for all chat. The lapel badge Derek was wearing said, 'Devilla', and Andy's, 'Angel', but whereas

Devilla was quaking in his high heels afraid of being recognised, Angel was as happy as Larry (sorry wrong gender!), and thoroughly enjoying this new experience, as were the others. For them it was a novelty, but not for Derek. They hadn't been warned by a wife to never do this sort of thing again, had they?

As they entered the old pub lounge, Zandra ushered them up to the bar to place their orders, bearing in mind that he was paying today, and he generously invited the locals to have one as well, which was much appreciated. The landlord had been warned that the group would be arriving for a meal and staying for the evening but Alexander had conveniently forgotten to say anything about their mode of dress, so 'Beega Jeemmy' was somewhat flummoxed!

Moving around in high heels for most of them was awkward, but they persevered. Spider, or rather Lizzie, as he would be called, just knew that, within five minutes, the skin of his right heel would have a blister, and he'd only walked into the limo and out of it again. This was a novelty, but a one off he'd already decided. He was fearful that he would bump into someone he knew. Being first to enter, he had stood dutifully at the bar awaiting the arrival of the others, trying to ignore the whistles and cheers from the regulars.

Sam, aka Bubbles, being American and a fairly recent incomer, found this all to be rather quaint; not a British custom he had ever heard of.

He had to smile at his father who was last to come through the door. Now he'd shaved off the beard, at least he looked the way his old man used to, other than a bit younger, but the black curly wig somehow didn't flatter him!

Tallulah acknowledged the welcome from the regulars by doing a very passable curtsy which brought another cheer. Theobald wasn't overly happy with the name given to him, but at least it beat 'Baldy', nor was it as bad as Hector's or Hammy's, so he made do.

No-one could possibly claim that they were a pretty sight. A lady becomes one by growing into the role from childhood, learning by her mistakes as she goes along. All that could be seen today was a row of 'mistakes', all standing in the most awkward positions, holding pints of beer...

There were good-natured ribald comments being thrown in all directions, by both the residents, and the visitors, as the eight 'luscious birds' sat down eventually to eat. Perhaps it was fortunate that there were no real females in the lounge that afternoon or tender ears might have been corrupted.

What wasn't realised by the visitors was that there was one on the premises; a normal female, and it was someone who was here many weekends to help out, when her other interests didn't interfere. She was in the kitchen, hard at work with the Pub's Chef. 'Beega Jeemy' had already taken the meal orders from everyone, but he didn't serve at the tables; he was busy enough looking after the bar and playing mine host...

"Where's Twister? You did say he would be here, didn't you?" Derek asked Alexander.

He was very careful never to call Twister 'Dad', or 'Father', or any of those affectionate pleasantries – Derek knew Twister couldn't cope with it.

Alexander looked at his watch.

"He knew when we were to be here and when we would be having food: at least Mabel, his secretary lady, did," he replied. "He was to be driving up from London and will be staying overnight at the hotel; must have been delayed in traffic. I told Mabel it was fancy dress and she said she would sort something out for him, so, he'll have his outfit on already."

Derek looked around the table. He was having difficulty relaxing. His friends, sitting beside him were thoroughly enjoying themselves. What idiots, he thought, dressed up in female clothes, full make-up; almost as if they did this every evening? What a bunch of pillocks! He was not at all comfortable. *If Sally ever finds out about this....*

"Gammon steak, for you, is that correct?" asked the voice at his shoulder. Derek looked up as he nodded, into the face of Christine – from the Gazette – Sally's replacement! What was she doing here? Thankfully he realised there was no recognition, as she moved to serve Spider.

"Fish and chips, madam?" she asked him.

"Yes, please," he replied and looked up.

"What the...!" said Spider, as he recognised the person he had been particularly careful to avoid getting involved with.

"Is there something wrong, madam? Did I give you the wrong one?" Her list was consulted. "It says: Lizzie – fish and chips... You are Lizzie aren't you?"

"No – I'm Spider, Christine! Don't you know me?" It spilled out of his mouth without thinking, and he gulped, and she looked at him again. "Anyway, what are you doing here? I've never seen you here before," he added, trying to appear nonchalant...

"Spider...? What are you...? This is my brother's pub. I help him at the weekends," she replied, giving him a funny look before going off to fetch the food for the others.

Derek sat smirking. This was more like it. He was beginning to enjoy himself now; it could be fun to see how Spider, the confirmed bachelor, would dig himself out of this...

"What...?" Spider blurted out of a full mouth. "What are you grinning at?"

"She fancies you, you know..." Derek replied knowingly, and started eating as the jolly noise continued all around.

It was a very thoughtful Spider who said very little during the remainder of the meal, and remained quiet until Christine returned to clear away empty plates. As she lifted his, he touched her hand. She hesitated, plate in mid-air.

"What are you doing tomorrow?" he asked her.

"Why, who wants to know?" she replied.

"I do, you sweet girl," was his rejoinder.

"What about your girlfriend, Penelope?"

"All a figment of Derek's fevered imagination..."

"Thought so."

"Tomorrow then?"

"My place, two o'clock!"

"Right," and he sat back in the seat with a big grin on his face as she left the area.

"Are you all right, Spider?" Derek asked, thereby breaking the rule of the day by not calling him, Lizzie. Derek was not grinning; he was worried for his friend. Was this the drink talking?

"I sure am, Devilla! Do you think I could miss this chance – did you not hear? Her brother owns the pub!"

They had finished the food and had just ordered another round of drinks when a taxi drew up in the forecourt. The door was opened by the driver, and out of it, moving very awkwardly, came a fluffy yellow chicken – man size!

Someone inside said, "Look outside!" and everyone did, to see the taxi pull away leaving the plump baby-hen standing all alone. It made its way towards the entrance door of the lounge. Inside, the place had gone silent.

Everyone watched the door...

Sally couldn't really complain about his clothing having been strewn everywhere, because that was her habit anyway. At least he hadn't disturbed her or Edwin as he came in, thank goodness, or she would not have been in such good spirits for this time in the morning.

The discarded clothing was lifted from the floor, piece by piece. Derek had obviously been enjoying himself last night with 'the boys'. She smiled to herself as she thought how stupid she was using that expression for the group Derek was with last night. They were a good crowd; a mixture of young and mature, amusing, and sensible when they needed to be; all good natured down-to-earth real men. Would saying they were 'lads' be better? Nooooo... I suppose at least being with that lot keeps my Derek on the straight and narrow. They are all good living blokes!

Nice, friendly, compassionate thoughts she was having this morning – until she lifted Derek's shirt – and saw the lipstick ...*the exact same shade as Sophie's!*

63

"It'll be a great night," said Andy.

"No thanks," said Derek, "I'm not into boxing."

"But it's not only the boxing. There's a meal and drinks and other entertainment. It's all blokes and it'll be a fun night, I'm sure. It was last year, anyway ...and you can sleep in my flat in my spare bedroom."

As he said that, the 'my', there was a twinge of guilt. It wasn't *his* flat or *his* spare bedroom – it was Sophie's, but she was to be away for Saturday and Sunday at her sister's, so Derek would never know it wasn't his: something to do with male pride and one-upmanship?

Andy had already made Derek aware that he and Sophie were in a steady relationship, but not that he, a big macho policeman, was actually living in a London flat belonging to his girlfriend, or, that occasionally, it was a home from which, every so often, ejection was being threatened because of his noisy habits.

Of course, there was no need for Sophie to know that Derek would be in the flat – not that she would object; it was just that macho thing again...

So, for the weekend under consideration the flat would be designated, by him, as *his*.

"You can travel down by train on Saturday morning and back home Sunday afternoon. It'll be a great evening..."

It was; Derek had to admit that. There were parts of the evening where he permitted his mind to wander because the painful-looking blows hitting an already-bloody face did not appeal to his sense of fun. However, the food was as good as Andy promised and, earlier, the comedian was funny; crude but funny, and the female singer was beautiful with a great singing voice and an excellent selection of music. He enjoyed those parts, but for him the boxing was not fun to watch.

Therefore, not surprisingly, Derek was one of the few not urging the gentlemen in the ring to kill each other. As the evening progressed, and the drink flowed, the noise and excitement increased, Derek found the alcohol, which was all at Andy's expense, to be more soporific than enervating. During the painful-looking bits he was drifting off, to think of things more pleasant than blood and guts.

He felt a tiny bit guilty sitting in this large male group, relaxing and enjoying the good things in life. He'd left Sally back in Newingsworth, feeling a bit upset at the prospect of coping on her own with ET and his grumpy behaviour at nights.

Sally certainly resented his visit to London, well, that was Derek's impression. It was almost as if she couldn't trust him to be let loose on his own in the big city. Why should she think that? He'd given her no recent reason to worry. However, it has to be admitted that alcohol was diminishing Derek's guilt, glass by glass.

Andy was being cautious about the quantity of drink he was consuming because he was on duty the following day, so there was a little extra for his friend. When the evening's entertainment was over Derek was pleased to be still able to stand and straighten his legs. It must have been sitting for several hours on the train that made them feel wobbly. The taxi took them all the way back across a London which seemed incredibly busy to Derek's drink-affected bleary eyes; so different from Newingsworth. At this early hour, Newingsworth would be dead.

Andy couldn't stop talking about how good the night had been. The only factor putting a damper on the proceedings was his next working shift, having lost out on the draw for the day off. His shift was to begin in roughly five hours and they were still in a taxi.

Sophie's plans had changed.

She left London that Saturday morning, saying cheerio to Andy, to drive to Cornwall, but on arrival had almost turned on her tail and returned, and she was tired. It had not been her intention to pay such a short visit but she was back in London by mid-evening.

It was disappointing that her sister had not mentioned that she and her husband were off to France by car for the week. The information was garnered from their next-door neighbour. It was a spur of the moment arrangement apparently – much as Sophie's had been to visit Cornwall. Sophie had wanted to surprise her sister, but it was she who'd been surprised.

Back in the flat, exhausted, she was tucked up in bed by eleven o'clock. She had taken the usual necessary precaution, knowing that Andy was planning to return after she was asleep, by putting earplugs in. It saved tempers becoming frayed...

The Metropolitan Police Annual function, which he attended last year for the first time, was where he would be tonight. When he returned, she knew he'd be surprised to see she was back; she also hoped he would be pleased to see her.

She fell asleep thinking nice thoughts, thoughts like appreciating how open and honest her Andy was, and that they had no secrets...

Walking up the two flights of stairs, sometimes two at a time if he felt particularly energetic, was usually routine when Andy returned to the flat. Tonight, with Derek hanging onto his arm as they came from the taxi, the stairs were not even considered. There was a perfectly good lift, especially when two males, one slightly more inebriated than the other, had to reach the second storey.

Derek started to giggle for no apparent reason – but it set Andy going too, and as they stumbled into the waiting elevator, it was Derek who stabbed at the button.

A few moments later the lift door opened and they stepped out into the corridor, it was a corridor unfamiliar to Andy. In slow motion, the thoughts in his befuddled brain suggested they might be on the wrong floor; and they were. They'd reached number five.

Try again.

Andy's own attempt returned them to the ground floor, before another very determined effort gave them success. He recognised the second floor corridor carpet, but his key to the flat became the next problem. It was somewhere in a pocket. If Sophie had not been away for the weekend he might have been brazen enough to ring the doorbell, even though it was now a quarter to three in the morning. She wouldn't have minded rising out of bed for him. Of course, he knew that she would only have heard the bell if she hadn't put earplugs in, but she wasn't there anyway...

"Can't find the key, Derek."

"Oh, alright," replied Derek, "Don't worry. I'll just go home then... Goodnight, I've had a wonderful..."

"Derek, you are in London. You can't go home tonight," slurred out Andy as he tried each pocket once again, "Ah-ha..."

"Shhhhhh...." hissed Derek. "It's late!"

Derek was the one who eventually succeeded in putting the key in the keyhole. The door was opened in a slightly quieter fashion than normal and ...they were in. Andy switched on the lights.

"Wow..." Derek was very impressed at the sight of Andy's flat, both in size and opulence, in comparison to Toozlethwaite Manor. He felt a real country bumpkin at this moment, a drunken country bumpkin at that too...

As Andy opened the door of the spare bedroom, Derek was suddenly desperate to undress and get into bed.

He knew he'd fall asleep instantly but, just as suddenly, he remembered his promise to phone his wife the moment he arrived in London.

He'd forgotten!

"I'll have to phone Sal," he anxiously told Andy, "She'll be worried about me..."

"Derek, she'll be asleep," said a very perceptive Andy, "and she'll not be happy if you do, at this time in the morning."

"No, no, no. ET will have wakened her. He always does."

"Derek ...*don't!*"

So, instead, Derek tumbled into bed and before Andy closed the door he was fast asleep.

Finding Sophie in the bed, when she should have been far away in Cornwall, was a shock to Andy's system, rather than just a surprise.

So much so that, when he rose to go off to work in the morning, he was careful to permit her to sleep on; he clean forgot to say that Derek was next door in the spare bedroom. Anyway she wouldn't have heard – earplugs!

Derek awoke in a strange bed in a room that was not immediately recognisable. It took time to come to the surface and recall the enjoyable night he'd had with his strange policeman buddy – and then he remembered that he had failed to phone Sally!

Don't panic, he told himself as he feverishly searched for his new acquisition – his iPhone. He'd already used it to speak to Sally and ET, while on the train when he was travelling south yesterday, the first time he'd tried out the 'Facetime' it worked a treat; they could see him, and he could see them. ET must have been able to make out it was him because he gurgled away and tried to grasp the phone. Sally even showed it to Jilly and she recognised him right away too – she growled...

He should have phoned her when he reached Andy's, if only to prove where he was, because, during the call on the train, she'd asked him again where he was staying; obviously worried that it might not be a nice place, after all it was a bloke's apartment he'd explained.

Well, he would put her mind at ease by phoning now and letting her see how nice the place was. It was almost unbelievable how clean and tidy and tasteful everything looked. Not at all what he'd expected of a big policeman's pad but then again, wasn't Andy good at needlework? Derek remembered the hankie in the *Torrid Hedgehog*; he was obviously more artistic than would first appear.

"Hello Derek, so you've deigned to phone at last," she said, and he could see little Edwin in her arms.

These phones were absolutely magnificent!

"Sorry, it was all a bit of a rush yesterday; didn't get the chance to ring. How are you managing, and are you coping without me?" Derek enquired.

In Toozlethwaite Manor, Sally hesitated. Should she admit that she normally had to cope without him even when he was with her, or should she be nice to him today? It was difficult trying to stop ET wriggling about while she struggled to operate this new smart-phone Derek bought for her. It hadn't been the best of nights!

"How is ET today? How is daddy's little fellow then? ET, can you see Daddy? Goo, goo, goo, goo, gooooo..."

"Derek, do you *have* to behave like an idiot? Anyway, how is the accommodation?"

"It is absolutely wonderful! See, you needn't have been concerned."

Just as he could see her and ET, she could see him, sitting in his underpants, hair a mess and needing a shave. Behind him on the bed was a lovely patterned duvet, and pretty pictures adorned the walls. Yes, the room did look surprising – quite sophisticated in fact...

"Well, that wasn't really my concern. Where is Andy anyway?"

"I'm not sure if he's here just now. He was starting work early and I think I heard the door close a little while ago, so I am on my own. He sends you his love though."

"It doesn't look very much like a single bloke's place..."

"Oh, so you can see it can you. That is really why I'm phoning you, to show you that everything is alright."

"Yes, I..."

Sally hesitated.

There was something in the background, something that moved; or rather it was someone, behind Derek's back. The door had opened and a figure walked into the room – and stopped suddenly.

Sophie panicked as she went in and saw – a burglar! How did he get in?

Andy was at work.

She was alone, but someone was sitting on her spare bed. She needed to dress; she hadn't a stitch on. The intruder was facing the other way and had neither seen nor heard her so Sophie backed out of the room again closing the door quietly. She had to phone the police immediately!

"What's wrong Sally?" asked Derek worriedly. "You look as if you've seen a ghost!"

Sally breathed deeply.

Keep calm, she tried telling herself. Just as she'd suspected all along! It's Sophie Clerkenwell-Brown! He's with that blonde, naked bimbo again!

"Derek," Sally said calmly, but with feeling, "We won't be here when you return..."

The call ended abruptly.

Why?

Poor Derek... He was shocked and could not understand.

He sat staring at the blank screen...

Did I say the wrong thing...?

Mac Black

Current occupation: a writer of humorous fiction. Previous working background: shipbuilding on the River Clyde, tyre manufacturing in Dundee and working in the food industry in Fife (in jobs that didn't make his hands too dirty).

He was born in Glasgow and lived there for about half a life before moving to Carnoustie and then to Cupar, his present home.

He has been married for a long time.